INTO THE
DARK FOREST

JEANINE FRICKE

STRATTON
—P R E S S—
Publishing Life

INTO THE DARK FOREST
Copyright © 2020 **Jeanine Fricke**

Stratton Press Publishing
831 N Tatnall Street Suite M #188,
Wilmington, DE 19801
www.stratton-press.com
1-888-323-7009

ISBN (Paperback): 978-1-64345-678-2
ISBN (Ebook): 978-1-64345-899-1

Printed in the United States of America

I wish to thank my husband, Dan Fricke, and my parents, Miles and LeAnn Winship, for their many hours of proofreading and for their continued support and encouragement. They gave me the courage to keep writing and submit my manuscript for publication. Thanks, also, to my good friend, Gail Hovland, who came to my rescue every time I had a problem with my computer, and to Karen Thaler, who helped me when I started to second-guess myself. Finally, thanks to Lynne Partelow, my longtime best friend, who inspired me to write about enduring friendship with all its ups and downs.

PROLOGUE

Sunday, October 27, 2013

The dark blue, late model Dodge Ram pickup pulled up in front of the 7-Eleven store at 1:15 in the afternoon. Five men climbed out of the extended cab truck.

"Be sure and lock the truck," said Cal, a dark-haired, thickset, acne-pitted man with a perpetually nasty scowl on his face and an equally nasty disposition. "We don't want nobody gittin' in there an' stealin' nothin'."

"You think I'm stupid or somethin', Cal?" the man named Pete retorted. "I know enough to lock the damn truck. And I don't need a moron like you tellin' me what to do." Pete was a large man with greasy blond hair and a jagged scar cutting a path from the hairline at his right temple almost to his mouth. He didn't look too smart, but looks were deceiving. He certainly wasn't a man of culture or good taste, but as he'd just told Cal, he wasn't stupid.

"Knock it off, you two!" A third man put himself between the two and pushed them apart. He was better dressed, neater-looking than either one of them. He was a fairly attractive man with thick, black hair, black-brown eyes, and a wide-but-not-too-wide mouth, obviously at least part Native American. "Keep your minds on why we're here. I'm tired of you two and your constant picking at each other." He lowered his voice. "We need to keep a low profile. We don't need people gawking at a couple of idiots who can't keep their tempers under control and their mouths shut."

"Hey, Joe, wait a minute—" Pete said.

"No, you wait," Joe hissed. "Any more of this and both of you are going to wish you'd never met me. Got it?" The dangerous glint in Joe's eyes told Pete he'd better get it.

"Yeah, sure, Joe," said Pete. "But I'll tell you this much. When this project is done, I'm outta here. I'm takin' my pay, and that's the last you'll see of me."

"Fine," Joe said. "I can live with that. What I can't live with is your big mouth!" He turned to Cal and said, "How 'bout you, Cal? Do you have anything to say to me?"

"Me? No. I'm good." Cal held up both hands, palms toward Joe, and backed up a few steps, as if to ward off an attack.

"Good. Then let's do what we came here to do and get out of here. We go in, and we buy what we need. No lifting anything. We pay for whatever we take. Last thing we want is for the cops to show up here and start asking questions."

He motioned to the other two men standing beside the bed of the pickup. "Trent, Sam, you two stay here and keep an eye out. If you see anything that looks like trouble—anything that even looks like a cop—you come get us."

"Right, Joe," Trent said. Trent and Sam were both of average build; Trent just a little taller than Sam. Both had dark hair. Trent's features were chiseled whereas Sam's were rounder and could tend to go toward fat if he weren't careful. What made Trent unforgettable was the myriad tattoos covering at least fifty percent of his body.

Sam's only tattoo was the much more stereotypical "Mom" inside a heart over his right bicep. He'd taken a lot of ribbing about it, but only once from each unfortunate man who made that mistake. "Without my mom, you would not have the pleasure of knowing me," he'd say, just before he pummeled them for their unkind remarks.

Joe, Pete, and Cal went inside the store. They split up, each going up and down separate aisles. They filled their baskets with anything they thought would be easy to cook and stave off hunger for the next several days. As an afterthought, Cal threw in several bags of cookies and a couple boxes of candy bars to satisfy his huge sweet tooth.

They approached the counter at the front of the store.

"You fellas aren't from around here, are you? You here to do a little hunting?" Ginny, the girl at the cash register, didn't look a day over seventeen though she was almost twenty-two.

"Yeah, that's right," Joe said. "How much do we owe you?"

"That'll be 73.57, please."

"Hold it a minute, Joe. We forgot the beer," Cal said.

"Hurry up and get it," Joe said.

Cal came back with four six-packs of Coors. Joe paid for everything, pocketed the receipt, and they headed for the door.

"You guys have a nice day," Ginny said. "And good hunting."

The three men let the door close behind them without responding and walked toward the truck. Ginny watched from the window. Something about them seemed off to her. She wrote their license plate number on the copy of their receipt and noted the make and color of the truck.

CHAPTER 1

Tuesday, March 10, 2015

Olivia sat on the hard, straight-backed chair with its metal arms and hard-as-a-rock vinyl cushion. She'd come to believe, over the last few days, that it was meant to make visitors uncomfortable enough that they wouldn't want to stay too long. The geometric-printed turquoise and brown curtains had been pulled open to let in what little light filtered down from the cloud-laden sky.

At least the walls, thank goodness, weren't the ugly institutional green she'd always, for some reason, associated with hospitals and prisons but were an up-to-date soft taupe, which had a quieting effect. They also lent an attractive background to the borrowed artwork on the wall opposite the bed.

Wires and tubes ran from a variety of machines, all helping to keep the patient alive. One machine monitored her heart. Two IVs ran life-saving fluids through long, clear tubes, feeding her the nutrients and antibiotics she needed. Another tube was connected to the oxygen source on the wall behind the bed and looped around her head, the nasal cannula gently blowing pure oxygen into her nose.

The ledge above the heat register below the window, which spanned almost the entire length of the wall, was nearly covered with cards, flowers, and balloons from well-meaning friends and acquaintances. The thought that they probably had no idea that their intended recipient may never even know they were there brought tears to Olivia's eyes.

The rails were up on both sides of the hospital bed, making it hard to reach her best friend's hand. Nevertheless, Olivia held on to it, as though by grasping it firmly enough, by squeezing it every so often, by occasionally giving just the slightest tug, she could pull her friend up and out of whatever abyss she'd tumbled into. Maybe Olivia could bring her back to the world of serene forests and awe-inspiring mountain views that were her life now.

Olivia picked up the Monday morning edition of *Missoula Reports* and read the headline at the top of the front page for the umpteenth time since she'd picked it up two days ago: "Ranger Hospitalized Following Humvee Hit-and-Run." The article that followed was accompanied by a picture of a smiling Alyssa in her ranger's uniform.

> Montana Fish and Wildlife Ranger, Alyssa Walton, is hospitalized and reported to be in critical condition following a hit-and-run accident on the corner of Main and Higgins in downtown Missoula early Saturday evening, March 7. Doctors say Walton suffered multiple life-threatening injuries when a black Humvee careened around the corner, jumped the curb, and ran her down. She is in the Critical Care Unit at City Hospital where doctors say they are unsure of her chances for survival.
>
> Witnesses say when the driver of the Humvee reached the corner at Main Street, he appeared to suddenly speed up and turn sharply, hitting Ranger Walton and barely missing her companion, Olivia Clayton.
>
> The driver of the Humvee was said to be wearing a faded denim jacket and a red plaid hunting cap.
>
> Police are searching the area for a late model black Humvee, with a damaged right front bumper. Anyone with information regarding

this incident is encouraged to contact Detective Sheldon at the Missoula Police Department. All identities will be kept confidential.

Olivia laid the paper in her lap and absentmindedly rubbed her fingers over the fading bruise on her right thigh. When she'd tried to push Alyssa out of the path of the Humvee bearing down on her, she'd lost her balance and fallen against the curb. She'd all but forgotten about her minor injury, except for the occasional moment when her leg started to ache a bit.

The article was so matter-of-fact, so impersonal. There'd been no mention of who Alyssa was, what kind of woman she was, what she'd endured in the last couple of years. Nothing was said about the fact that she'd received three commendations for work well done in the Montana Fish and Wildlife Service. There wasn't even a hint of personal information about her friend in the article.

She's just a statistic, Olivia thought. *No one cares. No, that's not right! I care. And I won't let that monster get away with what he's done to her.*

She dropped the paper into the trash can. There was nothing more in it she needed to know. No matter how many times she read the article, none of the facts changed. All the information she wanted was with the doctors and nurses who were attending to Alyssa while she lay in her hospital bed, unmoving, unknowing.

Olivia thought back to the last time she'd spoken with the doctor. He'd cautioned her not to get her hopes up. Alyssa had severe trauma to her brain, and the swelling was putting an alarming amount of pressure on it. In addition, the MRI and x-rays showed her pelvis was broken, as were both arms and her left leg. She'd lost a lot of blood from a lacerated femoral artery. If she were to wake up now, there'd be no way to protect her from the terrible pain she'd feel. In fact, he'd told her, they'd probably put her into a drug-induced coma to give her whatever relief from the pain they could. He finished by telling Olivia the chances of Alyssa's waking were slim to none, and that if she did, there was no telling what kind of condition she'd be in, given the injuries she'd sustained. He'd warned her that Alyssa may be in a vegetative state for however long she lived, but at this point, there was no way to know.

"Please don't sugarcoat it for me, Doctor." Olivia's voice dripped with sarcasm. "My best friend was run down by a drunk driver in a Humvee. She hasn't opened her eyes since she was brought here by ambulance three days ago. She hasn't so much as wiggled her finger or grimaced or, or…" She let her voice fade away and dropped her face into her hands. She struggled to suppress the tears of fear and frustration she'd held back for so long.

"I'm sorry," she said. "Did you know the day she was hit, March 7, was her birthday? She just turned forty-five. We'd been to dinner and were on our way to see a movie. We've celebrated our birthdays with dinner and a movie ever since we were freshmen in high school. We'd just stepped off the curb to cross the street when…" Once again, her voice died out with the horrifying memory of that huge vehicle plowing right over the limp body of her dearest friend, as though she were no more than a rag doll. That scene was one she'd never be able to erase from her mind completely.

She felt the doctor's hand on her shoulder when he told her he didn't know it was Alyssa's birthday. But his attempt at compassion appeared false when, though he'd said he was sorry, his bland expression showed no sympathy at all. He came across as even more detached when he told her they'd do everything they could to make her last days as comfortable as possible.

"*Last days? Last days?!*" Olivia angrily shoved the doctor's hand away and stood to face him. "You are never to repeat those words to me, or even in this room, again. Do you hear me? Do you *hear* me?" She shouted at the doctor, her face beet red and contorted with fear and frustration.

"I do," said the doctor, who remained calm, in spite of the nearly hysterical woman's face a mere six inches from his own. "But I think it's better for everyone, including Mrs. Walton, if you face reality now. Her injuries are severe enough that—"

"I don't want to hear how severe her injuries are," Olivia interrupted. "I want to hear you say that there's hope. She's strong, and she's a fighter. She always has been. She loves life and she's not ready to go yet. She's not ready. *I'm* not ready for her to go." Her voice died to a whisper. "Not now."

Olivia had slumped back down into the chair and turned away. That was the last time she'd seen the doctor today.

Now, five hours later, she gave her friend's limp, cold hand one more squeeze, rose, and walked to the window. She stared at the rooftops of the darkening city without really seeing them. The monitors attached to Alyssa kept up their persistent beeping. The bleak sky offered no answers. At the moment, all she had were questions. Questions and memories…

* * * * *

"Livvy! Livvy! Liv-veee!" Alyssa's voice was excited, high-pitched, as she tried to get Olivia's attention. It was the first time she'd ever had the nerve to hang by her knees on the cross bars of the swing set without hanging on, and Olivia didn't seem to be interested at all.

"Livvy, look! Look, Livvy! Will you *pul-leaze* look before I fall and break my head!"

That finally got Olivia's attention away from the anthill she'd been studying intently.

She ran over to the swing set and sat down so that her right-side-up face and Alyssa's upside-down face were nose to nose.

"That's great, Lissy," she said. "See, I told you there was nothing to be scared of. You just have to think you can do it, and then you can."

"Oh, that's what you always say," Alyssa replied.

The two ten-year-old girls were in the fourth grade together though they preferred to think of themselves as fifth-graders since this school year was almost over, and they were both certain they'd have good report cards. They didn't like to brag, but they considered themselves and each other the smartest kids in their class at Ben Franklin Elementary School in their small South Dakota town.

In fact, the two, who'd been best friends practically since they were in diapers, thought that, given the opportunity, they could someday rule the world. Lissy and Livvy—an unbeatable team. But that was only if they wanted to, of course. Who knew what would happen in thirteen or fourteen years? During the many long and decidedly serious conversations they'd had concerning their futures, they'd already determined that college was an absolute must if they were to meet the kind of men with whom they hoped to spend their lives and have huge families.

They both had dreams of fabulous, adventurous careers awaiting them, too. Olivia had decided six months ago that she wanted to be a doctor. She didn't know what kind yet, but she was positive medicine was in her future. Alyssa had fallen in love with the mountains and the lush green forest when her family vacationed in Yellowstone National Park the previous summer.

She'd decided to be a forest ranger and learn all about the forest and its inhabitants.

"Well, it's true, isn't it? Look at you. Are you still scared? No!"

Olivia clapped her hands with glee.

"I am doing it, aren't I?" Alyssa said and then added, "You know, you look funny upside down."

"I'm not upside down, you are," Olivia said, "and what do you mean I look funny? You're the one with frizzy orange hair dragging on the ground. Not to mention that your crazy freckles look even crazier when your face turns all red like that."

Alyssa's upside-down smile suddenly turned into a frown. "Now you're making fun of my hair and freckles, too?" She forgot, for a moment, how she was situated and started to cross her arms over her chest in defiance. In doing so, she lost her precarious toehold on the legs of the swing set and slipped off the bar, headfirst.

Olivia saw what was about to happen and instinctively stuck her legs out in front of her and reached up. When Alyssa dropped, Olivia was ready for her and caught her on her lap, her head cradled between her hands.

Olivia looked at her friend, who just lay there, not moving, for a long moment. *Oh, no!*

Her imagination got the better of her. *She can't be. She can't be!*

"Alyssa! Lissy! Please, please talk to me. I'm sorry I said your hair was frizzy and orange and you were covered with freckles. I'll take it all back, if you'll only talk to me! Please don't be dead!"

When Alyssa started to shake uncontrollably, Olivia was sure she was having a seizure.

She'd watched a dramatic episode about ambulance drivers on TV the night before, and the patient on the program had shaken the same way. She sat, terrified, and tried to remember what the EMTs on the program had done. Then, as she watched, she realized Alyssa wasn't seizing, but was trying hard not to laugh.

"I'm alive, silly." Alyssa struggled to suppress her giggles. "You just saved my life." She sat up and faced Olivia.

"Oh! You scared me so much." Olivia wrapped her arms around Alyssa's neck and gave her a huge hug. "Don't ever do that to me again. Promise!"

Alyssa pulled away from Olivia. "Now wasn't there something you wanted to say?"

"What? Oh, okay, I take it back. You know I don't really think your hair is frizzy and orange. I love your hair," she gushed, "and I think it's a beautiful shade of red, and it's not frizz, it's curls. And your freckles just make you look cuter. I'd give anything to have freckles like yours. All I got was this stupid birthmark." She pointed to the small heart-shaped red spot on her left arm.

"You're forgiven," Alyssa said. "I love your beautiful blond hair, too. And that birthmark looks just like the kiss of an angel."

The two girls giggled and, forgetting how close Alyssa had come to having, at the least, a bad headache, stood and started to dance around the swing set. After a couple minutes of cavorting like mischievous pixies, Alyssa came to an abrupt stop and faced Olivia.

"What?" The sudden transformation on her friend's face stopped Olivia in her tracks.

"I just happened to think." Alyssa's voice was grave. "You really did save my life just now. Oh my gosh! I could've died! I really could've fallen and broken my head or my neck or—I don't know. I might've been paralyzed for the rest of my life." She flung her arms around

Olivia's neck dramatically and practically sobbed, "Oh, Olivia! You're my hero! I owe you my life. And I'll never, ever forget it."

"Oh, come on, Lissy. I didn't do anything so great. You were slipping and I was there."

"No, seriously, I think you're a hero."

"Well, okay, if that's what you want to think," Olivia said, "but you know what I think? I think I'm hungry. Let's go see if Mom has any cookies for us." She grabbed Alyssa's hand and pulled her toward the house.

CHAPTER 2

Saturday, March 7, 2015

"And do you remember when Mr. Johnston made Marty Kale stand for an entire class period with his nose stuck to a piece of gum on the wall?" Olivia laughed at the memory of the class clown, who'd struggled to keep from laughing while maintaining contact between his nose and the concrete block wall.

"Oh, gosh, yes! Just because Marty smarted off to him about needing to chew gum because it helped him concentrate." Alyssa laughed with Olivia.

They were at a favorite restaurant in downtown Missoula. Here they could enjoy a delicious meal in a fun atmosphere without having to worry about being hit on by lonely men who used tired pickup lines to try to win them over.

It was Alyssa's birthday, and they were celebrating it in their customary fashion, with dinner and a movie, as they'd done for thirty years

They looked at each other across the table and simultaneously blurted out, "Miss Persons!"

A giggle found its way out of Alyssa's mouth, followed by a snort from Olivia, and then an out-and-out belly laugh from them both, as they remembered some of the antics of their sophomore geometry teacher.

"Do you remember the time she was sitting on the corner of her desk, and when she stood up, she stepped into the trash can and got it stuck on her foot?"

"And when she couldn't shake it off, she just clomped around the room with it still on her foot, pretending it wasn't there," Alyssa said. "I swear, I thought I'd die trying not to laugh! She looked so ridiculous!"

"Oh, I know!" Olivia said. "Then there was that time she had a hole in her pocket, and the cap on her packet of Tic Tacs was open. She left a trail of Tic Tacs everywhere she walked."

"Oh, and don't forget about the time…"

The two women continued reminiscing about fond and funny memories of their high school years, as they devoured their meals of Caesar salad, seafood crepes, fluffy croissants, and the house wine.

When they'd finished their entrees, all six of the waitresses gathered around their table, specifically selected for its location in the center of the room with a birthday cake. They encouraged all the patrons to join them in singing "Happy Birthday" to Alyssa, who promptly blushed bright red and lightly slugged her best friend on the arm.

As they enjoyed the rich German chocolate cake and a cup of coffee, talk turned to Alyssa's work.

"I had kind of a strange experience the other day," she said. "I was way up by Lone Man's Road. I had to put up a surveillance camera so we could keep an eye on the activities of some early-rising bears. This, mind you, is in early spring, and it's clear out in the middle of nowhere."

She paused to take another sip of coffee and then continued, "While I was up there, I ran into some guy I'd never seen before. I asked him how he was, and he seemed awfully nervous. We'd seen signs of someone staying near there a few weeks earlier when we went up to check trails. When I asked him if he was renting a cabin near the site, he said he and four of his buddies were vacationing up there."

"Vacationing at this time of year?" Olivia said. "Isn't that a little odd?"

"He said they'd all been laid off from their jobs in construction, and they'd decided to take a little time for R and R. I didn't have any reason not to believe him, so I just let it go at that and told him maybe I'd see him around." She took a bite of cake and another sip of coffee. "But ever since then, I've had this funny feeling about him that I just haven't been able to shake." Then she remembered something else about the man. "Oh, and I forgot to mention how creepy he looked."

"Creepy how?"

"He had a horrible, ugly scar from his mouth all the way to his temple. It gave him kind of a sinister appearance."

"Did you tell anyone else about meeting him?"

"Yes. Collin and I were out together a few days after that. We put up several more cameras and decided to check the one I'd mounted before. When we got there, we found several sets of footprints in the snow. We took the camera down and looked at the video. There were five men who seemed to be checking out the camera. It was odd. It seemed like they were trying to be sure they knew exactly where the camera was, and maybe what it was being used for, but they all tried to hide their faces with their hands or their hoods as they looked up at it, like they didn't want their faces to be identifiable."

"So what have you done about it?"

"Nothing, so far. Collin and I agreed we'd report it and then keep an eye out for anything that seemed out of place."

"Did you? Report it, I mean?"

"Yes. But just as I thought, since we had nothing else to go on, there wasn't much we could do about it. I guess we're just going to make it a point to be in that area a little more often and see if we find anything suspicious."

"Well, you just be careful. Sometimes I worry about you and wonder if maybe you shouldn't find yourself another line of work. Especially now that..." Olivia saw the pain in Alyssa's eyes, and her voice trailed off.

"I'm always careful," Alyssa said. "Besides, I'm sure there's nothing to this, anyway. It's probably just as the guy—I think he said his name was Pete—said. Five guys laid off and taking some time to regroup before looking for other jobs." She stopped and looked at Olivia, whose eyebrows were creased with concern. "I promise I'll be careful. But, Livvy, I can't give up my job as a ranger. It's pretty much my life now. It keeps the memories of Rob and the boys close. If I had to give it up, I just don't know what I'd do." Her voice broke and she stopped speaking.

"Hey! What are we doing? This is supposed to be a celebration. It's your birthday, and we have a movie to go to." Olivia picked up the tab for both meals, pushed back her chair, and grabbed Alyssa's hand. "Come on. The theater's just a short walk from here. Let's go so we can see the previews."

Alyssa left a generous tip on the table, and the two women walked to the front of the restaurant amid wishes of "happy birthday" and "have a great evening." As Olivia paid the bill, Alyssa thanked everyone for their good wishes. Then the two of them were on their way to the theater.

CHAPTER 3

Wednesday, March 11, 2015

Olivia arrived at the hospital later than she'd planned. She'd decided to stop by Alyssa's house on her way to water plants and check her mail. Alyssa had been edgy the last few days before she was run down. Olivia thought back to what her friend had told her the day of the accident. She wondered if something might show up in Alyssa's mail that could shed some light on her nervousness. She wondered if she should mention it to the police.

When she reached Alyssa's room, she pushed all thoughts of possible problems aside, determined to put forth a positive attitude when she was with Alyssa. She opened the door and saw a nurse busy changing one of the IV bags that had dripped steadily twenty-four hours a day for four days. Then, using a port in Alyssa's other hand, she injected a dose of something Olivia assumed to be an antibiotic. When she'd taken her vitals, the nurse gently administered a sponge bath to Alyssa's face, hands, and uninjured leg and straightened her sheets.

Olivia watched her friend's face intently, which elicited a sympathetic smile from the nurse and an almost imperceptible shake of her head.

"Did she have a good night?" Olivia asked the same question every day, hoping to hear a more encouraging answer soon.

"I just came on duty, but I guess it was uneventful," the nurse said.

"Do you think it helps her for me to be here? I mean, do you think she even knows? Can she hear me when I talk to her? What can I do to help her? There has to be something I can do."

Olivia knew the nurse probably couldn't tell her any more today than she could yesterday, but she was desperately grasping at straws to find some semblance of hope.

"We don't know if she hears us or not, but it doesn't hurt to try. Personally, I believe that anything positive we can say or do, even if it's just to hold her hand or brush her hair, has to help somehow." The nurse put a hand on Olivia's arm. "Talk to her. Read to her. Remind her how much she has to live for. I understand you're very close to her. Maybe you're the one person who can bring her out of this."

"Yes, we are close. We've been best friends for as long as I can remember. Our mothers were friends before we were born. We've been through everything together. School, boyfriends, successes, failures, marriages. We were each other's maid of honor. We supported each other. I don't think two people could be any closer without being attached at the hip. Lissy and Livvy, that's us."

"Does she have any family? I haven't seen anyone else up here with her besides you."

"No. Both her parents were killed in a car accident twenty years ago. She was an only child. And she lost her husband and both of her boys the same way just about two years ago. I'm all she has left. She's like a sister to me. I can't let her go. Not yet."

"Oh, I'm sorry to hear she's had such a tough time of it. She's very fortunate to have you. You hang in there, and if there's anything we can do for you, please let me or one of the other nurses know. And I want you to know that she, and you, will be in my prayers. Don't give up. There's always hope."

"Thank you so much." Olivia was near to tears at the nurse's kind words. "I'm sorry. I've been up here for four days, and I don't even know your name," she said, as the nurse turned to leave the room.

"It's Angie." The nurse pointed to the dry-erase board on the wall.

"Oh, I hadn't even noticed that. Is Angie short for Angela?"

"Yes, it is. I'll be back later. Meantime, you take care," Angie said and walked away down the hall.

Angela, like an angel. The corners of Olivia's mouth turned up slightly.

She pulled the uncomfortable chair as close to the bed as she could get it and took Alyssa's right hand in both of her own, careful to avoid bumping the cast on her arm.

"Lissy, honey, it's Livvy. It's time for you to wake up now. You've been asleep long enough. It's time to open your eyes and come back to me." She patted Alyssa's hand and laid it on the sheet beside her. She stood and brushed a stray hair from Alyssa's face.

"You've always had such a time taming this mop of yours, haven't you? I remember you used to get so frustrated trying to get it to straighten out and lie flat. Then you decided to cut it all off once. Remember that disaster? Oh, it was funny! You looked like a porcupine with cork-screwy red quills sticking out all over your head. You almost killed me for telling you that at the time. I'd be thrilled to have you sit up in that bed right now and tell me off again. Come on, Lissy. Let's hear it. I just insulted your first haircut."

She watched Alyssa's face for any sign of a reaction but could see nothing there. Her eyes remained tightly closed, and her face was placid.

"Nothing? Okay, then how about this..."

She talked to Alyssa for a full hour. She didn't know if she heard anything but hoped she did. As long as her friend was alive and breathing on her own, she wouldn't let go of hope. When her throat started to ache and she was too hoarse to talk anymore, she stood by the window watching the traffic below a few minutes and then decided to get a breath of fresh air.

She walked out the hospital door and deeply inhaled the hint of spring in the crisp mountain air. Spring, when the air was fresh and full of promises...

* * * * *

The late afternoon sun poured through the window of Olivia's bedroom on this mid-April day.

Olivia and Alyssa were busy doing their hair and makeup and getting dressed before their dates picked them up for the senior prom.

"Oh, Lissy, you look gorgeous! Turn around for me so I can see the back."

Olivia watched as Alyssa spun around in her low-heeled soft green pumps to give her a look at the back of her gown. As she turned, the light caught the sequins that adorned the strapless pale green bodice and cascaded down the soft cream-colored skirt. They almost matched the shine in Alyssa's green eyes.

"It's perfect," Olivia said. "Now let's get your hair done."

Olivia picked up a brush and went to work on Alyssa's hair. She'd practiced on her several times, to be sure she could get it just right for prom night. She worked diligently for half an hour, brushing and separating locks of the lustrous, dark red hair with natural golden highlights. Little by little, she managed to get each lock piled on top of Alyssa's head until she had it exactly the way she wanted it. "Just a bit of hair spray, and voilà!"

Olivia gave Alyssa a hand mirror and turned her on the stool so she could see the back of her head. Alyssa declared that her new, glamorous hairdo was perfect. "It looks like I spent a fortune and a whole afternoon at the beauty parlor. Thank you so much!" Olivia accepted Alyssa's hug and told her she was gorgeous.

"Now, it's my turn," Olivia said. She let Alyssa take her by the shoulders and head her toward the closet. She reached in and took out the gown she'd chosen for the evening. It was a robin's egg blue satin with an empire waste, narrow ribbon straps, and slightly flared skirt trimmed with iridescent sequins that shimmered with every color of the rainbow when she moved.

She slipped it over her head, and Alyssa zipped up the back for her. Olivia stepped into the pair of silver heels she'd chosen and picked up the matching silver clutch purse. She turned to critique herself in the mirror.

"I guess I'll do," she said, "once I get my hair done." She'd opted to go with a much simpler style since her long blond hair was straight and easier to manage than Alyssa's naturally curly hair. She sat down at the vanity and pulled just the sides of her long mane back into a partial ponytail. Just a little curl on the ends with her curling iron and she'd achieved the look she wanted. She fastened it with a rhinestone-laden barrette in the shape of a butterfly. When she was done, she stood and turned so Alyssa could appraise her.

"What do you think?" she asked her friend, who assured her that she looked absolutely magical and would knock the socks off her date when he saw her.

"Really? You think I'm okay?" Olivia had never been as sure of her looks as a lot of the other, more popular girls seemed to be. She thought her face was too angular and her eyes were too far apart. Her mouth was wide, and her nose turned up slightly. All in all, she didn't think she had the classic good looks other girls had—the kind of looks that caused boys to turn their heads when they walked by.

"I think you're more than okay. You look beautiful. Just like Cinderella."

Olivia hooked her arm through Alyssa's elbow and said, "Let's go show our folks how stunning we both look." They giggled and together they went downstairs to model for their parents, who'd agreed to sit back and let the girls get ready on their own and surprise them.

When they glided into the living room where all four parents waited, both fathers wolf-whistled, and both mothers' hands flew to their cheeks in obvious delight at how their daughters looked.

"Well, what do you think?" Olivia looked at her parents for their approval. She rolled her eyes when her dad suggested she wear a good, durable sweater over her gown. He winked at her mom as he said it, a gesture not wasted on his daughter.

"Oh, Dad." Olivia kissed him on the cheek. "This dress doesn't call for durable."

"And you, young lady," Alyssa's dad said to his daughter. "What's holding that thing up? Maybe we should rig up something to make sure it stays up. What do you think?"

"Oh, Daddy, come on. What do you really think?" Alyssa said.

"I think both our little girls have grown up to be beautiful young women. I suppose it was inevitable."

The two girls listened to their fathers' back-and-forth banter about the dangers of having such gorgeous daughters, the money they'd spent on their dresses, and all the "doodads" to go with them, and whether they should let the girls, looking as they did, go out with the two teenaged boys.

Again, Olivia rolled her eyes at Alyssa, who reciprocated in kind. The two men went on a little longer until Olivia's mom, Anne, finally interrupted. "You two stop giving these girls a hard time."

"That's right," said Alyssa's mom, Janet. "Come on, let's get a few pictures of each of them before their dates get here. Then we'll get some with the boys quick before they have to leave."

After five or six pictures, Mike and Robbie showed up in tandem at the front door, each looking quite handsome in his tux and carrying beautiful corsages to adorn their dates' dresses.

Several pictures later, each accompanied by "oohs" and "aahs" and compliments for each couple, the four teens were out the door amidst choruses of "have fun, but behave" and "drive carefully."

They assured them they would and were off in Mike's dad's new BMW.

They arrived just in time for the grand march. The boys escorted their dates to the long tables set for dinner, which was served by members of the sophomore class. They chatted and laughed and enjoyed their meal. After dinner, the whole crowd moved to the other end of the gym, which had been decorated in the theme of "Starry, Starry Night" for the dance.

It was the most romantic night either Olivia or Alyssa had thus far experienced, and one neither of them would ever forget.

CHAPTER 4

Thursday, March 12, 2015
Afternoon

"You know, I'm getting a little tired of sitting here watching you sleep. The least you could do is wake up long enough to tell me to shut up. I've been going on for days now, talking myself blue in the face." Olivia sighed and gently lay Alyssa's hand down on the bed.

She looked up as the nurse who'd spoken with her the day before came in to check on Alyssa. "Hello, there. Remember me?"

"Of course. Angie, right? I want to thank you for what you said yesterday. You did give me hope. And I'm going to be here every day for as long as she needs me." Olivia nodded toward the pale woman lying on the bed, eyes closed tightly to the world.

Her attention shifted back to Angie when the nurse said, "You know, you asked me if I thought she could hear you? Well, I do. I think she knows you're here, and I think that's why she's hung on for as long as she has. It's been almost a full week now, hasn't it?"

"Yes," Olivia said. "She was hit on the seventh and this is the twelfth, isn't it? So yes, a week ago, day after tomorrow."

"Did they ever find the guy who hit her?" Angie straightened the bed covers around her patient and adjusted the pillow under her head.

"Not the last I heard," Olivia said. "You'd think a black Humvee with a huge dent in the front bumper wouldn't be that hard to find, but I guess there are more of them around than I thought. The one we want seems to have disappeared from the face of the earth."

"Well, they'll find him sooner or later. He'll have to get it fixed sometime."

"I sure hope so. And when they do find him, I'm hoping to have a few minutes alone with him. I want him to know who he hit—what she's like, what her dreams are, how she's struggled. And how she's managed to stay vibrant, caring, and loving to everyone she knows, in spite of what she's been through. And then, I want to hurt him and make him suffer, just like he's made her suffer."

"I'm sure you feel that way now," Angie said, "but don't let your anger eat you up and make you do things you'll regret later. Tell him about her, what kind of person she is. In the cold light of day, when he's stone sober, he'll know what he's done. And if he has any conscience at all, he'll suffer when he figures it out."

"I suppose you're right," Olivia said. "I just need to vent. I want to take all my frustration out on someone, and right now, I can't think of anyone better, whoever he is."

When Angie said she'd probably see her again the next day and left to tend to her other patients, Olivia turned back to Alyssa. She sat on the hard chair and reached for Alyssa's hand.

As she did, she thought she felt just the slightest twitch in Alyssa's thumb.

"Do that again, Lissy," she said. "Move your thumb again."

Nothing.

"Come on, I know you're in there. You can do it. Move your thumb for me, Lissy. Please?"

Another small movement. Olivia jumped out of the chair. "Good girl, Lissy! I knew you could do it!"

She ran to the door and looked up and down the hall. She didn't see Angie anywhere, so she ran back to Alyssa's bed and pushed the call button that hung over the rail.

An interminably long two minutes later, Angie came back into the room. "What is it? Can I get you something?"

"No. No, not for me. I felt it! I felt her thumb move! Watch!" Olivia picked up Alyssa's hand again and gently squeezed it. "Now, Lissy, do it again. Move your thumb just one more time for me, okay?"

She waited. At first nothing happened, and then, just as Angie opened her mouth to say something, Lissy's thumb moved back and forth over Olivia's finger.

"Did you see that? Her thumb moved. She did it!"

"Yes, I did," Angie said, "but don't get your hopes up too high, too soon. It's a good sign, but you can't expect too much yet." She told Olivia she'd be sure to alert the doctor and left her alone with Alyssa again.

It is a good sign. I knew she could do it. She's going to be okay. Olivia leaned back in her chair. Her eyes closed, her head dropped, and for the first time in days she slept soundly. Two hours later, she woke when another nurse came in to check Alyssa's vital signs. She rubbed her stiff neck and left the room to stretch her legs. When she came back, the nurse was gone, and the curtains had been closed against the sunshine.

Olivia went straight to the window. "Oh, no you don't." She pulled the drapes open.

"Lissy needs to feel that sunshine on her face, and she needs to see it when she opens her eyes."

Alyssa had told her that ever since she'd lost Rob and the boys, she'd felt like she needed the sunshine. She felt claustrophobic and depressed when she couldn't see the sky. She almost never closed the curtains at home during the day. Only in the evenings to keep people from peering in when the lights were on.

"That's better." Olivia smiled. "That's much better."

As she watched out the window, Olivia saw a procession of cars turn the corner a block away. The car in the lead had crepe paper streamers on the antenna and long strings of tin cans dangling from the rear bumper and bouncing noisily down the street…

* * * * *

Olivia's hands pressed gently on Alyssa's shoulders in an attempt to stop her nervous pacing. "Lissy, why are you fidgeting? You're about to walk down the aisle and marry the man of your dreams. I told you way back in high school that you two were meant for each other. All anyone had to do was look at the two of you together at prom. You've always been the perfect couple."

She took Alyssa's bouquet so she could adjust her bra strap. Then Alyssa went back to her pacing, stopping each time she passed the full-length mirror to inspect her hair or her face or her gown.

"Lissy, for heaven's sake, sit down! You're making me tired with your pacing. Why are you so nervous, anyway?"

"I'm not nervous about *being* married, I'm nervous about *getting* married. I'm so afraid I'm going to screw up and say the wrong thing, or break out in giggles, or worse yet, in tears. I want this day to be perfect, but I know something's going to go wrong."

"Don't be silly. This is your day, and it will be perfect. Just look at it so far." Olivia was right. The weather was beautiful. Blue skies, mild temperatures, no wind, no rain. The flowers were all delivered on time. The caterers were already set up in the reception hall. The band was set up for the reception following the ceremony.

"And you," she spread her arms toward her friend, "you look like an angel. Rob is going to think he died and went to heaven. Now, let's see. Do you have your something old, something new, something borrowed, and something blue?"

Olivia smiled as Alyssa held up her arm. The bracelet she'd given Alyssa for her sixteenth birthday was something old. Something new was her wedding gown, and something borrowed were the diamond earrings her mother had lent her for the occasion.

"The only thing I'm missing is something blue," Alyssa said.

"Did I hear you say you need something blue?" Alyssa's mom came into the room at that moment. "Do you think this will do?" She held out a beautiful baby blue handkerchief with exquisite lace trim around the edges. "Your dad gave me this when we were going together. I've kept it in my treasure box, waiting to give it to my daughter on her wedding day."

"Oh, Mom! It's beautiful! I'll use it for my something blue, but it will be borrowed, too. I couldn't take this away from you. It's yours from Daddy."

"But I want you to have it now, and your dad approves. So please take it, and maybe you'll have a daughter to pass it on to someday."

"Thank you, Mom. Now you'd better go before you make me cry. I don't want to have to start all over on my makeup." Alyssa hugged her mom carefully, so as not to crush her corsage.

Alyssa's mom left to be ushered to her seat in the sanctuary. Olivia patted an imaginary wrinkle out of Alyssa's gown and said, "Okay, I think we're set. Are you ready to become Mrs. Robert Walton?"

CHAPTER 5

Thursday, March 12, 2015
Evening

Olivia had no sooner arrived home from her long vigil at the hospital than her cell phone rang. She dug it out of her purse and pressed the call button to answer.

"Hello, this is Olivia." She stifled a yawn and tried to sound alert.

"Hello, Mrs. Clayton. This is Detective Sheldon from the Missoula Police Department. I just wanted to let you know we're still actively looking for the person who ran down your friend last weekend."

"You mean the drunk who ran her over and then took off?"

"Actually, there's some question as to whether or not that's accurate. We've talked to four eyewitnesses." He went on to explain that the witnesses said it didn't look to them as though the driver was drunk. They saw him driving slowly on the intersecting street before he turned the corner and jumped the curb. He seemed to be keeping a close eye out for something, as though he expected it to come around that corner. Then he suddenly floored the gas pedal, took the corner at breakneck speed, and left the scene as fast as he could after running down Alyssa.

"What?" Olivia's eyebrows arched and her jaw dropped. Suddenly she felt weak in the knees. She sat down hard onto the nearest chair. "Do you mean to tell me someone we don't even know deliberately tried to run over one or both of us? I find that awfully hard to believe. Why would anyone want to hurt—or worse—either one of us? Are you sure he wasn't after someone else, and we just got in the way?" She rubbed her free hand over her eyes and was aware that she was trembling.

"You said 'we.'"

"What?" Olivia didn't follow him.

"You said, 'someone *we* don't even know.' How do you know Mrs. Walton doesn't know him?"

"I guess I'm just assuming. Why would someone she knows try to kill her?" Olivia shook her head. "I don't know anyone who owns a Humvee. In fact, I don't know that many people around here at all. I haven't lived here very long. I suppose it's possible Alyssa knows who it is, but I can't imagine she wouldn't have told me about anyone who'd been threatening her. We tell each other everything, and she's never mentioned any enemies or any disagreements with anyone."

"Well, I wouldn't get too upset about it yet," Sheldon said. "We'll keep looking for that Humvee. It has to turn up sooner or later. And when it does, we'll get some answers."

"So you don't think I need to be worried?" Olivia said.

"No, I don't think so at this point. Of course, if you do notice anyone suspicious hanging around you or the hospital, please don't hesitate to call us immediately. Even though we can't positively say you're in any danger right now, we can't rule out the possibility either, and it's better to be safe than sorry." He paused for a moment and then asked, "How is Mrs. Walton doing? Has she come around or said anything at all?"

"No. She hasn't opened her eyes yet. But she did move her thumb three times, once on her own and twice when I asked her to do it again. I'm taking that as a positive sign. She'll wake up any day now. And if she has anything important to say, I'll be sure to let you know."

"Sounds good. I'll be expecting to hear from you then," Sheldon said.

"Thank you, Detective, for bringing me up to date. Oh, and by the way, it's Ms. Clayton now. My husband and I were divorced about six months ago."

"Oh, sorry. I don't remember your telling me that before."

"I probably didn't. I guess at the time I was more concerned for Alyssa, and I didn't think it was important. It doesn't matter, anyway. It doesn't have anything to do with what happened," she said. "Again, thanks for the update. We'll keep in touch."

Olivia hung up her phone and left it on the table while she went to pour herself a glass of wine. She picked up her phone on her way back to the living room. Kicking off her shoes, she tucked her legs under her as she sat down in the huge overstuffed chair across from the fireplace.

She put the phone down on the end table and took a long sip from her glass.

"Aah, that's good," she said to the empty room. "I needed this." She leaned her head against the pillowed back of the chair, closed her eyes, and let the stillness of the house envelope her. She thought about what Detective Sheldon had told her. It was a little unsettling, yes, but at the same time she just couldn't begin to imagine why anyone would want to harm Alyssa. Or her.

Maybe it was meant for me, and they got the wrong person. She shivered a little in her chair. Then she smiled to herself and shrugged off the terrible thought. There was no reason anyone would be after her like that. She was tired and stressed and letting her imagination run away with her. And she was almost as positive there couldn't be anyone after Alyssa either.

Except…Olivia again remembered how concerned Alyssa had seemed the few days before her "accident." And the strange man she'd run into on the job several days ago. *Why didn't I remember to tell Detective Sheldon about that? Well, I'll have to call him first thing in the morning.*

Reluctantly, Olivia rose from her comfortable chair and made her way back to the kitchen.

She checked the plants lining the wide windowsill over the sink. They were still moist from being watered four days ago. She'd have to remember to check them again in two or three days.

She dug through the refrigerator and debated what to have for supper. Something quick, easy, and tasty. Finally, she settled on a Reuben sandwich. She started to pull out the makings for it: dark rye bread, sauerkraut, Swiss cheese, thin-sliced corned beef, mayonnaise, and Dijon mustard. She put the bread in the toaster and drained the sauerkraut. She took a plate out of the cupboard and grabbed a knife from the drawer below it. Her toast popped up, and she started to build her sandwich. Finally, she heated it a bit in the microwave to melt the cheese and heat the sauerkraut. She added a few potato chips and a crispy dill pickle to her plate, poured a little more wine into her glass, and went back to the living room.

She settled once more into her big, comfy chair and picked up the TV remote. She surfed the channels, hoping to find something light and entertaining to watch. Finally, she opted for an old Dean Martin and Jerry Lewis movie. She took a big bite out of her sandwich. Oh, but it did feel good to be home.

CHAPTER 6

Friday, March 13, 2015

Olivia got up feeling refreshed. She'd slept soundly all night. She completed her morning routine and then left for the hospital. She took a detour on her way to check things at Alyssa's house again. The plants were still fine, having been thoroughly watered the last time she was there. The crocuses were beginning to poke their heads through the soil.

Wow, I almost forgot that spring is just around the corner. I'll have to remember to tell Lissy her flowers are coming up.

She checked the mailbox and found several items in it, three of which were catalogs.

There also were bills from a credit card company and the satellite TV service. She didn't see anything that looked suspicious. Certainly nothing that would cause Alyssa to be overly concerned.

What if I should run across something suspicious in Lissy's mail? It's against the law for me to open it. But what if she can't open it herself and it's something that could help? And what about email? Is that illegal, too?

Olivia wondered if she should bring it up to Detective Sheldon. Should they be snooping through Alyssa's personal business?

Of course we should, if it means figuring out what's going on. She could still be in danger.

But Olivia had never known Alyssa's passwords. She decided she'd definitely talk to Sheldon about it soon. There were people in the police department who had ways of figuring those things out.

The thought of talking to the detective again suddenly appealed to her. Olivia had met him only once in person, on the day Alyssa was injured. She remembered briefly thinking at the time that she wouldn't mind getting to know him a little better under different circumstances. He was tall and nicely built. Trim, but muscular. He had slightly wavy, dark brown hair with a few gold highlights and a little dusting of gray at the temples. His facial features were slightly chiseled, though not hard. And his piercing blue eyes gave her the impression they could look right into her mind and read her thoughts.

When she arrived at the hospital, Olivia happened to glance at the gift shop window.

There on the top shelf, right in front, was a cute little stuffed bear. It wore a forest ranger's uniform and held a sign that read, "Only YOU Can Prevent Frowny Faces (by getting better soon)!" It was kind of hokey, she knew, but it fit, considering that Alyssa had studied forestry and then became a forest ranger in the beautiful Rocky Mountains of western Montana. She went in, took it off the shelf in the window, and handed it to the volunteer behind the counter.

"He's cute, isn't he?" The woman, whose name tag read Gladys, smiled warmly at Olivia.

"Yes, he is. My friend is in the hospital, and she happens to be a forest ranger. I thought she'd get a kick out of this when she wakes up."

"Oh, is your friend the one I've heard about? That poor woman who was hit by one of those big Army-type vehicles? How is she doing, dear?" Gladys looked sympathetically at Olivia, as though she were the one who needed her compassion.

"I'm not really sure. I haven't made it up there to see her yet today. But she did wiggle her thumb yesterday. So I'm hopeful that she'll come out of it okay."

"I'm sure she will. I'll be praying for her," Gladys said.

Olivia murmured her thanks to Gladys and headed for the elevator. She pushed four and immediately felt herself being conveyed upward to where the Critical Care Unit was. She turned right as she disembarked from the elevator and followed the long hallway to Alyssa's room, 426, which was the last one at the end of the hall. Her steps were silent on the carpeted floor. The only sound she made was the soft whisper of the sleeves of her raincoat as her arms swung at her sides.

It would be simple for someone to sneak in here and not be seen or heard. He'd just have to make sure everyone was busy and be quick about it.

The idea chilled her when she thought about the possibility that Alyssa's "accident" hadn't been that at all, but a deliberate attempt on her life.

I definitely need to talk to Detective Sheldon.

When she came to Alyssa's room, she tapped softly on the partially opened door in case the nurses were busy working with their patient. No one answered, so she pushed the door farther open and went in. Everything looked pretty much the same as it had the day before, except the nurse's name on the dry erase board had been changed from Angela to Ellen. Hadn't Angie said she'd see her today? Olivia guessed she must be working a later shift.

She went to the corner and retrieved the chair for which she'd almost developed a healthy hatred. She pulled it over beside the bed and reached for her friend's hand.

"Hey, you. How ya doing this morning? I thought you'd be sitting up in bed demanding a steak dinner and pecan pie by now. Tell you what, though. As soon as you get out of here and are up to it, that's exactly what you're going to get. It'll be all your favorites—a big, thick steak with onions and mushroom gravy, twice-baked potato, garlicky asparagus, and pecan pie for dessert, with whipped cream, of course. All made by the best chef you know—me!"

She remembered the gift she'd picked up and was still holding in her left hand. She held it up in front of Alyssa. "If you'd open your eyes right now, you'd see this cute little guy who came to visit you and tell you to get better. Please, Lissy. Please open your eyes for me. I need to know you'll be okay." Olivia's voice broke on a sob, and she quickly turned away.

It took her a moment to regain her composure. Then she turned back to face Alyssa again. "I've stopped by your place a couple times to check on things. I watered your plants and brought in your mail. I phoned the utility company and explained your situation, so they're okay with not getting paid right away. And I'll call about your credit card and TV service. So you see, you don't have to worry about anything but getting better."

Olivia sat back down and watched Alyssa's face. She was hoping to see her eyes open or even a slight movement under her eyelids. She picked up her hand again. "Alyssa, can you move your thumb for me again like you did yesterday? Or squeeze my hand? Anything, Lissy. I'll take anything. Open your eyes, and tell me to shut up and let you sleep in peace. Just, please, snap out of this, Lissy."

"You keep talking to her that way, she's likely to do just that." A short, buxom nurse bustled into the room. "You must be Olivia. Angie filled me in on you. I'm Ellen. I'll be here until the two o'clock shift change. Then Angie'll be back."

She hustled over and started to take Alyssa's vital signs. "All her vitals are very good today, and she's still breathing on her own. All good things. Have you talked to the doctor?"

"Not for a couple days," Olivia said. "Why? Is there something new?"

Olivia listened carefully as Ellen filled her in on what the doctor had said. The swelling on her brain had gone down some. He'd ordered a CT scan, plus x-rays on both arms to be sure those broken bones were healing the way they should. He also had said that if Alyssa continued to hold her own, and the swelling kept going down, he hoped to send her to surgery in a few days to repair her shattered pelvis. It was too risky to try to do it while she was comatose.

"I hadn't even been thinking about that, I guess," Olivia said. "I've been so worried about her not waking up from the coma, I guess I forgot about her other injuries. But what you're telling me sounds good, doesn't it? I mean, the swelling going down and all? That means she's going to come out of it and be okay, right?"

"It means she has a better chance of it," Ellen said. "There's always hope. Never let go of that," she told Olivia.

"That's the same thing Angie told me yesterday. Just keep telling me, please. I need to hear it."

When Ellen finished smoothing Alyssa's sheets and checking her IV bag, she gave Olivia's arm a squeeze. "You're a good friend. You hang in there, okay?"

"Thank you," Olivia said. "I will."

Just that small bit of good news lifted Olivia's spirits considerably. Enough, in fact, that she felt she could leave Alyssa's side long enough to go down to the cafeteria and treat herself to one of their famous eclairs and a cup of coffee. She grabbed her purse, patted Alyssa's hand, and told her she'd be back before Alyssa knew she'd been gone. Then she left the room and headed for the elevator.

As she walked down the hall, she wasn't paying much attention to the people around her.

She'd learned that visitors and patients, alike, tended to prefer anonymity, so she tried to avoid eye contact. She started to scoot around an empty gurney that had been left against the wall and bumped into someone she hadn't noticed.

"Oh, I'm sorry. Excuse me," she said.

The man just grunted something and brushed past her. Olivia watched as he continued down the hall. *How rude.* The very next moment, she was horrified to see him turn into Alyssa's room. *He doesn't belong in there!*

"Wait! Stop! Someone stop that man! He's not supposed to be in there! Stop him!" She ran toward Alyssa's room, not waiting to see if anyone had heard her. She burst into the room just in time to see him tampering with Alyssa's IV.

"No!" She flew at the man, who was so startled he almost lost his footing. But before she could stop him, he regained his balance and was on his way out the door. Ellen, who'd heard Olivia's shouts, ran into the room. He shoved her hard, and she hit the wall behind her while trying to grab his arm at the same time. He jerked his arm away and sprinted for the emergency exit door.

"Call security!" Ellen yelled back to the nurses' station. "There's a man heading for the emergency exit on fourth floor west."

"Ellen, he's done something to Alyssa's IV!" Olivia said. "You've got to stop it now. I saw him doing something to it. I don't know if he put something in it or what, but stop it. Now!"

Ellen immediately shut down the IV. She disconnected the port in in Alyssa's hand, removed the bag from its hook, and set it on the table beside the bed.

"I'll give this to the lab for testing. If he put something in it, we'll know soon enough, and we'll give the results to the police. Meantime, I'll go get another bag. Will you stay here and keep an eye on her for a few minutes?"

"Of course," Olivia said. "Wild horses couldn't drag me out of here now."

Ellen rushed off to get another IV bag. Olivia, shaking down to her boots, sank into the chair, fighting to control her trembling hands.

"Oh, Lissy. Who was that? I wish you'd wake up and tell me what's going on."

As soon as Ellen got back, she was going to call Detective Sheldon. This had to be dealt with by someone much more capable than she was. She sat on the edge of the hard chair and tried to calm her nerves.

Ellen returned with the new IV. Before she hooked it up, she took a blood sample. Then she checked Alyssa's vitals, hooked up the IV, and told Olivia all seemed to be well. "I'll tell you what the blood tests show as soon as we get the results."

Fifteen minutes later, Detective Sheldon and Olivia stood outside Alyssa's room while Olivia told him exactly what had happened.

He shook his head and said, "Hospital security never even got a glimpse of the guy. Can you give me a description of him?"

"Not much of one, I'm afraid. He was wearing a dark hooded sweatshirt. He kept his hood pulled forward and his face down, so I really couldn't see it. Other than that, he looked pretty ordinary. Blue jeans, cowboy boots. I'm pretty sure he was white. But that's about it."

"Was he tall or short? Heavy or thin? Did he say anything at all?"

"No. He just kind of grunted when I slammed into him. He was average height—maybe around five-ten or so, and not heavy, but not thin either. Maybe around a 175 pounds. Oh, and there was a tattoo on the back of his right hand. And he smelled of wood smoke. I'm sorry I can't tell you anything else. It all happened so fast."

"You're doing fine, Ms. Clayton. Everything you can tell us will help." Sheldon patted her shoulder, guiding her back into Alyssa's room at the same time. "I'm going to have a man posted outside her room at all times. For now, only hospital personnel, you, and I will be admitted. Would you feel better if I had someone watching your place, as well?"

Olivia thought for a moment before replying. "No, I don't think it's necessary. I honestly can't think of any reason someone would be after me."

"Well, if you change your mind, be sure to let me know. After all, you couldn't think of any reason someone would be after Mrs. Walton either," the detective said.

"Oh! That reminds me. I wanted to tell you something she told me just before she was hurt." Olivia repeated what Alyssa had told her about meeting the stranger and thinking his story sounded odd. "The guy told Alyssa that he and some of his buddies were on vacation, and they were staying in a cabin near where she ran into him."

"Vacation in March in Montana?"

"That's why she thought it sounded funny. He told her they'd been laid off from their jobs and were out here for some R and R. But I got the feeling Alyssa wasn't buying his story," Olivia said.

"What did she do about it?"

"Well, nothing, really." Olivia told him what Alyssa had told her about the surveillance camera she'd mounted and the boot tracks she'd found under it a few days later. She mentioned the five men Alyssa and Collin had seen on the playback, and the fact that the men seemed quite interested in the camera, but that, in spite of their interest, they managed to keep their faces hidden. "Since they had no reason to doubt the guy's story, they decided to leave them alone, report it, and keep an eye open for trouble, or anything else that looked suspicious."

"Do you know the name of the ranger who was with Mrs. Walton that day?"

"Hmm...Let me think. I'm sure she mentioned it to me. Was it Colton or Colby or...No, it was Collin. That's it, Collin. I think she's mentioned working with him a few times before. She said they got along pretty well together. Before, of course, she was always partnered with Rob, her husband, who was a ranger, too. So it was a double blow to her when Rob was killed. She not only lost her husband, she lost her trusted partner of many years, too."

"Must have been really hard on her," Sheldon said. "Well, I think I'd better get moving. I'll want to talk to Collin. You don't happen to know his last name, do you?"

"No, I'm sorry. I don't think Alyssa ever mentioned it. But I know she was working from Ranger Station Four, so I'll bet you could go there and find him." She paused for a moment and then said, "I'm sorry I didn't tell you this sooner. I guess I haven't been thinking straight since all this happened. Anyway, can you look into it? I thought maybe you'd be able to check her phone and email messages, too. Maybe Collin was able to get some information on the guys on the video. I didn't think I should go snooping, and besides, I don't have the slightest idea how to hack someone's email. But you can get into them somehow, can't you?"

"We have a couple people in the department who can. In the meantime, I can check things out with her superiors and see if she mentioned any kind of trouble to them. Thanks for filling me in on this, Ms. Clayton. I'll get on it right away."

"You're welcome. And again, I'm sorry I didn't think to tell you sooner. Oh, and please, call me Olivia or Livvy. Ms. Clayton sounds so stiff, and since we're going to be seeing a bit of each other, I think we can be a little less formal, can't we?"

"Okay, Livvy. And you can call me Shel."

A chuckle escaped Olivia's lips. "Shel Sheldon?" She apologized for laughing at his name, and her cheeks and ears flushed bright red.

"Shel's a nickname. You know, short for Sheldon. I never use my first name."

"Why not?"

"Let's just say my parents had a warped sense of humor and let it go at that."

They spoke for a few more minutes, and then Shel said he needed to get back to the station to get the ball rolling on their search for the intruder.

"You take care, and try to get some rest yourself," he said.

"I will," she said. "In fact, I'm thinking of asking the nurse for a cot so I can be here all the time." She hated to admit it, but she was feeling a little apprehensive about going to her empty house alone after what had happened here today. She'd feel much safer here with a policeman standing guard right outside the door.

"I'll stay in touch," Shel said. "And remember, if you think of anything else…"

"I'll let you know," Olivia said. "And, yes, I definitely will stay here tonight. I don't want her to be alone."

Shel thanked her again for filling him in about things, cautioned her to be careful, and left for the police station.

Olivia looked down at the still, pale woman in the bed. "You're not alone, Lissy, I'm here."

* * * * *

Olivia held Alyssa's hand as another contraction contorted her face. She knew Alyssa was upset that Rob wasn't there with her. They'd taken the Lamaze classes together so that he could be with her when their first baby was born. But now it seemed Rob was nowhere to be found.

"You're not alone, Lissy. I'm here. I'm sure Rob will be here soon, too. Just keep breathing and thinking about what this is all for. I'll stay with you until he comes or they kick me out."

"I know, and I'm so glad, Livvy. If Rob can't be here, I wouldn't want it to be anyone but you. I'm so glad you were able to make the trip. Oh, I wish this were over right now!"

"It'll be over soon, Lissy. Just hang in there." Olivia knew that what Alyssa had really wanted to say was she wished her mom could be here instead, but both her mom and dad had died in a terrible car accident four months earlier. They would never get to see their first grandchild.

"Well, how's the mom-to-be doing?" A cheerful young nurse practically danced into Alyssa's room.

After checking her patient, she said, "Guess what? I think it's time to have a baby!" She pushed the call button hung on the bed rail, and in a few moments, there were two nurse's aides there ready to help. They put the side rails up, told Olivia she could follow them as far as the maternity waiting room, and wheeled Alyssa out of the room and down the hall.

"Wait! What about Rob?" Alyssa clutched at Olivia's arm.

"I'll let him know just as soon as he gets here." Olivia extracted her arm from Alyssa's grip. "You just concentrate on having that baby. We'll both be here waiting for you when you come back."

"I guess...I don't...have any...choice." Alyssa panted and blew, panted and blew.

"Nope," said the nurse. "The doctor's waiting for us, and that baby isn't waiting for anyone." She told Olivia she'd let her know as soon as the new little Walton had arrived. Ten minutes later, a harried Rob rushed into the waiting room. "Where is she?"

"They took her in about ten minutes ago. Where were you? We tried calling several times and couldn't get through."

"I had to deal with a group of angry campers who didn't think they had to pay attention to the 'No Fires' signs," he said. "I thought it was going to get ugly there for a while, but they finally gave in, packed up, and left. Too bad they had to cut their stay short when a simple camp stove could've solved the whole problem."

The fire index had been so high with the dry weather Montana had been suffering that a single stray spark could put the whole forest in flames.

Rob and Alyssa's wedding took place two weeks after their college graduation. They both applied for, and acquired, jobs that took them to western Montana. They fell in love with the area and made it their permanent home. They both were determined to do their part to keep the environment and the people who enjoyed it safe.

Now, still flushed from his mad rush to get to the hospital, Rob said, "Anyway, I'm here now, and I suppose I'm too late."

Olivia told him Alyssa had asked for him, but that their baby wasn't going to wait for its daddy to show up. "It probably won't be much longer now," she said.

Another ten minutes later, the nurse came into the waiting room with a little blue-blanketed bundle in her arms. She looked at Rob and said, "Are you the proud papa of this Baby Boy Walton?"

When Rob, who was temporarily speechless, nodded his head, she gently lay the baby in his outstretched arms. "A boy? I have a son?" His face was all smiles.

"You sure do," the nurse said. "As of 3:25 p.m. on August 4, 1995. He's a handsome little guy, too."

"What about Alyssa? Is she okay? Can I see her?"

"Sure. Come on. I'll take you to her room. It'll be a few minutes before they get her in there, but we can get you three comfortable while you're waiting. Meantime, you can get acquainted with this little guy."

She led them back to Alyssa's room and brought in an extra chair.

"Do you want me to leave, Rob?" Olivia didn't want to horn in on Alyssa and Rob's first time together with their newborn son.

"No way. Alyssa would skin me alive me if you did. Here, do you want to hold him?"

"I'd love to, if you don't mind," she said. She took the baby from Rob's arms and smiled at the sweet little face, which was, she thought, a spitting image of Rob's. "Oh, he's beautiful. I think he looks just like you, Rob."

"Really? You think so?" Rob beamed from ear to ear.

A few minutes later, Alyssa was wheeled into the room, tired, but radiant. She smiled at them and then turned her gaze to the baby in Olivia's arms.

"Hi, honey," Rob said. He rose and went to kiss and hold his wife. "Did you see him? We have a beautiful baby boy."

"Boys aren't beautiful, they're handsome," Alyssa said. "Jeremy Robert Walton. Sounds pretty good, doesn't it? And, no." Her voice was firm. "We will not call him JR for short. By the way, where were you? We tried to call you several times."

He apologized for not being there when she needed him and explained what had happened. She nodded her head in understanding and said, "I'll forgive you this time, but don't let it happen again." She winked at Olivia and flashed a smile toward her husband.

Olivia stood up and took the baby to his mother. "Here, Mama, I think he wants you," she said, though the sleeping infant couldn't have cared less at that moment. Alyssa reached out and took her son. She snuggled him up against her.

Twenty-five months later, on Wednesday, September 17, 1997, they did it all again, and another Baby Boy Walton joined the family. This time Rob was there, as well as Olivia. They named the new arrival Oliver, the closest Alyssa could come to Olivia for a boy, which thrilled Olivia. His middle name was Jackson, after Alyssa's father.

Despite the women's best-laid plans to both get married, have two kids, and raise them side by side, Olivia and her husband, Kyle, had never been able to have children. Kyle blamed Olivia, though the doctors could find no reason Olivia shouldn't be able to get pregnant, and eventually, the stress had led to a separation and, finally, divorce. To compensate, Olivia dubbed herself "Aunt Livvy" and doted on Alyssa and Rob's boys. Alyssa and Rob named her the boys' godmother and guardian, and she stayed involved with their active lives as much as she could.

The career aspect of Olivia's life hadn't gone as she'd dreamed it would either. She'd decided she wouldn't be able to handle working with sick or injured people, especially children, and opted for a different career altogether. She double-majored in American literature and creative writing in college and got a job as a junior editor for a magazine in Omaha right after she graduated.

Kyle had taken a position as plant manager for a major x-ray film manufacturer in Oregon soon after they were married, so they relocated there. After the divorce, Olivia hadn't wanted to stay in Oregon alone, so she applied for, and was awarded, a job as senior editor for a well-known book publishing company. The best thing about it was that she could live wherever she wanted and, with the miracle of computers, work from home. Since Alyssa already lived in Montana, Olivia decided to pick up and move there. Once again, she and Alyssa were close, not just in spirit, but also in proximity.

CHAPTER 7

Saturday, March 14, 2015

The morning had dawned sunny and calm. Above-normal temperatures were predicted for the next few days. The fresh mountain air lifted Olivia's spirits. She inhaled the odor of the pine trees in the park across the street from the hospital. After spending the night on a cot, she needed to get the kinks out of her aching back. She also needed a shower and a fresh change of clothes. The night had been uneventful, and Officer John James assured her that he wouldn't leave his post by Alyssa's door until his replacement arrived.

Thus reassured, Olivia headed for home. On the way, she stopped by a favorite pastry shop and picked out a variety of fresh-baked goodies to take back to the hospital with her. The hardworking nurses and diligent police officers deserved a treat.

At home, she put a fresh pot of coffee on to brew while she was in the shower. She let the hot water flow over her and gradually felt her muscles relax. After toweling off and blow-drying her hair, she pulled on a pair of clean jeans, a comfortable cotton sweater, and throwing convention to the wind, her white canvas shoes.

Who cares if it's not Memorial Day yet? It's almost spring, it's warm outside, and these shoes are comfy. Besides, does anyone really follow that no-white-shoes-until-Memorial-Day rule anymore?

She went to the kitchen and sat down with the morning paper, a cream-filled croissant, and a cup of hot coffee. It felt good to sit at her own table in the peace and quiet. She skimmed the headlines and the top stories and then turned to the crossword puzzle. After finishing that, she pushed the paper aside and wondered what today would bring.

Maybe I should start thinking about getting a little work done today.

Her boss, at the publisher's home office in New York City, had been apprised of the situation with Alyssa and had agreed that Olivia could take a few weeks off to be with her if she needed to. But now, after only a week, Olivia felt the pressure of deadlines pushing in on her. She decided to take some work with her to the hospital. She was starting to run out of things to talk about to Alyssa anyway.

She picked up her laptop and gathered the typewritten pages stacked on her desk. She put them in her briefcase, poured herself another cup of coffee in a spill-proof mug, and was ready to go. She left her house after making sure all the lights were off and the doors and windows were closed and locked. Usually she didn't worry about the windows so much, but now she felt the need to be a little more cautious.

She didn't think it was necessary to stop by Alyssa's since she'd done it the day before. She headed straight for the hospital. Gratefully, she pulled into a parking place that was close to the front entrance, and juggling her purse, briefcase, box of pastries, and coffee, she made her way inside and to the elevator. Luckily, there was someone already waiting for it who was happy to push four for her. She leaned against the wall of the elevator cab and mentally prepared herself for whatever would happen today.

When she stopped by the nurses' station, Olivia found both Angie and Ellen behind the desk, along with two other nurses she didn't know. "I brought you a treat," she said. "And if you have a small plate or napkin, I can take a couple to the officer at Alyssa's door."

She waited while Ellen went to the break room and came back with two small plates, a few napkins, and a cup of hot coffee. "I thought maybe Officer James would like some coffee to go with his. That poor man has been on his feet the whole night long."

"Is there any reason he can't sit down?"

"I offered to get him a chair," Ellen said, "but he turned it down. Said if he sat, he'd probably doze off, so he preferred to stand. His replacement should be here within a half hour. Maybe you should take some donuts for him, too." She added a couple more to the plate, put everything on a tray, and handed it to Olivia. "Thanks so much for this," she said. "It's nice to be appreciated."

"I really do appreciate you. All of you. You work hard, and you care about the people you're tending to, as well as for those who have to sit and wait. You give me hope, and that's what I need right now."

"You hang on to that hope, Olivia, and never let it go."

"I won't." Olivia promised to let them know if she needed anything and turned toward Alyssa's room.

When she reached it, she offered the plate of pastries to Officer James. "There are a couple here for your replacement, too," she told him. "I just want you to know how much I appreciate what you're doing. It means a lot to me."

The officer thanked her and said his replacement, Officer Evan Kendall, would be there soon. He assured her he was a good cop, and that she and Alyssa would both be safe with him standing guard.

Olivia thanked him and went into the room where Alyssa still lay in the same position with the monitors beeping away steadily. She put her briefcase, purse, and coffee on the small table in the corner. Then she went to the window and opened the curtains. It was a shame, she thought, that the window couldn't be opened. It would be so nice for Alyssa to be able to feel and smell the fresh spring air.

Before she sat down to work, she went to Alyssa's side. She picked up her hand, surprised to feel a warmth in it that hadn't been there before.

"Good morning, sunshine," she said. "And how is the patient today?

It's a glorious spring day outside. The sun is shining, the air is warm, and your crocuses are coming up. The pine trees in the park smell wonderful. I wish you could smell them. If you open your eyes, you can see how blue the sky is. And then, before you know it, we'll have you up and out of that bed and into a chair by the window, so you can watch the city below. Oh, Lissy, you don't want to miss all of this. This is life, and you love life.

"Let's try something different today. Let's see if you can give me a little smile. You don't have to work too hard to do that. Just lift the corners of your mouth a tiny bit for me. You have the most beautiful smile I've ever seen." She watched. Five seconds. Ten seconds. Then, to her delight and amazement, Alyssa's mouth turned up a bit at the corners.

"Yes! Lissy, you did it! I knew you were in there. Now we have to work harder to bring the rest of you back. Don't go anywhere. I have to get a nurse. You be ready to show her what you just did, okay?"

Olivia could barely contain her excitement. She ran down to the nurses' station. Angie and Ellen both looked up from the charts they'd been updating to see Olivia's smiling, hopeful face.

"She did it! I asked her to smile for me, just a little bit, and she did it! You have to come see this." She couldn't wait for them to come out from behind the desk. She took off back toward Alyssa's room. Ten seconds later, both nurses caught up to her there.

"Okay, Lissy, they're here. Angie and Ellen want to see that beautiful smile of yours. Can you do it for us one more time?"

They all watched. They could tell she was trying. It took some effort, but after a few moments, Alyssa managed another small smile.

Olivia beamed at Angie and Ellen. She felt as proud as she thought a mother must feel when her baby took her first steps. The two nurses smiled back at her, and Ellen told her that her encouragement was the best medicine Alyssa could have.

Angie spoke to Alyssa. She told her that Olivia had been with her day and night, talking to her and holding her hand. She said, "We've all been waiting for you to wake up and open your eyes. You just hang in there, listen to her, and we'll do all the rest with you, okay? We have the medicine. You have to have the will."

"You're not alone, Lissy," Olivia said. "The doctors and nurses are taking good care of you, and I'll be here for you for as long as you need me to be. And once you're better, and I know you're going to be okay, I'm going after the guy who did this to you. I'll find him, and he'll pay for this."

As she looked down at her friend's face, Olivia thought she saw Alyssa's lips move. Was she trying to say something? "What, Lissy? What are you trying to tell me?"

"St-stay 'way," came the hoarse whisper. "St-stay a-way."

"Stay away? Fat chance, Lissy. I'm here for you, and I always will be. Now you need to rest a bit. I'm going to be right over there in the corner doing a little work. Now that I know you're on your way back, I have some deadlines to meet. I'll check on you every so often. Oh, it's so good to know you're coming back to us!" She squeezed her hand and gently laid it back on the bed.

Angie and Ellen both smiled at Olivia. Every once in a while, they saw miracles—or near miracles, anyway—at their jobs. This was one of them. Or it might just have been the power of love and friendship. Either way, it was the reason they did the job they did. They checked Alyssa's IV and smoothed her sheets before they left the room.

Olivia sat down at the table, put her head in her hands, and sobbed. But they were tears of joy, relief, and pure exhaustion that she cried, not tears of grief. She let herself feel it for a while and then went to the sink and splashed some cool water on her face. Alyssa was going to be okay. She was going to be okay!

An hour later, Olivia shoved aside her laptop and put the manuscript she'd been working on back in her briefcase. The story she was reading was mediocre at best. It was more suitable for a paperback romance novel than a high-quality hardcover book. One of those dime a dozen stories: girl meets boy, they fall in love, have some kind of a crisis and fall out of love, discover they can't live without each other, make up, and live happily ever after. She'd decided about a fourth of the way into it that she could not, in all good conscience, recommend their company publish this book.

She felt sorry for the author because obviously, she'd worked hard to put her thoughts into words, and Olivia knew firsthand how difficult it was to become a published author. She'd written a few books for children herself, and she'd had to force herself to ignore the scores of rejection slips she'd received before someone finally agreed to publish them. She decided she'd write a short personal note to this unlucky aspiring author and offer some encouragement, and maybe a little bit of advice, even though it wasn't really part of her job.

For now, though, she put work aside and stood up. She glanced out the window just in time to see Detective Sheldon getting out of a gray midsize sedan. She thought she saw something odd in the front window and then realized it was the red dome-shaped beacon light he used when in pursuit or on his way to the scene of an accident or crime. She wondered if cops really slapped them onto the tops of their cars the way they always did on TV, or if they just kept them on the dashboard. *Maybe I'll have to ask him.*

When he came in and spoke to Olivia, however, she forgot all about the red light. "Good morning, Ms. Clayton," he said. "Actually, I guess it's afternoon."

"Remember, it's Livvy," she said. "What are you doing here? Did you find him?"

"Sorry, not yet. We will, though. He can't hide forever. No, I'm on my lunch break and thought I'd stop up and see how she was doing. Any change yet?"

"As a matter of fact, there has been a change, just this morning. First, she smiled for me, and then we got her to do it again for Ellen and Angie. And—you won't believe this—she tried to tell me something. It sounded like she said, 'stay away,' but I don't think that's what she said, because I can't imagine why she'd want me to stay away. Whatever it was, I'm taking it as a promising sign. I honestly believe she's going to come through this and be a hundred percent back to her old self in no time."

Olivia suddenly realized she'd been rambling. "I'm sorry. I didn't mean to go on so much. It was such a relief to finally get something from her, I guess I needed to tell someone."

"Don't apologize. You've had a rough week or so. You've been a real trooper coming here day after day, talking to her and encouraging her. You've kept a lot bottled up inside for a long time. It's about time you let some of it out." He gave her a sympathetic smile and said, "Actually, I came here with an ulterior motive. I was hoping I could talk you into having lunch with me."

"I suppose since there's an officer outside her door I could go down to the cafeteria for a little while," she said.

"Actually, I was thinking of getting you out of here. There's a little café not too far from here. Not much for atmosphere, but they serve the best fresh-caught trout you'll ever have at a restaurant. And as you said, my officer is right outside her door. Nothing is going to happen while you're gone."

"Okay, you talked me into it," Olivia said. "Just let me get my purse." She picked up her purse and stopped by Alyssa's bed. "I won't be gone long, Lissy. I'm just going to get a bite of lunch, and be right back. Maybe when I get back, we can have a little chat."

"Ready?" Shel took Olivia's elbow to guide her out of the room.

When they got outside, Olivia stopped on the sidewalk for a moment.

"Something wrong?"

"No, I just wanted to take in the day for a minute. The sunshine feels so good. Do you smell those pine trees? I've been sitting in that room for so long, I'd almost forgotten that spring is almost here. It feels good." She smiled at him and said, "Let's go. All of a sudden I have a craving for fresh-caught trout."

"I'm parked over there." He pointed to the right, and she saw the gray sedan just five or six cars down from where she'd parked hers.

He opened the passenger door for her, and she got in.

"This is the first time I've ever ridden in a police car," she said.

"Just be glad you're in the front seat and not the back."

"So tell me. If you were in pursuit of someone, would you take this red light and slap it onto the roof of your car like they do on TV? I always wondered how they did that and managed to keep their eyes on the road and on the bad guys all at the same time."

"Actually, we used to do that, but now most of us just keep it on the dashboard. It's still visible, and it's safer not to be messing with it when we're driving at high speeds. Some cops still like to put it on the roof. Maybe they think it's more visible that way, but personally, I like leaving it right where it is."

"You must live a very interesting life. Always something different going on and new people to meet," she said.

"It can get pretty dull sometimes. Following lead after lead down dead-end roads. Having to read through volumes of reports and interviews. Sometimes I'm at the station all night, and I've been known to wear the same clothes for more than forty-eight hours at a stretch. And don't forget, a lot of the people I meet don't have characters of the highest caliber."

"I guess I hadn't thought of that," she said.

"Of course, there is the occasional exception." He smiled at her. "Once in a while, I get to meet an attractive woman with a tender heart and a brain. And when I do, I like to invite her to my favorite café for lunch."

Olivia didn't know quite how to respond to that, so she just sat quietly for a moment.

"Maybe I shouldn't have said that," Shel said.

"Oh, no. It's fine," she said. "I appreciate the compliment. It's just that right now I feel like all my thoughts and energy should be focused on Lissy."

"That's okay. We'll have time when things get back to normal for you," he said. "But you have to promise me that you'll let me call you then. I really would like to get to know you better."

"I'd be upset if you didn't call," she said, and she realized she meant it.

Shel pulled up in front of the café. A big painted sign in front read "FLYING EAGLE CAFÉ" and sported a wood carving of a bald eagle with its wings spread wide and a large trout in its mouth. Olivia started to open her car door, but Shel had already gotten out and come around to her side to open it for her. It had been so long since anyone had done that for her, she'd forgotten what it was like to have a man help her out of a car.

When they walked into the café, a petite waitress with glossy, pitch-black hair, glowing brown-red skin, and the high cheekbones of the native Americans that lived in the area waved familiarly at Shel.

"Your usual table is ready, Shel. I'll be over in a couple seconds to take your order."

"Thanks, Dawn," he said and led Olivia to the booth in the far-right corner.

They slid onto benches opposite each other. True to her word, Dawn was there almost immediately with her order pad and pencil in hand.

"We're going to have the trout special," Shel said. "I'll have hash browns and coleslaw with mine. Livvy, what would you like?"

"That sounds good to me, too," she said.

"Wow! A woman who will eat hash browns with me. You're not afraid of the calories? Not that you need to be," he hastened to add.

"Oh, I'll probably regret it tomorrow when I can't fasten my jeans, but every once in a while, you know, you just have to give in to temptation and treat yourself. I love hash browns, and I haven't had them for ages."

They were quiet for a few minutes while Dawn busily set down glasses of cold water with crushed ice tinkling against the glass and silverware wrapped in a paper napkin.

"Coffee for either of you?" she asked.

"Please," Olivia and Shel answered at the same time.

"Cream or sugar?"

"No, thanks, just black," they again both said simultaneously. They looked at each other and started laughing. To her embarrassment, once she started, Olivia couldn't stop.

"Oh, please. Make me stop! I don't know why that struck me as so funny. People must think I'm on the edge of hysterics. I guess you're right. I have been keeping things bottled up inside me for too long." She let out one last little giggle and then looked away from Shel, afraid that if she looked at him, she'd burst out laughing again.

"No, it's great to hear you laugh. You haven't had much to laugh about for a while. It's nice to see you loosen up a bit."

They talked a little about the weather and the high school track team. When their meals came, they stopped talking and dug into their food.

"Mm! You were right. This is absolutely the best trout I've ever eaten. They must do pretty good business if all their food is this good. I'm surprised they don't have a bigger place."

Shel explained that the Flying Eagle was a family-owned business that had been there for three generations. The family preferred to keep it smaller and maintain the atmosphere of a well-known, comfortable establishment that flourished on its reputation for its friendliness, as well as its food. Dawn's family lived comfortably enough, and they had a faithful group of customers who'd been coming there for years.

"Dawn's full name is Dawn Sky Flies with Eagles, by the way. My grandpa was friends with Dawn's grandpa, and my dad was friends with her dad. Most of their family lives on the reservation near here, but Dawn's immediate family moved into town several years ago. It was easier for them to live in town since their business is here."

"Dawn Sky. What a pretty name." Olivia took another bite. "What reservation is it?"

"The Flathead reservation. It's a consolidation of the Salish and Kootenai tribes."

"I've always loved learning about Native American culture," Olivia said. "I love their music and their dances. And I love their relationship to the earth and the sky and the water. I think if all of us lived with the same respect that most Native Americans have for those things and for other living beings, the world would be a far better place."

"I tend to agree with you there," Shel said. "Oh, there are some problems with them, but there are problems with the white people, too. And blacks, Mexicans, and Asians. No race or ethnic group is without its problems."

"That's so true," Olivia said. "Well, anyway," she said, moving the subject back to a less serious topic, "they can add another faithful customer to their list now. I can't believe I've never heard of this place, as good as it is. Thank you for introducing me to it." Olivia took another bite of the delicious meal. "I was hungrier than I thought I was," she said. "The hospital cafeteria food isn't bad, but it doesn't compare to this."

They finished their meals, and Dawn came over to see if they wanted dessert.

"I really couldn't eat another bite," Olivia said. "I'm stuffed! But it was delicious, and I will be back. And I'll be bringing a friend with me, too, just as soon as she's able to get around on her own again."

Shel paid for the meal, and Olivia insisted on leaving a tip for Dawn. They left the café, and Shel suggested a walk to counteract the huge meal they'd just consumed. Olivia consented but said it would have to be a short one. She didn't want to be away from the hospital much longer. They walked a few blocks, looking in store windows and just enjoying each other's company.

"There's something I thought of that I meant to ask you," Olivia said. "There must be security cameras in the hospital. Did any of them pick up the guy that was in Alyssa's room? I'm sure you probably already thought of it, but I was just wondering."

Shel told her the police had checked them, but because the intruder had kept his hood pulled up and over his face as far as he could get it, and kept his head down, the cameras were no help to them this time. The cameras in the parking ramps hadn't caught anything either. The man evidently hadn't left a vehicle in there. He'd either walked or parked far enough away from the hospital that he wouldn't be noticed. "I'm pretty sure he wouldn't be driving that Humvee around here either. So we have no idea what kind of vehicle we're looking for." Shel looked frustrated, and Olivia felt a bit sorry for him. His was not an easy job.

They walked back to his car, and he drove her to the hospital.

"Thanks for lunch and for the company, too. I've been talking so much the last several days with no one talking back to me most of the time, that I'm getting tired of hearing my own voice. I think I've come close to losing it a few times. My mind, I mean, not my voice."

"You're very welcome. And thank you for joining me. Lunch is much better when you share it with a beautiful woman. Now, go see Alyssa. But remember to take care of yourself, too. We aren't going to let anything happen to her. And I'll keep you informed when anything new comes up." He gave her an encouraging smile, and she smiled back at him and told him she'd see him soon.

When she got to Alyssa's room, Olivia sat down in the chair by the bed and told her about her lunch with Shel. "I don't suppose you'd really call it a date," she said, "but it was nice. He's easy to talk to, and just between you, me, and the bed rail, he's easy on the eyes, too. I think you'd like him. I want you to meet him, Lissy, so wake up, please."

She sat for a few more minutes and thought about how strange life could be. Here she was, at one of the worst times of her life, her best friend lying in a hospital bed critically injured and even, at one point, close to death, and along came a man she was pretty sure she could get seriously interested in. However, as she'd told Shel, now was just not the right time. Maybe when Alyssa was better. It was something else to give her hope.

Now if only she could find a way to help Alyssa put her devastating past behind her and find some hope for the future...

* * * * *

Olivia didn't know how Alyssa had managed to make it through the triple funeral service.

She'd sat watching her closest friend, whose face was etched with unfathomable grief. It had taken everything Olivia had, but she finally managed to get the exhausted woman to allow herself to be put to bed.

She thought back to six days ago, before the unthinkable had happened. She'd been chatting on the phone with Lissy, who was telling her of her plans for the weekend. Robbie and the boys were on a three-day fishing trip at Georgetown Lake, about an hour and a half southeast of Missoula. They'd been looking forward to this trip for a long time.

So had Lissy. She and Robbie had made a deal. She'd let them go fishing, and he'd let her shop for new furniture for the living room. They'd just finished painting it, and now the furniture and drapes looked dowdy. He'd told her he trusted her taste and that if she found something she liked, she should go ahead and buy it.

"I'm so ready to do this, Livvy. Do you know how long we've had that furniture? We got it when I was expecting Jeremy. More than eighteen years ago. I think we're due new stuff, don't you?"

"I'd say so," Olivia said. "What are you going to be looking for?"

"I'm thinking modern rustic. The post-and-beam structure of the house just cries for it. I've been looking at sites on the Internet and at every catalog I can get my hands on. There's some truly beautiful stuff out there. Of course, the more rustic you get, the more money you pay. I'm not going to take unfair advantage of Rob's generosity, but I'm not going super cheap either. If I choose carefully, maybe the new furniture will last another eighteen years, heaven forbid!"

She laughed and told Olivia if she intended to accomplish anything, she'd better get going. They said goodbye and promised to speak again soon.

The next thing Olivia had heard from Alyssa was that Rob and the boys had been killed in a head-on collision. The high school kid driving on the wrong side of I-90 had been high on drugs. He, too, had been killed instantly. The sheriff's deputy who had come to the house to give the news to Alyssa had said that death had come quickly to all four victims. Both vehicles had been so mangled they were unrecognizable. The only way they'd been able to identify the victims was by the license plates.

Alyssa promptly fainted when she heard the news. The deputy had sent his partner to bring the next-door neighbor to be with her. The neighbor, an elderly woman who'd been like a surrogate grandmother to the boys, held Alyssa and rocked back and forth, back and forth with her, all the time telling her that someday—a long time from now—she'd begin to feel better again.

When she was able to compose herself enough, Alyssa had called Olivia, who said she'd be on the next plane to Missoula. Olivia arrived in Missoula at nine-thirty that evening. She hailed a cab and gave the driver Alyssa's address.

Olivia had to bite her tongue to keep from telling the cab driver to shut up when, trying to be friendly, he started to tell her about the terrible tragedy near Missoula that morning. "The father was a forest ranger. I feel sorry for the wife. Can't imagine what she must be going through."

I can. Hell. She's going through Hell. As much as Olivia wanted to tell the driver to stop talking, she realized he couldn't possibly know he was talking about people who were very dear to her. She kept silent the rest of the way to Alyssa's.

The driver pulled up in front of Alyssa's and wished Olivia an enjoyable stay. She murmured "thanks" to him and paid the cab fare. She waited while he got her luggage out of the trunk and told him she could manage it from there.

She walked the length of the sidewalk to Alyssa, who'd seen the cab pull up to the curb and was waiting for her on the doorstep. Olivia dropped her luggage and wrapped her arms around her friend. She felt Lissy's trembling body and knew she was at the end of her rope.

"Come on. Let's get you to bed. We can talk tomorrow, whenever you're ready."

She led Alyssa upstairs to what had been Rob's and her bedroom, but it now offered no comfort or escape to the woman who would occupy it alone. One look at the queen-sized bed and Alyssa sobbed heartbreakingly. "Oh, Livvy! I can't sleep here. I don't know if I'll ever be able to again. I just know I can't tonight."

"It's okay," Olivia said. "You can sleep in the guest room. I'll sleep downstairs on the sofa. I'll still be able to hear you if you need anything." She led Alyssa down the hall to the comfortably appointed room she'd stayed in on several previous, much happier visits. She found her friend's night clothes in the highboy next to the window in the master bedroom and took them down the hall to her. When Alyssa was ready, Olivia helped her into bed and told her if she needed anything during the night, all she had to do was call out.

She brushed a strand of hair from Alyssa's eyes and told her to rest well and she would see her in the morning. When she started to pull the bedroom door closed behind her, Alyssa cried out, saying she didn't want it closed. She asked Olivia to leave the hall light on for her. Olivia did as she was asked, and left the door open about halfway. Instead of the bright ceiling light, she switched on a small lamp on the hall table, thinking it would be easier for Alyssa to sleep with a dimmer light.

Then she found sheets and a blanket and pillow in the hall closet and made up a bed of sorts for herself on the living room sofa. The new sofa that Rob and the boys would never see.

Somehow, the two women made it through the next several days. Though her heart was breaking, too, Olivia made most of the funeral arrangements, at Alyssa's request. Alyssa told her what songs and flowers she wanted for the service. Though Olivia was glad to be able to help, she was also glad when the whole ordeal was over.

Rob had wanted to be cremated when his time came, and as he and Alyssa had agreed, his ashes were to be kept until Alyssa's could join his. Then they would be scattered together. Alyssa said they'd never talked about what should be done with the boys' ashes. She hadn't planned to outlive her sons. But she knew they were both free spirits who loved the forest as much as she and

Rob did, and she couldn't think of a better way to honor them than to have them cremated as well, and spread their ashes over one of their favorite spots overlooking the Bitterroot Valley.

Olivia stayed with Alyssa for two weeks. Then she had to get back home to Kyle and to her job. She promised Alyssa she'd be back in a few months, or sooner if she was needed. They cried when they said their goodbyes. Olivia didn't know how she did it, but somehow Alyssa managed a smile and said, "Thank you for everything. I wouldn't have made it through this without you."

"You be strong, Lissy," Olivia said. "And you take care of yourself, you hear?"

Alyssa nodded. "I will. I'll miss you, Livvy. The house is just so big and empty now." Her vacant eyes and the empty, hopeless look on her face almost made Olivia change her mind and stay a bit longer, but she knew Alyssa would have to start the healing process on her own. She'd be there, though, in spirit; and she'd be available by phone, if Alyssa needed her.

"I know," Olivia said. "It's going to take some time, Lissy, but it will get easier. And I'm only a phone call away if you need me, no matter what time it is. And you can email or text me any time, too."

The cab driver, who'd been waiting for the last five minutes, honked his horn. Olivia gave her friend one last big hug, picked up her bags, and started down the sidewalk. She turned for one last look at her friend, but Alyssa had already gone back into the house and shut the door against the world. Olivia climbed into the cab and told the driver to take her to the airport.

Life regained some sense of normalcy. Olivia noticed an undercurrent of sadness about Alyssa for a long time after that horrific day, but eventually, she started sounding more like her old self each time they spoke on the phone. Olivia sensed that her old friend was on her way back to the world of the living.

CHAPTER 8

Sunday, March 15, 2015
Morning

Today promised to be as nice as the day before. Olivia again had spent the night on the cot in Alyssa's room. She knew Alyssa was safe with the officers keeping watch outside her room twenty-four hours a day, but she wanted to stay close in case there were any more improvements in her condition.

However, nothing had happened through the night, and despite the uncomfortable accommodations, she managed to get a fairly good night's sleep. She'd become so inured to the normal sounds and activities of the hospital, she could tune them out by now.

She picked up her bag and went into the bathroom. Normally, visitors weren't supposed to use the restrooms in patients' rooms, but Angie had said that as long as Alyssa didn't need it, it was okay. Olivia appreciated not having to go all the way up the hall to the public restrooms near the elevators to dress and do her face.

She looked in the mirror. She was shocked to see the face that looked back at her. In spite of the good night's rest she'd had, her eyes were dull, and there were huge dark circles under them.

Guess this is why they make concealer, she thought.

She washed her face and patted it dry then started rummaging through her makeup case. She usually didn't wear much makeup— just light foundation, a touch of blush, and a bit of mascara. Today, however, she thought it was going to take a little more than that to make her look and feel human again.

After putting on her face, she pulled on the same slim jeans she'd worn the previous day, along with a fresh turquoise-and-purple plaid western-styled shirt. The shirt accentuated the blue of her eyes and, she thought, made them look a little less lackluster. When she felt she looked as good as she was going to look, she put her things back in her bag and went to say good morning to Alyssa.

Her friend still hadn't moved or opened her eyes, but Olivia was not as disheartened by this fact as she might have been, had she not heard those few whispered words from Alyssa the day before.

Besides, she reminded herself, if Alyssa woke up and tried to move, the pain from her broken pelvis would be excruciating, and she could end up doing more damage to it.

"Good morning, sleepyhead," Olivia said. "It looks like another gorgeous day out there. I'm going to ask the nurses and aids not to keep closing your curtains during the day. I know how much you love the sunshine on your face. I wish we could move your bed closer to the window, but I'm afraid with all these monitors and IVs hooked up to you, it's not possible. I guess if you want to see the sunshine, you'll have to open your eyes and prove to them you don't need all these gadgets anymore."

She squeezed Alyssa's hand and told her she was going to leave her for just a little while. She needed to get some breakfast. For a hospital, she thought the food wasn't too bad. A gooey cinnamon roll, a hard-boiled egg, and some strong black coffee sounded good. "I'll be back before you know it, I promise."

She left the room and nodded to the officer, who was starting to look a little weary. *I'd better bring a cup of good strong coffee back for him, too.*

The elevator door was open when she reached it, and she was pleasantly surprised to see Detective Sheldon just about to step through it. He seemed a little surprised to see her, too.

"Good morning," Olivia said. "I was heading down to the cafeteria for a quick bite. Can I talk you into joining me? I'll even buy this time."

"Well, now, I can hardly pass up an offer like that, can I?" He stepped to the side to let her in, and they waited while two nurses and an orderly joined them.

"Going down?" As soon as she said it, Olivia realized that it was a silly question since they were on the top floor.

"Cafeteria, please," one of the nurses said.

"Popular place this morning," Shel said. "That's where we're headed, too."

Olivia pushed one, the door closed, and the elevator whirred its way down.

Once they'd chosen what they wanted from the cafeteria line, Alyssa paid for both meals, and they made their way to a table for two next to the windows. Shel pulled her chair out for her.

She set the tray down on the table and took her seat.

"Thank you," she said. "I'm not used to such treatment. It's been a long time since anyone has opened a door or pulled a chair out for me."

"I like to think that chivalry is not dead," he said. "There are certain things my parents pretty much ingrained into me, and one of them was how to treat a lady."

"Well, then, I thank your parents, too."

They were quiet for a few minutes while they ate their breakfast. Olivia was surprised at how comfortable she was with the silence. She didn't feel like she had to try to make small talk with him all the time.

When all that was left was their coffee, Shel cleared his throat and said, "I guess now is a good time to tell you why I'm here."

"Have you found him or learned anything new?"

"We have. I mean, we haven't found the guy who hit Mrs. Walton, or the one you saw in her room either, but we do have some news. The test results from the IV he tampered with are in. There was enough cocaine in it to kill a horse. We think Mrs. Walton may have stumbled onto a drug ring, or possibly a group of arms dealers, who think an overdose is a surefire way to get rid of a potential witness."

"Drugs?" Olivia's eyes opened wide in astonishment. "Alyssa stumbled on to someone dealing drugs?"

"Or maybe guns. We don't know anything for sure yet."

Over the last few decades, the more remote areas of Montana had held a certain appeal to people who wanted to carry out their illegal activities. The sparsely populated areas also provided ideal hiding places for certain notorious people, not the least of whom was Theodore John "Ted" Kaczynski, better known as "the Unibomber." Kaczynski hid out in a remote cabin near Lincoln, Montana, where he had no running water or electricity and taught himself to be a survivalist. But the forest didn't hide only the people, but also their equipment and buildings.

Now Shel said, "Sure would help if she could wake up and talk to me. We still don't have any solid leads on the situation. I'm kind of at a stand-still until she wakes up and gives me some answers."

"Shel, do you think that guy Alyssa ran into up by Lone Man's Road is involved? Maybe that's why they were so interested in that camera she mounted. They might feel threatened by her, and that's why they tried to kill her. And they'll probably try again, won't they? We have to find them before they can get to her again."

"Not we, Livvy, as in you and I. We as in my fellow police officers and I. I don't want you setting yourself up as a target, too. You let us do the dirty work, okay?"

When she didn't answer him right away, he repeated himself. "Okay? Promise me you'll stay away?"

"Stay away!" Olivia's eyes widened with the dawning of realization. "That's what Lissy was trying to tell me the other day—to stay away from the bad guys. She didn't want me to stay away from her. Oh, I wish she'd wake up and tell us what's going on!"

"I'm pretty confident she will," Shel said. "It may just take a little more time."

"Speaking of time," Olivia said, looking at her watch, "I think I've been away long enough. Would you like to come back up with me and see if the doctor had anything to say this morning? He should have been by on his rounds by now."

"Sounds like a good idea."

When they got back to Alyssa's room, a new nurse was busy with the morning routine of taking her vitals, checking the IV, and straightening the bed and the room.

"Good morning," she said. "I'm Jen. I'll be Alyssa's nurse this morning." She looked at Olivia and said, "You I recognize because I was in here during the night to check on our patient. You were sound asleep on your cot." She turned to Shel and said, "You, however, I don't know, and I'm not sure you should be in here."

"He's okay," Olivia said as Shel pulled out his badge to show the nurse. She introduced the two, explaining to Jen who Shel was and why he was there. "Trust me, if I didn't think he were okay, he wouldn't be in here."

"Sorry," said Jen. "I just wanted to be sure. I have strict orders that only certain people are allowed in this room."

"Thanks for being cautious," Olivia said. "Can you tell me if the doctor has been in yet and if he had anything new to report?"

"Actually, you just missed him by about fifteen minutes. Let me look at her chart, and I can tell you exactly what he said." She picked up the chart from the table at the end of the bed.

"Well, this looks like good news."

"What is it?"

"Dr. Cameron says he thinks she's ready for surgery to repair her pelvis. He'll have the orthopedic surgeon look at her MRI and review her progress, and then they'll make the decision."

"Oh, that is good news! That means she's getting better. Do you know when the surgeon will be here?"

"How does right now sound?"

Olivia whirled around at the sound of an unfamiliar male voice.

"Didn't mean to startle you," said a rather short, yet athletically-built man with graying hair at his temples. He had a report in his left hand and a stethoscope draped around his neck. He extended his right hand to her. "I'm Dr. Stevens, the orthopedic surgeon Dr. Cameron called in."

Olivia shook his hand and introduced herself. "I'm Olivia Clayton. I'm the closest thing she has to family." She gestured toward Shel, introducing him to the surgeon, repeating what she'd just told Jen.

Olivia noticed how Shel towered over the doctor as the two men shook hands. Then the doctor asked them both to step out of the room for a few minutes so he could examine his patient.

"No problem," said Olivia. She and Shel left the room while Jen stayed to assist the doctor. They walked toward the elevator where Shel took her hand and told her he needed to get back to work. He reminded her to call him when she had news about Alyssa's surgery.

"I will. I promise," Olivia said. "Oh, I hope it's good news."

"I have a feeling it will be," Shel said.

"Is that the famous gut instinct cops claim to have?"

"That's what it is," he said. He let go of her hand. "Take care and have a good day. I'll talk to you soon."

"You have a good day, too," she said.

He stepped into the elevator and pushed one. He waved goodbye as the doors closed between them.

Oh, I can't believe this! Lissy's getting better, and I think I'm falling for Shel. What's more, I think he might be just as interested in me. Maybe things are going to be okay.

CHAPTER 9

Saturday, January 11, 2014

Joe and the four men with him stomped the snow off their feet as they walked across the front porch of the log cabin. Joe cringed when he heard Cal start his incessant moaning again, this time about how cold it was. He wondered if Cal would ever be happy about anything. He never seemed to stop complaining about their current situation. It was too cold and too far from civilization. There was no good TV reception, much less cable or a satellite hookup. On the coldest days, the pipes froze, and they were on their knees with a blow torch, thawing them out so they wouldn't burst.

Now, for the umpteenth time, Cal was griping about the location of this operation. He thought someplace warm, like Florida or Arizona, would've been better. And for the umpteenth time, Joe said, "No, they wouldn't. I told you, we're here for exactly the reasons you don't want to be here. Have you noticed the crowds around here? All those nosy busybodies looking at us and wondering who we are and what we're up to?"

He sneered with contempt when Cal said, "No, I ain't seen nobody, Joe," before it dawned on him that Joe was being sarcastic.

When Cal slouched down onto the couch and put his feet up on the coffee table, Joe scowled him and said, "Get those wet boots off that table, you idiot. We don't want to have to pay for damages when we leave. If there are any, it's all coming out of your pocket."

Grudgingly, Cal dropped his feet to the floor, giving Joe a dirty look behind his back.

"Whose turn is it to do the cooking tonight?" Joe looked at Trent, who'd been watching the scene between Joe and Cal play out. The smug smile on Trent's face told Joe he'd been enjoying the conflict between the two men. He reminded himself to keep an eye on Trent. *I have a feeling he's a powder keg, ready to go off at the slightest provocation.*

"Pete's cooking tonight," said Trent.

Joe called Trent, Cal, and Sam to join him at the table while Pete worked on supper. It hadn't been a particularly fun drive to the little hoe-dunk town forty miles north of here where Joe had rented a post office box under an assumed name. That, however, was where they'd had to go to pick up the plans for the compound that would be under construction as soon as the snow cleared and the ground thawed, if it ever did. And as soon as the boss got the "legalities" worked out and gave them the go-ahead.

The construction of the compound was the only reason Joe tolerated Pete and Cal.

Especially Pete. He was good at reading blueprints and swinging a hammer. When it came to construction, he knew what he was doing. He was a complete idiot in a lot of ways, but Joe had to admit he'd already proved himself useful on a couple of other smaller projects they'd completed.

As soon as the compound was finished, Joe would be finished with Pete. He'd leave, and Joe wouldn't care if he never saw him again. He wasn't worried about Pete running off at the mouth. Joe had enough information to hold over his head for a long time.

Cal, a journeyman electrician, would be useful as well. It would be his responsibility to get the compound hooked up to the solar panels and generators that would supply it with power.

The idea was to stay off the grid. No purchased electricity, gas, phone lines, or water. He also knew enough about plumbing to make himself useful in that area. Joe would keep Cal around to keep up the maintenance on the compound's systems. Once all the amenities were in—power, heat, water, swimming pool, and all the other luxuries that were in the plans—he had no doubts that Cal would be quite content to stay put and take full advantage of them. Hopefully, his constant complaining would come to an end then, too.

Trent and Sam would stay, too. Now they were there to help with the construction, but their main job in the future would be security. They also would do any "dirty work" that needed doing, such as silencing certain people when they needed it—whether temporarily or permanently. Joe liked keeping his hands clean of that type of work. In his line of business, he needed men he could count on for certain things, and he believed Trent and Sam were the right kind of men.

Joe's current job was supervising the building of the compound. When that was done, he'd run the business end of the operation. He wasn't particularly happy about having to babysit these four, but the pay was good, and this way he knew things would be done the way they should be.

He cringed when Cal, who was coming awfully close to whining, asked him yet again why they'd had to come here so early, saying he just didn't get it.

"It's not for you to get," Joe said. "Just quit worrying about it, and learn to live with it, will you? I'm getting sick of listening to you moan and complain all the time."

Actually, quite a bit had been accomplished since the five men had arrived in Missoula back in October. The twenty-five acres on which the compound would stand were now completely surrounded by an eight-foot-high chain-link fence, no small task considering the size and geography of the plot of land. A pole barn, where supplies would be stored when they were able to get them, had been erected next.

When the time came for the construction of the actual headquarters and the individual cottages, a small army of men would arrive to help. These would be men from inside the operation who'd worked on numerous such projects, both in the United States and in South America. Joe would oversee every aspect. He wasn't really looking forward to this either, but the rewards were great, so he tolerated the unpleasant parts of his job and looked forward to the not-too-distant future.

His thoughts were interrupted when Pete called out from the kitchen that supper was ready. Evidently Pete was hungry. He sat down at the table with a heaping plate of hot dogs, beans, buttered bread, and a cold beer, and dug in with gusto.

"Did you save anything for the rest of us?" Joe glared at Pete and started piling his own plate with food.

CHAPTER 10

Friday, February 27, 2015

Joe feigned patience as Pete related his meeting with the woman near their cabin a little while ago. He described her as wearing a park ranger's uniform and having curly red hair. Joe wondered if she was the same woman who'd stopped Trent and Cal for littering the previous fall.

"All I know is she knows I'm here now," Pete said.

"How does she know you're here now, Pete? I told you to be careful." Joe's features tightened, and his fists clenched at his sides.

"I was being careful, I swear. I was just out lookin' around, and I happened to glance off to my right, and there she was. She had some kinda equipment with her that she was hangin' on a tree. I think it might have been one of those motion-sensor cameras they use to watch the deer and the bears and stuff, you know?"

"Did she say anything to you?"

"Just asked me how I was doin', that's all."

"You sure that's all?"

"Well, that and if I was the one rentin' the cabin here."

"What did you tell her?"

"I told her me and four of my buddies were up here for a little a vacation." Obviously, Pete believed it was a brilliant explanation.

Joe, however, did not. "You what? You idiot! Who's going to believe that five men would be taking a vacation, from October 'til March?"

"Well, I kinda made her think that we'd all been laid off when the place we worked for went under. I told her we were in the construction business. I think she bought it."

"You think she bought it? You damn well better hope she bought it." Joe pounded his fist on the table and sprang to his feet. "I wouldn't have, I know that."

"Yeah, but there's no reason for her to think anything else, is there, Joe?"

"Maybe not, but I'll bet we see her out here again. I think she may already have been keeping an eye on us. That's why I had Trent and Sam follow her a few times. If she wasn't suspicious before, she sure as heck is now. You know what that means?"

"Well..."

"It means," Joe said, poking a finger at Pete's chest, "that we'd better start looking like we're on vacation. We'd better get some licenses and do a little fishing. We'll take some nature hikes, do a little bird-watching. Whatever you want to do to make her a little less suspicious than she probably already is. Do you think you can manage that?"

"Sure, Joe," Pete said. He rubbed the spot Joe had been poking while thinking there were things other than birds he'd rather watch. They'd been here for four months now, and the only times they ever went anywhere was to pick up supplies, either for themselves or for the compound that would be under construction again as soon as the weather permitted. Pete would have given anything to see a good action movie or visit one of the local bars and pick up a girl for a good time. But Joe wouldn't allow it. They needed to keep a low profile, he'd said.

"What about the rest of you guys? You think you can act like you're enjoying yourselves, just relaxing and having a little fun?"

"No problem, Joe," Cal said. "As long as we don't have nothin' to do right now anyway, we might as well have a little fun while we're stuck out here."

"Good. Meantime, I guess I'd better try to find out just who she is."

Pete, eager to get back on Joe's good side, offered to do that for him, but Joe shoved his offer aside. "No. You've already messed things up enough. I think I'll take a little ride over to the rangers' station tomorrow and do a little snooping around. If she's there, I'll try to strike up a conversation with her and find out if she suspects anything. If she does, I'll try to persuade her she has nothing to worry about."

"I'm sorry, Joe," Pete said. "I didn't know what I should tell her. I didn't think it'd hurt to let her think we were just a bunch of guys out here for a good time."

"Your problem is that you didn't think at all. But I guess what's done is done. Forget it for now, and let's make a few plans so she'll think we're here to relax."

They found seven or eight fishing poles, and even some ice fishing equipment, in a small room behind the kitchen, along with a couple tackle boxes. There also were a few sets of snowshoes and some cross-country skis. Joe had tried cross-country skiing before and had found that he'd enjoyed it, but he doubted any of the others would. They'd probably go more for ice fishing or hunting small game like rabbits or squirrels.

"It shouldn't be too hard to make her believe we're here to enjoy ourselves" Joe said. "When I go to the rangers' station tomorrow, I'll ask where we can get some good bait and where the best place for fishing is near here. I'll ask for some maps of the area, too. Hopefully, they won't wonder why we've been here so long and are just now asking."

"Joe, do you want me to go back and get rid of that camera? I know exactly where she put it," said Pete, still trying to get himself back in Joe's good graces.

"Sure, Pete, you do that." Joe's voice dripped with sarcasm. "You don't think that will make her even more suspicious? No, I do not want you to do anything with that camera, but I do want you to show all of us where it is so we all know how to avoid it. And from now on, whenever any of us go anywhere, we keep our eyes peeled for things like that. Even if you aren't doing anything suspicious, there's no reason to let them see what we look like."

"Right," Cal said. "Now, who's cooking tonight? I'm starving."
Joe gave Cal a dirty look but didn't say anything more.

"I am," Trent said. "How does scrambled eggs and bacon sound?"

"Like breakfast," Cal said, "but I'm just hungry enough to eat it for supper."

Trent got busy in the kitchen. He scrambled up a dozen eggs, fried a pound of bacon, and piled several slices of toast onto a plate. In about fifteen minutes, the five men were sitting around the table chowing down.

CHAPTER 11

Monday, March 2, 2015

Alyssa arrived at Ranger Station Number Four a little before eight in the morning. She had a few more cameras to mount near a couple campgrounds and public viewing places. There had been reports of at least two bears that had ventured too close to areas used by campers and tourists. In order to catch them, the rangers first needed to find out what their habits were: where they were showing up most frequently, if they were only going after garbage, how many of them there were, how old and how big they were, and whether they were black bears or grizzlies. It was still a little early for them to be coming out of hibernation, but occasionally, one did come out earlier and start foraging for food. Montana Fish and Wildlife rangers didn't want them to become a nuisance or a danger. The decision had been made to go ahead and check out the potential for problems before the forest was crawling with hikers, campers, and fishermen.

Alyssa had started with just the one camera three days ago because she'd planned to be in the area anyway. Today she'd be working with a partner, Collin Wilson. She liked Collin and would be glad to have his company; although, it still took some getting used to working with someone other than Rob. Sometimes she ran into a problem that was more easily handled with two people. A couple of weeks before, she'd been on her way to check the flooding of a fast-running creek and had come up on a tree that had fallen across the road. She'd had to call back to the station and request help to move it. It would have saved time had she been working with a partner to begin with that day.

She also wanted to check on the camera she'd installed the other day. She doubted it had caught anything of interest yet, but it was worth checking anyway. You never knew.

Alyssa and Collin strapped on their side arms, checked their ammunition, and made sure there was a rifle with plenty of ammo in the Jeep they'd be using. They hoped never to have to use their weapons, but they had to be ready in case it became necessary.

Knowing they'd be away from the station and in remote areas for the better part of the day, they packed some rations, a couple gallons of water, and a small cooler with Coke and a couple juice boxes in it. They also made sure there were an ax, shovel, tarp, rope, two heavy-duty flashlights, matches, a camera, binoculars, blankets, a tow chain, and a first-aid kit in the back end of the Jeep.

"I think we're good to go," Alyssa said. He agreed, and after letting the dispatcher at the station know where they were headed, they drove out of the parking lot. As they were leaving, they passed a blue Dodge Ram pickup with only the driver in it.

"I haven't seen that one around here before, have you?" Collin asked.

"Nope. Don't think so. Tourist season seems to be starting a little early this year."

Collin looked at her questioningly, so she told him about meeting the strange man in the forest when she mounted the first camera.

"Vacation in March?" Collin seemed dubious when Alyssa told him that part of the story.

"I know. It seemed a little odd to me, too, but since I had no reason to doubt him, I had to let him go."

"Where are they staying?"

"They're renting Mike Sloan's cabin way up by Lone Man's Road."

"Wow, they're really in it for the peace and quiet, aren't they? That's way out in the middle of nowhere."

"That's what I thought, but like I said, I had no reason to check him out. Maybe we'll swing by there today and see what we can see," Alyssa said.

It took them nearly an hour to reach their first destination. In places, the trail was still covered with snow or ice. In others, the mud made it hard to get through without getting stuck. They even had to stop a couple times to move a fallen tree from across the trail before they could continue.

Their first stop was a campground off the beaten track, used mostly by seasoned woodsmen, rather than novice campers or tourists. There were no power hookups, no water other than what could be carried up from the stream, and no outhouses. It was strictly an area for tent camping.

However, there were four or five fire pits with heavy iron grates over them, and a couple large trash cans. The latter were what interested the bears. Alyssa and Collin climbed out of their Jeep and walked around the campground, looking for signs of bears. There were no tracks or bear scat in the snow, and the trash cans were intact, lids still on them and clamped down tightly.

"Looks good here," Collin said. "At least with the snow still on the ground it's easy to tell if anything's been moving around here."

"It does make our job easier," Alyssa said. "Let's go ahead and mount a camera here anyway. That tree over there looks like a good place to put one." She pointed to a tall ponderosa pine whose branches started about ten feet above the ground.

Collin retrieved a camera and the mounting equipment from the back of the Jeep. He went over to the designated tree and set the camera down carefully. Each one of them cost the Forestry Department close to $400. They were equipped with night vision capabilities and would run for almost a year on one set of batteries. The mounting equipment consisted of a strap through a slot in the back of the camera, which encircled the tree. This eliminated the need to pound nails into the bark.

Collin placed the strap about eight feet or so above the ground and picked up the camera.

He slid the strap through the camera's mounting slot and then fastened the two ends of the strap together. He made sure it was good and snug, so as not to slide down the trunk of the tree.

"One down," he said.

"Great," Alyssa said. "Shall we go on to the next spot?"

Twenty minutes later, they pulled into another campground. Very much like the first one, it also was primitive and meant for tent camping only. They walked the perimeters of this site as they had the first, with the same results. It didn't look like there'd been any activity around here for quite a while.

The next three sites were spaced farther apart. It took nearly three more hours to reach all the areas they wanted to check. The third and fourth sites were set up for RVs and campers with electric hookups. The fifth was another tents-only campsite. Finally, they were finished mounting the cameras at all five sites. They hadn't seen anything suspicious at any of these locations.

"Well, that's that," Collin said. "Do you still want to go on over and check out the one you put up the other day? We're probably about forty-five minutes away from there now, don't you think?"

"Sounds about right, given the condition of the trails," Alyssa said. "We probably should check it out since no one will be back up here to check on things for another week or so."

They climbed into the Jeep. The temperature had dropped a few degrees, and Alyssa was glad there was a good heater in the vehicle. She also was glad they used Jeep Renegades now rather than the Wranglers they used in the "old" days. With the hard top and insulation, they were much warmer. They also were a little more bear-proof, which you could see if you looked at the roofs of a couple of the Jeeps back at the station. They had some nasty scratches from some very sharp, very long claws. If those roofs had been made of canvas, the rangers who'd been in the Jeeps could've been seriously hurt, or worse.

"Okay," Collin said. "All set?"

"Yep," Alyssa answered. She fastened her seat belt with a solid snap. "Let's go. Looks like it's going to be well after dark by the time we get back, so we don't want to dawdle."

Collin turned the Jeep around and drove back the way they'd come for about forty minutes.

"Next trail, turn right," Alyssa said. "It's about three-quarters of a mile in from there."

They drove until they saw the sign: "Lone Man's Rd." Collin turned right onto it and followed the narrow trail for three-quarters of a mile.

"Stop here," Alyssa said. "See, you can still see my tracks." She pointed ahead at the ground.

Collin stopped the Jeep, and they climbed out. They stretched their legs a bit and looked around at their surroundings.

"It's over here," Alyssa said. She started toward the tree where she'd mounted the camera. She looked down at the ground and whistled lowly.

"Look at this. There are a lot of tracks here," she said. "Only they aren't bear tracks."

They picked out six different sets of boot prints in the snow. Five of those sets came from the opposite direction from which Alyssa and Collin had come. The sixth smaller set led back toward where Collin had parked the Jeep.

Alyssa pointed out the smaller set. "Those are my prints. Let's walk in a little farther." She patted her sidearm for reassurance, and the two of them set out. They followed the tracks in the snow for about fifteen minutes. Whoever had made them evidently hadn't been concerned about leaving a trail.

"They lead Sloan's cabin below the ridge up there," Collin said. He pointed to the north where they could see a tendril of smoke rising above the treetops.

"The guy I ran into here yesterday said there were a few of them renting a cabin up here. But I wonder why they were so interested in the camera," Alyssa said.

"I don't know, but let's take a look at it and see what we've got."

They walked back to where the camera was mounted. He unhooked the strap and took the camera down. He pushed play, and they watched as one man, careful to keep his face shielded with one hand, pointed upwards toward the camera with the other. The four others on the video all looked up, also being sure their faces weren't visible, and nodded. One man said something to the others. Then they all turned of one accord and headed back into the forest the way they'd come.

"Well, that was interesting," Collin said. "It sure looked to me like they didn't want anyone to see their faces."

"Yes, and that doesn't make sense, does it? Even if we couldn't see their faces, we could still follow their tracks up to the cabin and easily find out who they are that way."

"True. Maybe they didn't expect anyone to be back here so soon and were hoping it would snow before then and cover up their tracks."

"Makes sense," Alyssa said.

"I think we should report this and keep an eye on these guys," Collin said. He strapped the camera back up on the tree.

"I agree." Alyssa nodded at him, and they turned back toward the Jeep. "It's getting colder. It'll be dark soon, too. I say we head back to the station and return here in a few days."

"Good idea," Collin said.

They each grabbed a drink and a snack from the back seat of the Jeep and then climbed into the front.

"Here we go," Collin said. He started the Jeep and turned it around.

CHAPTER 12

Sunday, March 15, 2015
Evening

Though Olivia knew Alyssa would be safe at the hospital, she opted to stay there on the cot in her room another night. The surgery to repair Alyssa's pelvis had been scheduled for early the next morning, and Olivia wanted to be there when they took her in. Maybe Alyssa didn't know she was here, but then again, maybe she did. Maybe she actually had heard everything Olivia had said to her in her comatose state. At any rate, Olivia wasn't about to not be there to send her best friend off for major surgery.

Nurses and lab technicians came and went most of the afternoon, drawing blood, keeping a close eye on Alyssa's vital signs, and making sure everything that needed to be done before the surgery was done. They nodded and smiled at Olivia, who was at the table in the corner trying, without much success, to concentrate on her work.

She was having a hard time thinking about manuscripts. She replayed in her mind what Shel had told her about that Humvee: how it had moved slowly down the street, the driver seemingly looking for someone or something, and then purposefully speeding up, jumping the curb, and running down Alyssa in the process. It certainly didn't sound like it had been an accident to Olivia. What she couldn't figure out was how a perfect stranger could possibly know where they would be at that precise time.

Unless someone's been watching Alyssa or me, or both of us. Think, Olivia. Think! Find the pieces of the puzzle and put them together.

No matter how hard she tried, though, Olivia couldn't fit the pieces together. She resolved to put her mind to the task until she came up with some answers.

Then she remembered Shel's admonition to stay away and let him and his men handle it.

Easier said than done, she thought, *but that's what they're trained to do. I'm just a book editor.*

In the meantime, her job would be right here by Alyssa's side. Alyssa, with whom she'd been through all the major events of her life. Alyssa, whose parents had died right before her first son was born. Alyssa, who'd lost her husband and both sons only a couple years ago. Alyssa, who had lifted Olivia out of her depression after the divorce. Nothing would keep Olivia from seeing her friend through what lay ahead for as long as she was needed.

Olivia shoved aside the manuscript she'd been staring at blankly for the last twenty minutes and got out her notepad and pen. She started a list of things she needed to know if she were to take Alyssa home with her until she was able to fend for herself. Would she need a nurse part-time? Would Olivia be able to help her with her physical therapy at home, or would she need to be brought into town for that? How many times a week would she need to have therapy? Would Alyssa need to be on a special diet for any length of time? Would she need to have a hospital bed brought home?

Whatever it took, Olivia was prepared to do it. She knew that had it been her lying in that bed, Alyssa would've done the same for her. They'd grown up side by side, more like sisters than friends. Olivia honestly didn't know how she would've gone on had Alyssa not survived this ordeal. She knew she still had a long way to go, but she was confident now that Alyssa eventually would be okay.

Olivia rose from her makeshift desk, walked across the room, and looked down at Alyssa's face. She looked quite peaceful. The bruises on her face had almost completely faded away. Her broken arms and leg were healing well, the doctor had said, and normal circulation had returned to her fingers, so her hands no longer felt icy to Olivia's touch.

Olivia took the hairbrush she'd brought from Alyssa's house. Gently, she brushed the long, naturally curly hair.

She's always hated her hair. I've given her such a hard time about it at times, always teasing her. What she doesn't know is how much I really love it. That fiery red color is so lively. No other color would suit her personality.

All the time she brushed Alyssa's hair, Olivia spoke to her. She talked about what they'd do when Olivia was up and around on her own two feet again. She talked about going camping.

"I'll even learn how to cook over a campfire," she said.

She talked about going to the Grand Canyon, someplace neither of them had ever been.

She spoke of going to the Black Hills in South Dakota to see Mt. Rushmore. They'd both been there as young girls with their parents, but they'd talked about wanting to see it again, now that they were old enough to appreciate it. "There's so much to do yet, Lissy! And we're going to do as much of it as we can once you're ready."

She put the brush away and leaned over to hug Alyssa as well as she could over the bed rail. "I'll be right back. I'm just going to go outside for some fresh air and try to clear my head a little. Maybe by the time I get back you'll be awake."

She'd discovered a small balcony positioned off the families' waiting room on this level.

She went out and rested her arms on the railing. The sun was just starting to drop behind the mountain to the west of Missoula. It was almost too dark to see anything, but when she glanced down toward the park across the street, she saw what she thought looked like a red SUV parked in the small drive-in space near the horseshoe court. With the amber-colored sodium streetlights, however, she couldn't tell for sure whether the vehicle was red or brown.

I really don't like those yellow lights. They make everything look spooky, she thought.

Suddenly, she realized the temperature had taken a dip, and she was beginning to feel a little cooler than was comfortable. She turned and went back inside.

When she got back with the cup of tea she'd grabbed from the nurses' station on her way, Alyssa's eyes were still closed. Olivia sighed and wondered, for the hundredth time, how long she'd have to wait.

Waiting is always the hardest part.

CHAPTER 13

Wednesday, September 3, 2014

Olivia's divorce was finalized on August 5. She knew she didn't want to stay in Portland where she'd have a chance of running into Kyle and his new "friend" every time she turned a corner.

As soon as Kyle asked her for a divorce, Olivia started looking for a different job. When a major publisher in New York offered her the position of senior editor, she couldn't turn it down, especially since they'd said she could work from anywhere in the country, as long as she had a good computer. Now all she had to do was decide where she wanted to live.

When Alyssa suggested she move to Missoula, pointing out that she could work from home just as well there as in Portland, or anywhere else, Olivia thought, *Why not?* She'd been impressed with Missoula since the first time she'd visited there. *Beautiful country, plenty of cultural entertainment, wonderful people, and best of all— Lissy. I'd have her support and love if I moved to Missoula, and she'd have the same from me.* She couldn't think of any other place she'd rather live. "Okay! That's exactly what I'll do," she'd said.

The next week she took Thursday and Friday off and flew to Montana for a long weekend.

She enlisted Lissy's help in finding a house. Her house in Portland, which she'd received as part of the divorce settlement, was already on the market, so when she found a place she liked, she made the purchase of it contingent on the sale of her house within a month.

The house she found was on the outskirts of town, set back among the pines about halfway up a rocky ridge, with forests butting up against the backyard. In fact, the property included some forested land, which added to its appeal. The view was spectacular, and she'd have plenty of privacy here. Her driveway was more like a narrow country road at three-quarters of a mile long.

The realtor had given her the name of a man who would clear the snow for her when she needed it and grade the dirt in the summer when it was rutted.

The house itself wasn't huge, at two thousand square feet, but it was plenty big enough for Olivia; and even though there was no basement, there was plenty of storage space in the attached garage. All the walls had been painted recently in a soft, creamy Navajo white, and the whole place had been scrubbed immaculately clean. It was move-in ready, which Olivia appreciated greatly.

There were three bedrooms, one of which she would use as an office, and another as a guest room. The updated kitchen boasted beautiful hickory cabinets and brand-new black appliances. She hadn't been too sure of the appliances at first, but in the end, she'd decided they fit the decor, and she liked them after all. The living room had a vaulted ceiling, which extended into the dining room and kitchen. Tall windows across the front wall of the living room offered a view of the city below, as well as the mountains on the other side of town. There also were a full bathroom for guests, and a beautiful bathroom, as well as a large walk-in closet off the master bedroom. Most important to her, there was room for her baby grand piano.

She particularly loved her master bathroom. It had a long vanity with two sinks and lots of counter space. There was a good-sized linen closet. The toilet sat in its own little room. A separate, glass-enclosed shower shared the view with a huge soaker tub, which sat next to a large window that looked out onto the back of her property. Someone had been quite artistic with the tile surrounding the shower. A mosaic forest scene, with a waterfall cascading over the built-in seat into an aqua pool on the shower floor made Olivia feel like she was showering in the middle of the forest. It was meant to be relaxing, and it was. She was enchanted by it.

The previous owners had put in some beautiful flower gardens, including one large one in the front yard that was full of random plantings of wildflowers indigenous to the area, including lupine, Queen Anne's lace, Indian paintbrush, and bitterroot, the official flower of the state of Montana.

The flower beds and lawn in the backyard butted up against the stand of evergreen trees where the forested part of her five-acre plot of land started. She'd been delighted to find that a crystal clear little creek ran right through her property. There was an abundance of wildlife that she could watch from the deck off her kitchen or from just about any window in the house.

The outside of the house was charming. It had cedar siding and a front porch just made for a couple of Adirondack rocking chairs and a porch swing. Hooks for hanging planters were lined up along the beam that supported the porch roof. A rock-lined cedar chip-cushioned path wound its way from the driveway to the front steps. On each side of the path there were undulating flower beds with more native flowers and some magnificent yucca plants. Lilac bushes grew in the front yard, as well as a few large blue spruce trees. Along the west side of the driveway were chokecherry bushes, from which she hoped she could produce some delicious chokecherry jelly and syrup. The scents she'd inhaled the first time she saw the place had almost sold her on the house before she'd even seen the inside of it.

The other great selling point was the awesome view from the front porch. The landscapers had been heedful when placing the trees and bushes in the yard, so as not to block the views to the north, west, and east. She also was able to see much of the road below her property from there.

The house in Portland had sold a week and a half after Olivia made the offer on the Missoula house. She'd packed up everything she owned, rented a U-Haul truck, and said goodbye to Portland. Now, finally, she was ready to be on her way.

"I'm ready to hit the road." Olivia had called to let Alyssa know when she was leaving.

She'd wrapped up the last of the many details involved with moving and was anxious to be on her way at last.

"I can hardly wait," Alyssa said. "When do you think you'll get here?"

"It's about an eight-and-a-half-hour drive from Portland to Missoula. I'm getting a little later start than I thought, and I really don't think I want to try to negotiate the passes in this truck after dark. I thought I'd probably go as far as Moses Lake, Washington, today and stay there for the night. I should get in there before dark easily and be able to get a good night's rest. Then it's only a little more than four hours' drive tomorrow. If I get out of there at a decent time, I should be in Missoula by early afternoon. Of course, this all depends on how fast I feel I can drive the truck, especially since I'm pulling my car behind it."

Originally, Olivia had thought she'd sell her car and buy something else when she was settled in Missoula. However, since her house sold so fast, she really didn't have time to sell the car, so she'd checked into towing it on a trailer behind the U-Haul truck. She'd been reassured that it wouldn't be as daunting a task as she was afraid it would be, so she'd decided to try it.

"You're a lot braver than I'd be," Alyssa said. "I'm not sure I'd want to try it at all. I'll say a prayer that you don't have any mechanical problems or meet up with any bad drivers on the road. And, Livvy, please be careful. I don't want to lose you, too."

"I promise," Olivia said. "I'm not worried about it, really. In fact, I'm thinking of it as a huge adventure. There was a time when I didn't think I'd ever do something like this on my own. But I think I've changed in some ways over the last several months. For the better. I'll see you tomorrow!"

She hung up her cell phone, checked the charge on it, took one last look around the house, and left, locking the front door for the last time ever. She didn't look back as she walked out to the truck.

CHAPTER 14

Tuesday, March 17, 2015
Morning

"How is she doing?" Olivia was speaking with Dr. Stevens, who'd just finished operating on Alyssa's fractured pelvis.

"She's doing well, considering everything she's been through," he said. "You know, it's almost a miracle she's made it this far. And then to have major reconstructive surgery on top of everything, well, I think she's one tough lady." He continued, telling Olivia that when he got a look at Alyssa's injuries, he found that they weren't quite as devastating as he first thought. He'd put in three pins, cleaned out the bone fragments, and stitched up some torn ligaments. "She won't be in as much pain when she wakes up now."

"That's good news," Olivia said. "Will she be able to walk normally and go back to work soon?"

"I think with physical and occupational therapy, she'll be up and walking in a couple months, and she should be able to return to work eventually."

A short while later, when Angie came in to get Alyssa's bed ready for her, Olivia told her what the doctor said.

"Yes," Angie said. "I'm so happy for her. And for you," she added. "It's been pretty tough on you, too, these last couple of weeks, hasn't it?"

"I don't mind. I know she'd do the same thing for me if the tables were turned."

"I'm sure she would. Friendships like the one you two have are one in a million." Angie smiled and patted Olivia's arm. "She'll be in recovery for another hour or so. Then I'll be back to get her settled in. Now, I'd better finish up in here and see to the rest of my patients." She hummed a catchy little tune to herself as she went about her work.

Olivia planned to dig into her own work right after she had some breakfast. Since Alyssa wouldn't be back for a while yet, she decided to go down to the cafeteria for a quick bite. She smiled at the police officer at the door and asked him if he'd like anything from the cafeteria. He gratefully told her a cup of black coffee sounded wonderful.

"Can do," Olivia said and strolled toward the elevator.

After her breakfast of scrambled eggs, English muffin with locally harvested honey, orange juice, and coffee, she paid for another cup of coffee and went back to the fourth floor.

The officer thanked her for getting the coffee for him and tried to pay her for it. She waved him off, saying it was the least she could do for him.

It has to be hard to stand here like that all night or all day long. Good thing they divide the day into three eight-hour shifts. Even then, I don't think I could do it.

She didn't stop to think that she had, indeed, been doing something very much like that, only with the additional stress of concern for her friend. She didn't think of it as a job, nor as a sacrifice. To her it was just what good friends did for each other.

Glancing out the window when she entered Alyssa's room, she saw that there were some rather ominous-looking clouds off to the west. The weatherman had predicted the possibility of an early spring storm today, and it looked like he was right.

While Olivia was in the cafeteria, Alyssa had been returned to her room. Olivia adjusted the light covers over her. "I'm back, Lissy. I'll be over by the window working again today. If you need me, just call me," she said, wondering if it might actually happen today.

She took the laptop and manuscript out of her briefcase, and she settled into reading the draft of a new novel by another novice author. This one kept her attention better than the last one she'd started to read. She kept reading, making editorial marks and suggestions as she read. The book had a good story line and strong dialogue. Luckily, it was interesting enough that she didn't even mind that it was a romance novel that took place in the days of the Old West. Normally, she didn't care for Westerns, but the romantic twist, along with a bit of the history of the Old West, made this one easier for her to digest mentally.

In fact, she was so engrossed in the pages she was reading, she hadn't even noticed how black the sky had become. A gust of wind straight out of the west came up hard enough to rattle the window a bit. Then a sudden bolt of lightning struck, so close that it temporarily blinded her, and thunder followed almost on top of it. She jumped back from the window.

"What?" A troubled cry from behind her caused her to turn around.

Alyssa's eyes were wide open, and she looked frantically around the room.

"Lissy! Lissy, it's okay," Olivia said as she rushed to the side of the bed. "It's just a thunderstorm. You're safe. You're in the hospital, and I'm here with you. You're safe."

"Livvy?" Alyssa's eyes seemed to clear a little as she struggled to focus on the face looking down at her. Her voice was raspy as she asked, "What happened? Why am I here?"

"We'll talk all about that later," Olivia said. "Right now, I'm just so thankful that you're finally awake. And you're talking to me, and you know who I am."

"Of course, I know who you are," Alyssa croaked, a little irritably. "Why wouldn't I?"

"You've been through a lot in the last couple weeks, sweetie," Olivia told her. "I promise I'll fill you in later. But for now, I think I'd better call the nurse. She'll be happy to see you with your eyes open, too." Olivia pressed the call button.

Another bolt of lightning split the clouds, and another loud boom of thunder rolled across the sky. Worry creased Alyssa's face, and her fingers fidgeted with agitation.

"Sounds like that's close enough to start a forest fire," she said. "I need to get out there and help."

"You won't be going anywhere for a while," Olivia said. "You're going to have to stay here until the doctors say it's okay for you to go home. And then, you'll come stay with me for a while until they say it's okay for you to go back to work."

Angie came through the door and abruptly stopped when she heard Olivia having an actual two-sided conversation with her patient.

"Well, look who finally decided to wake up and smell the flowers!" she said happily. "It's good to see your eyes open. How are you feeling?"

"Like I was hit by a truck," Alyssa said, even though at this point she didn't remember that that was exactly what had happened to her. She grimaced as she tried to raise a hand to her head and discovered that she couldn't.

Olivia glanced across the bed to Angie, who shook her head from side to side, indicating that this wasn't a good time to go into it. No need to upset Alyssa with that news now.

"Well, with the bump on your head and the other injuries you sustained, I imagine that's about how I'd expect you to feel," Angie said. "I want to check your vitals now. And then we'll see what else we can do to make you more comfortable."

"My hips and back hurt," Lissy said. "Why can't I move?"

"Because you're in a brace. We don't want you to move," Angie said. "You had reconstructive surgery on your pelvis this morning, so it's important to keep you still for the next few weeks. You're going to be pretty uncomfortable for a while, I'm afraid, but we'll be able to give you some good meds that will keep most of the pain at bay."

Olivia noticed the confusion that furrowed Alyssa's brow. "I'm sure you don't remember it yet, Lissy, but we'll get all that sorted out for you in time." She noticed that Alyssa looked down at her arms, aware for the first time that they both were in casts.

"I don't remember much of anything after having dinner with you yesterday, Livvy."

"That was ten days ago. Like Angie said, you had a pretty nasty bump on your head. You've been pretty much out of it since then. But you're back now, and you're going to be just fine." She asked if there was anything she could do for her.

Alyssa said she was thirsty and asked for something to drink. Olivia looked at Angie, who nodded and said Alyssa could have a few sips of water but needed to take it slowly until her stomach was used to having something in it again.

Olivia poured water into the cup on the bedside table, put a straw through the hole in the lid, and held the cup for her friend while she sipped through the straw.

Olivia barely heard the whispered "thank you" from Alyssa as she closed her eyes and was off to sleep again—this time a natural sleep from which she knew her friend would awaken again soon enough.

CHAPTER 15

Tuesday, March 17, 2015
Evening

Olivia had decided to spend the night at home instead of on the uncomfortable cot at the hospital. Now that Alyssa was conscious and seemed to be getting better by the moment, she felt a little more relaxed about leaving her under the watchful eyes of the police officers and nurses.

She'd stopped by the grocery store on her way home to pick up a few things she knew she needed. The last time she'd been home she'd checked the refrigerator and noticed that a few things had been in there so long they could almost walk away under their own power.

Let's see…Bread, milk, eggs, grapes, a couple meats, lettuce, tomatoes, some cheese, and some fresh veggies. Looks like that's about it.

She pushed her cart up to the front and started putting her selections on the grocery conveyor.

"Evening," the boy at the register said. "Did you find everything okay?"

"Yes, thank you," Olivia said. She wrote out a check and handed it over to him.

"Thank you for shopping at Kwik Shop," the boy said. He handed her the receipt. "Do you need some help getting these to your car?"

"No, thanks. I think I can manage it." Olivia smiled at him and said, "Have a nice day."

She pushed her cart with the two bags of groceries through the automatic door.

As she walked past the outdoor stand full of potted tulips, daffodils, and crocuses, the red SUV two rows over from her car barely registered in her mind. Even if she had noticed it, Missoula was full of vehicles just like it. A lot of people here preferred four-wheel drive. In fact, she was seriously considering buying one for herself. It probably would make navigating her long, steep driveway a lot easier in the winter.

She loaded her groceries into the trunk and shoved the cart into the cart return stand. She smiled to herself as she got into her car. She looked forward to spending an evening at home by herself. She pulled into traffic and turned toward home.

No manuscripts tonight either. I'm just going to put my feet up, relax, and try not to think of anything.

She pushed a little harder on the gas pedal. Home and a glass of wine couldn't come too soon.

Olivia finally pulled off the road and started up her driveway. She unloaded the bags from the trunk and took them to the house, leaving her briefcase and purse on the front seat of the car. She put the groceries on the counter next to the sink and went back out to retrieve her briefcase and purse. As she straightened from reaching for the case on the passenger's seat, she caught a glimpse of a red SUV passing by the bottom of her driveway.

Popular color for SUVs, she thought. *I wonder how many of those there are in Missoula.*

* * * * *

The two men in the front seat of the SUV watched her load her groceries into the trunk and get behind the wheel.

"You're absolutely sure? We can't afford any more mistakes," Joe said.

"I'm positive. I'd never forget her," Trent said. "She was a wildcat flyin' at me the way she did. I was lucky to get out of there with everything intact."

"Okay. Let's follow her. See where she goes. Knowing where she lives might come in handy one of these days."

When Olivia turned into her driveway, the red SUV, which had hung back a considerable distance to this point, kept going and came to a stop around a curve about half a mile farther up the road.

"Okay, so it looks like that's her home sweet home. We just might have to teach her a lesson one of these days, if she gets in our way again," Joe said, a cruel smile on his face. "Come on. Let's get back to the cabin."

* * * * *

Olivia barely made it back inside when she heard the kitchen phone ring. She snatched it up quickly and said, "Hello, this is Olivia."

"Olivia, I'm so glad I caught you. I tried your cell phone, but you must have it turned off."

Olivia recognized the voice on the other end of the line as belonging to her boss, Georgia.

"Oh, it needs to be charged. I forgot to do it while I was at the hospital. Thanks for reminding me."

"How's your friend doing?"

Olivia filled Georgia in on Alyssa's progress. "I'm so relieved and thankful that she's going to be okay," she said.

"That's great," Georgia said. "How are you doing? I hope you're not wearing yourself too thin."

"No, I'm fine, but I'm looking forward to sleeping in my own bed tonight. I spent the last couple nights on a cot at the hospital. I haven't had a chance to tell you the latest." She gave Georgia an abbreviated version of the incident with Alyssa's IV. "I caught him in the act. Almost had him, too, but the slippery snake got away. He put enough cocaine in that IV to kill a horse," she said. "There's a police officer standing guard outside her door twenty-four hours a day now, but I still felt like I should be there."

Georgia expressed her relief that Olivia had been able to avert disaster. Then she changed the subject. "How are you coming with those manuscripts I sent you a few weeks ago?"

Olivia told her she was about halfway into the second one, which she thought held a little more promise than the first. She explained that the author of the first one had made a good effort, but that she thought it would need quite a lot of fine-tuning and at least fifty or sixty more pages to be of interest to their company. "I meant to send the author a personal note, but it slipped my mind."

Georgia agreed with Olivia's recommendation about the first manuscript and told her she'd already sent a letter to the author explaining the problems. "Anyway," she said, "I wanted to check in and see how things were going." She told Olivia she could reassign projects to other editors if Olivia wanted her to.

"Thanks, but I think I'll be alright. Alyssa's going to be in the hospital for a few more weeks. I've been working from there." She told Georgia of her plans to bring Alyssa home with her to care of her there and mentioned that the doctors had said it probably would be a few months before she was ready to go back to work.

They chatted a few more minutes about trivial things before ending their conversation. Olivia hung up the phone and went back to putting away her groceries.

She made herself a simple meal of mac and cheese from a box with a small salad on the side. She poured a glass of wine and padded stocking-footed into the living room where she settled into her big chair for an evening of mindless television viewing.

Two hours of silly sitcoms later, she yawned, turned off the TV, and locked the doors before heading to bed. Tomorrow was another day—and the day after that, and the day after that.

She wondered if they'd be any different than the past ten days had been.

Two minutes after her head hit the pillow, she was sound asleep.

CHAPTER 16

Thursday, September 4, 2014

Olivia made good time on her drive from Portland to Missoula by way of Moses Lake.

After the first half-hour or so, she'd gotten used to having the extra length and weight of the trailer carrying her car following her down the Interstate. Normally, she was a bit more of an aggressive driver, but since she didn't have a deadline to meet, she decided to take it easy. Most of the way she was able to drive right at the speed limit, slowing only for sharper turns or steeper descents through some of the passes in the rugged Rocky Mountains.

She found herself enjoying the drive. Since she wasn't pushing herself to hurry, and had only her driving to think about for the time being, she was able to enjoy the beautiful scenery across the three states she was traversing. She'd always flown over Washington, Idaho, and Montana on her previous visits, thus missing the beauty of the area. Now she was awestricken by the massive rock formations, deep green forests, crystal clear lakes, and pristine rivers.

Suddenly she felt happier than she had in a long time. In fact, she found herself smiling for the first time since her divorce.

She called Alyssa when she was within about half an hour from Missoula. "I should be there by about two thirty," she said. "Rather than my driving this thing all the way through town, I think I'll take the second exit and skirt around town so I can go straight to the house. Do you want to meet me there?"

"Sure. Can do. I've got today and the next two days off, so I'm free to help you get settled."

"Oh, Lissy, you didn't have to take your vacation time to work for me."

"If I don't use it, I lose it," Alyssa said. "Besides, it won't be work. It'll be fun. Exhausting, mind-numbing, muscle-taxing fun." They both laughed, said they would see each other in about half an hour or so, and hung up.

Olivia smiled at the thought of seeing her new home and getting settled into it. She'd felt a bit restless and aimless since her divorce. Now, with a new job and a new home close to Alyssa, she was beginning to believe she had a brighter future ahead of her.

Thirty-five minutes later, Olivia pulled up in front of her new house. She turned off the engine and sat in the driveway looking at the house and yard.

This is it, Olivia Clayton. This is your new start in life. It's do or die now, kiddo.

Shaking herself out of her reverie, she opened the door and climbed down from the truck. She dug the house keys out of her purse and walked up the front steps.

"Here goes everything!" she said out loud and turned the key in the lock.

When she was inside, she stood in the middle of the living room and looked around. It was just as nice as she remembered its being. She walked through each room, picturing what pieces of furniture would go here and what would go there. She didn't have a lot of big pieces of furniture.

When she'd sold the house in Portland, she'd sold most of the furniture with it. Too many painful memories were associated with it. She and Kyle had picked out most of it together, back in the good days they'd shared. So the furniture, and even some of the art they'd collected, stayed with the house—except for her baby grand piano, an antique rocking chair that had belonged to her grandmother, and the bedroom set that had been hers since she was a junior in college. The latter, which consisted of a queen-sized bed, dresser, and highboy chest, would be fine for the guest room.

She would never let go of the chair. She was very young when her grandma died, but she remembered snuggling on her lap in that chair, listening to stories made up by her grandma, just for her. Nor would she ever give up her piano. Music had always been important to her. No matter what kind of mood she was in, she could count on her music to pick her up or calm her down. She already missed being able to play since the piano, which had been dismantled to be moved, had to be the first thing on the truck. She hadn't been able to play for several days now, and her fingers itched to move over the keys.

She'd also kept the dishes, pots and pans, and other kitchen necessities that Kyle had left with her. She'd decided she'd buy any other items she needed, such as living room and dining room furniture, when she got into the house and knew exactly what kinds of pieces she wanted. Her new place was an entirely different style and called for a different decor. She thought it needed something a bit more "Montana-ish."

She'd just walked back into the living room when she heard tires crunching on the gravel in the driveway. She went to the door and was thrilled to see Alyssa getting out of her car. She ran down the steps to greet her. They met in a huge bear hug.

"I'm so glad you're here at last!" Alyssa said. "Come on. Let's go look at your house."

"I just did that," Olivia said, "but I can do it again. Come on in."

The two walked arm in arm to the house, and when they were inside, Alyssa said, "Oh, Livvy, I think you're going to be very happy here. It's a wonderful house, and once your things are in here, it's going to be so homey and cozy." Then she changed gears and said, "Did you have lunch yet? I wasn't sure if you would've eaten on the road or not, so I packed a picnic for us. I thought we could sit on your front porch and enjoy the view while we eat."

Olivia, who'd had only a cheese sandwich while driving, had been listening to her stomach growl for the last half hour. A picnic on her new porch sounded wonderful. She waited while Alyssa went out to her car and brought her picnic basket back to the house. She opened the basket to take a look while Alyssa went back for a couple lawn chairs from the trunk of her car.

They sat down in the chairs and started pulling food out of the basket. Alyssa had packed still-warm fried chicken, cold potato salad, crunchy dill pickles, fruit salad, and a bottle of white Zinfandel wine. Olivia balanced most of it on her lap while Alyssa turned the large picnic basket upside down to use for a table.

"This looks like a feast," Olivia said and dug into the fried chicken.

"I'm hungry, too. I didn't want to eat until you got here, so we could have your first meal in your new home together."

"I'm glad you waited. This is really special, Lissy." They ate most of the rest of the meal in a companionable silence, glad just to be together and enjoying the marvelous view.

When they were finished, and almost too full to move, Olivia brushed her hands on the front of her jeans and said, "Well, partner, are you ready to work?"

CHAPTER 17

Monday, September 15, 2014

"Done!" Olivia stood with her hands on her hips and looked around the living room. "What do you think, Lissy?"

Eleven days after moving into her new home, the last of the pictures were on the walls.

Her new furniture had been delivered the week before. The men she'd hired from the moving company in town, to unload and reassemble her piano, had come and gone the day after she'd arrived as well. The shelves on each side of the rock fireplace were filled with books and favorite knickknacks and even a few plants had found a new home.

"I think it looks great," Alyssa said. "It's warm and welcoming and comfortable, Livvy. I think you did a marvelous job decorating it. The furniture you bought is perfect. The whole living room decor is set off by that mountain view through those huge front windows."

"We did it, Lissy. You helped a lot with all of it. I could never have done it all by myself."

"Okay. We did it. I still think it looks marvelous."

"Me, too," Olivia said. "I think we deserve to treat ourselves, don't you?" She went into the kitchen and came back in a few minutes with a tray of cheeses and crackers, accompanied by an unopened bottle of white Zin. "Care to join me in a glass of wine?"

"Wouldn't it be a little crowded for the two of us?" Alyssa managed to look apologetic when she told the old joke. Both of them hooted as though they'd never heard that one before.

"We must be more worn out than we thought we were," Olivia said. "I stopped thinking that one was funny years ago."

Alyssa put on a phony frown. "Well, now you've gone and hurt my feelings," she said. Her frown quickly changed to a smile, and she took one of the chairs by the fireplace. "I'll leave the big chair for you. Not that I think you need a bigger chair, but I know that's the one you were looking forward to having in here, so you could curl up in it with your manuscripts."

"Ooh," said Olivia, as she sank down into the overstuffed chair. "It is comfy. I'm really glad I didn't talk myself out of it, even though it cost almost half again as much as the other two chairs together."

"You're lucky you make enough money at your job to be able to live the way you want to," Alyssa said. "A lot of recently divorced women end up with no house, no furniture, nothing. I still can't believe you didn't take any alimony from Kyle."

"I didn't want it," Olivia said. "The house and furniture were enough. If I got a check from him every month, it would just keep memories alive that I'd rather not ever think of again. Selling the house and furniture gave me what I needed to get this place. And I do make enough with my job to meet my monthly expenses and still have some left to enjoy myself."

"Sometimes I wish I could get away from my memories," Alyssa said. "But then I realize I don't ever want to forget. I finally was able to give Rob's and the boys' clothes to Goodwill. It took me several months before I could let go of them. But then I realized I didn't need them to keep their memories with me."

"I know it's been hard for you, Lissy, but I'm really proud of the way you've carried on since the accident. A lot of people would have just given up after what you've been through in the last few years. You are a strong lady, Alyssa Walton. I hope you know that."

"What are we doing talking about our depressing pasts like this? We both have a lot to look forward to, new adventures to experience, places to go. Montana is a big state, and I've only seen a relatively small piece of it." Alyssa stopped talking and gazed out the large front window for a couple moments. "What do you say we go on a camping trip together next summer sometime?"

"I think that sounds like a wonderful idea," Olivia agreed. "But promise me we won't go where there are bears or mountain lions."

"Can't promise you that," Alyssa said, "but you won't have to worry about them. Ranger Lissy will keep you safe from the big scary animals."

"Okay, okay! I forgot for a moment to whom I was speaking." Olivia laughed, and it felt good to be able to do so.

They finished up their snack, put the half-empty bottle of wine in the refrigerator, and wiped imaginary crumbs on the fronts of their jeans.

"Let's take a little hike," Olivia suggested. "I still haven't seen all my property properly." She giggled girlishly at the way her last sentence sounded. "Property properly. Say that fast three times!"

"You must be more tired than I thought. You're getting goofy. I think some fresh air would be a good idea. Shall we?"

"Yes, let's!"

They left by way of the patio doors off the kitchen. They stood on the deck for a few minutes, taking in the beautiful surroundings. The chrysanthemums were in full bloom now, and the deciduous trees had started taking on their fall colors. Red, orange, and gold leaves joined the varying shades of green pine needles in the forest.

"Isn't it beautiful?" Olivia sighed. "I still can't believe it's mine."

"It is lovely," Alyssa said. "If I didn't get to work in this environment five days a week, I think I'd be envious. I don't think I'll ever grow tired of this. You're lucky to have found this place, Livvy."

"I think you're very lucky, too, in some ways, Lissy. You dreamed of being a forest ranger for as long as I can remember, and you made your dream come true. One of the best things that can happen in someone's lifetime is that she's happy in her job."

"I am lucky in that respect," Alyssa said. "Not so lucky in other areas of my life. But that's enough. No more self-pity today. Let's go for a hike."

They went down the steps leading to the backyard and headed toward the tree line. As they passed under a tall oak tree, a large black-and-white bird took flight from its perch high up in its branches.

"Oh, a magpie!" Alyssa said. "I love those birds. I know they're obnoxious and raucous, but they're so pretty, and they have so much personality. I'm a little surprised to see one up here. They usually like to be in a more open area. I guess as long as he has a place at the edge of the trees to build his nest, he must figure your yard is open enough. Did you know they mate for life? And they actually have a funeral of sorts when another magpie dies."

"I never heard of birds having funerals before. Seems kind of strange," Olivia said. "They are striking-looking birds though."

"They are related to both the crow and the jay," Alyssa said. "They can be kind of ornery. They'll steal your food if you're not careful. They aren't afraid of people and can be pests at times. But I still like them."

"If I hang around with you long enough, I have a feeling I'll learn volumes about the forest and all the little critters in it."

"Just stick with me, kid," Alyssa said. "I'll take you places you never expected to go."

"Well, I'm going to take you up on that right now. Let's explore my woods a little, shall we?" Olivia hooked her arm through Alyssa's, and they started toward the trees.

About twenty yards into the trees, they came upon what looked like a game trail. It was deep enough into the forest that the darkness made it almost invisible unless one was being very observant. Alyssa had been pointing out certain things to Olivia, like poison ivy, wild berry bushes, and mushrooms that were edible, if Olivia wanted to collect them, and that was how they happened to notice the trail.

"Let's follow this game trail for a little way and see where it takes us, shall we?"

"I'm game if you are," Olivia said, and then added, "pun intended." She followed closely behind her friend, only slightly nervous about the prospect of bears and other wild animals in the vicinity.

They spoke quietly as they hiked. Alyssa pointed out anything she thought would interest Olivia along the way.

About fifteen minutes later, Alyssa stopped in the middle of the trail and held a finger to her lips. "Shh! See that dark spot in the side of the mountain there?" She spoke softly and pointed to where she wanted Olivia to look.

Olivia hadn't yet spotted the cave. There was thick brush all around and in front of it, which effectively hid it from the untrained eye. Then, as she stared in the direction Alyssa pointed, she started to discern the darker, slightly rounded shape of the cave entrance.

"Yes, I see it," Olivia whispered back.

"Could be a bear's den. Be very quiet and we'll see if we can sneak a peek inside."

Olivia stood openmouthed, as Alyssa slowly and cautiously worked her way through the brush until she was about six feet in front of the opening. She motioned for Olivia to stay put and tiptoed to the mouth of the cave.

"What are you doing?" Olivia hissed. "Are you nuts? Do you want to get yourself killed?" She'd temporarily forgotten that her friend knew how to handle herself in these woods.

"Stay put and be quiet," Alyssa said. "I just want to check it out. It's good to know if there's anything living this close to your house."

She continued sneaking closer to the cave, and when she got to the opening, she took a small flashlight from her pocket and shone it into the cave. She could tell by the beam of her light bouncing off the back wall that the cave wasn't very deep. And it didn't look as though anything had inhabited it for quite a long time. She motioned to Olivia to come and take a look for herself.

"Are you sure it's safe?" Olivia kept her voice at a whisper.

"Would I steer you wrong? Come on and have a look."

Olivia gathered her nerves and joined Alyssa at the mouth of the small cave.

"See, nothing in here," Alyssa said. "This could be a handy spot to keep in mind just in case you ever find yourself caught in a sudden downpour out here. We should come back here someday soon and stock it with some firewood and a few supplies."

"Oh, that sounds intriguing," Olivia said. "A little hideaway all my own. And yours, too, of course, if you ever need one."

"We'll do that one of these days then," Alyssa said, "but right now, I think we'd better be going back down. I don't think you want to be caught in here when it gets dark. And it is getting late in the afternoon."

She led the way back down the trail. Going down, Olivia thought the trail seemed a little steeper than it had when they were climbing up it. The leaves and pine needles underfoot were damp and slightly slippery. She found she had to sidestep in places to keep from gaining too much momentum. Soon they were back at the edge of the forest in Olivia's backyard.

"Whew! That was a workout," Olivia said.

"It was a bit of a climb, wasn't it?"

"Yes, but I loved it. And finding that cave was such fun. I like your idea of stocking it with a few survival items, too. Be prepared. That's my motto," she said.

"Since when?"

"Okay, so it's my new motto!"

CHAPTER 18

Friday, October 31, 2014

"How do I look?" Olivia's face was a ghostly white with wrinkles drawn in with a brown eyebrow pencil. She wore a flowing, shiny, blue satin robe and a droopy, blue, pointed hat sporting yellow stars. In one hand she carried a wizard's wand, and in the other a large black pot filled with wrapped candies.

"Terrifying! How 'bout me?" Alyssa face was covered with green makeup, and she wore a long black robe and tall pointed hat. On the very tip of her nose was a huge plastic wart. "Should I cackle when I open the door?" She put on the evilest evil expression she could muster and squawked what she thought was a wicked laugh, but it came out more like a silly giggle.

"I wouldn't want to meet up with you in a dark alley. I hope we don't scare the little kids too much when they come to trick-or-treat here. But then, what's the point of Halloween if it's not to get a little spooked?"

"Oh, I think this is going to be fun, Livvy. I haven't dressed up for Halloween since I took Jeremy and Oliver trick-or-treating when…" Her voice trailed off, and for a moment she was lost in in the past, a sad, wistful expression on her face and her eyes suddenly moist with tears.

Olivia wanted this evening to be fun for her friend. She changed the subject quickly.

"Hey, do you remember when the two of us dressed like circus performers when we were in third grade? I went as a bareback rider with my stick horse, Magic. I wore pink sequined tights and a blue tutu. You went as a clown. It was right after you'd gotten your hair cut that time, and it was perfect for clown hair. And you had a big red nose that actually honked, and huge, floppy shoes that kept tripping you up."

They both laughed at the memory, and the mood they'd been in all day while preparing for this evening was restored. After the stressful couple of years they'd each had, they'd decided to go all out for Halloween this year.

They'd talked about how special the night had been when they were young. There was one house on their block that was turned into a haunted castle every year. Because it was owned by someone everyone on the block knew, parents weren't reluctant to let their kids go through it.

Spaghetti "brains," peeled grape "eyeballs," cold liver for—what else?—liver. Warmed tomato juice in a bucket, with bits of dog food floating around in it, made convincing "fish blood stew." By the time they got through the "Hall of Gore," with its black cats, skeletons, witches, spiders, bats, and spooky music, they were shaking in their shoes, even though they knew who really lived there and what everything really was.

Olivia and Alyssa had decided they didn't want to go that far this Halloween, but they'd still managed to fix up Alyssa's front yard and porch. On each side of the far end of the sidewalk, two huge pumpkins with carved hideous faces flanked a chicken wire tunnel that ran the length of the sidewalk. It was covered with black tarps, and orange lights were strung along the inside of it. Silky spiderwebs tickled the unsuspecting trick-or-treater's face, and the occasional huge rubber spider or bat dangled down in opportune places. They'd had a great time shopping at the Party Place downtown where the clerk who waited on them must have thought they were crazy. A CD of spooky music and sound effects added even more atmosphere. At the end of the tunnel were a pair of grinning plastic skeletons that danced and rattled to the music. It had taken them all day to construct it, but the overall effect, they thought, was pretty darned scary.

"How many kids do you think we'll have?" Olivia, who still was not familiar with Alyssa's neighborhood, had no idea what to expect.

"Well, last year I think I counted about sixty, although some of those may have been second-timers," Alyssa said. "This is a family-friendly neighborhood. That's why Rob and I moved into this house. Lots of kids around. I know most of them. Can't wait to see what they think of this."

At six o'clock they turned on the yellow-bulbed porch lights, the sound-effects CD, and the strings of lights in the tunnel, just as the first group of trick-or-treaters arrived at the front sidewalk.

"Whoa! Look at this!" one little boy said.

"Awesome!" said another.

The third was younger and more hesitant. "I'm not sure I wanna go in there."

In the end, however, all three entered the tunnel and were rewarded with goodies at the other end of it. Overall, the evening was a huge success, and Olivia and Alyssa had as much fun as the kids did. They were kept busy until about nine thirty. Then they turned off the lights and music.

"How much candy is left?" Olivia hoped there were still a few pieces of her favorite kind in the pot.

"Let's see. One, two, three…Um, I count just nine pieces here. Wow! They didn't leave much for us, did they?"

"I think they all loved it though, don't you? Even the older kids got a kick out of it. I heard a lot of positive comments from parents, too."

"So did I," Alyssa said. "It was fun, but I'm not sure I'd want to do it again."

"Too late," Olivia replied. "I heard someone say he wondered what we'd do next year. I think we're stuck."

The two women laughed and sat down hard on Alyssa's sofa. "I'm pooped."

Olivia nodded in agreement. "Me, too. I think I'd better help you get this cleaned up and then head for home and get some sleep."

"Why don't you stay here tonight? This stuff can wait until morning. I don't feel like being alone." In a singsong voice that

Olivia knew all too well, Alyssa said, "If you stay, I'll make my famous buttermilk pancakes with homemade chokecherry syrup for breakfast."

"That's bribery."

"You betcha!" Alyssa grinned.

"Okay, throw in hot sausage with those pancakes, and you've got a deal."

"Deal!" Alyssa said, and they shook hands on it. She locked the front door and then suggested a cup of hot cocoa and popcorn while they watched a movie on TV.

Olivia flipped through the channels. She noted all the spooky movies that were being aired. "Do you want scary, funny, or romantic tonight?"

Alyssa, who'd gone into the kitchen to get their snack ready, said, "Not scary. I know how you get with those. Do you remember what happened when we watched *Nightmare on Elm Street*? You literally threw yourself on the floor and covered your eyes," Alyssa teased. "Is there something funny or romantic anywhere?"

"How 'bout a romantic comedy? There's a Doris Day and Rock Hudson movie on. I'm pretty sure I've seen it before, but I can always watch their movies. They just don't make them like that anymore."

"That sounds good. The cocoa and popcorn are almost ready."

As Alyssa walked back into the living room, she glanced at the front window. "Oh, I forgot to close the drapes." She set her tray down and went over to pull the cord, looking out the window as she did so. "Hmm…That's odd," she said. "That same red SUV has been parked out there before. At least, I think it's the same one."

"Does it belong to one of the neighbors?"

"No. No one around here has a red one, that I know of. It's funny though. I'm pretty sure I've seen this one somewhere before. I just can't place it."

"Well, close the curtains and come away from the window," said Olivia. "Who knows how many red SUVs there are in town? It's probably a parent waiting for his or her late trick-or-treaters to come back. Or do you think it's the boogeyman man?"

"Yes, that's what it is. It is Halloween after all!" Alyssa laughed and passed a large bowl of popcorn to Olivia, who promptly dug in and declared it was the best popcorn she'd ever eaten.

Alyssa picked at her popcorn slowly, a look of concentration on her face. "I know I've seen that SUV somewhere, or one very much like it." She thought for a moment more and then snapped her fingers.

"I know! I've run into one a couple times at work. I stopped one about a month ago. I was out doing routine checks of campsites, and there was a red vehicle in front of me. I don't know if they didn't see me, or if they just didn't care, but they tossed a big bag of trash out the window. It broke open, and trash flew everywhere. So I pulled them over and asked them to go back and pick it up. They were very apologetic and contrite. They seemed pretty phony to me, but I made sure they cleaned up their mess and let them go with a warning."

She absentmindedly took another bite of popcorn and said, "That was just a couple guys that time. I figured they were campers, though of a different ilk than I'm used to seeing around here. They were kind of rough-looking and pretty crude."

After taking a sip of cocoa, she continued, "Then, about a week and a half ago, I saw what I thought was the same SUV, but there were two different men in it this time. They were way up in the middle of nowhere. I couldn't figure out what they'd be doing there, so I followed them a short time.

"I think they caught sight of me in their rearview mirror because they pulled over and waited for me to catch up with them. They waved me over, and when I got out of my Jeep, they asked me if there was a problem and why I was following them. I told them I hadn't been following them, they just happened to be ahead of me. I said I was heading up to check on a report of poaching in the area."

"Was it them? Were they the poachers?"

"No. There really weren't any poachers. I just said that so they wouldn't be suspicious."

"Oh. So then what happened?"

"Nothing, really. I asked them where they were from, and they said they were from Kansas. They told me they'd never been to Montana before, and they wanted to check out the fishing here. At the time, something about them made me a little suspicious, but there was nothing concrete I could put a finger on, so I just told them to be careful, and I asked them to let us know if they heard or saw anyone that might be poaching."

"Did you ever see them again?"

"I'm not sure. I've seen a few red SUVs since then, but like you said, those aren't all that uncommon in Missoula. A couple times I had the feeling I was being followed, and when I checked my mirror, I saw one, a few cars behind me. But again, that's not uncommon." She took another handful of popcorn and said, "Oh, it was probably all just coincidence. Sometimes I let my imagination run away with me."

"You're probably right, Lissy. I wouldn't worry too much about it. But if it gets weird, I think you should report it to someone."

They turned their attention back to the movie and forgot about red SUVs and strange men.

Two hours later, both women were asleep. Alyssa was curled up in her favorite chair, and Olivia had stretched out on the sofa. Neither one had seen the face peering through the small window in the door.

CHAPTER 19

Wednesday, March 18, 2015

When Olivia arrived at the hospital in the morning, she stopped at the cafeteria to pick up a cup of coffee and a couple donuts. She'd skipped breakfast because she'd been anxious to get up to see Alyssa.

When the elevator reached the fourth floor, she stepped out and turned right. As she rounded the corner in the hallway, she noticed a man walking ahead of her.

I wonder who that is. I don't remember ever seeing him here before. Something about him doesn't seem right.

As she watched, the man stopped and looked around. She quickly ducked into a nook where there was a nurses' mini-station set up with a small desk, computer, and phone. She carefully peeked out and saw the man start walking toward the end of the hall again—toward Alyssa's room. When he stopped at the door and spoke to the guard, she noticed that he was wearing a surgical mask. But why? Masks weren't required for Alyssa's room. The hairs on the back of her neck stood up. Now she saw what was bothering her about him. The cuffs of his blue jeans stuck out from beneath the light green scrubs he was wearing, and below those were the toes of a pair of dirty, scuffed cowboy boots.

"Wait! Don't let him in there!" Officer James looked at her as she started running toward Alyssa's room. "He doesn't belong here. Look at his legs and his feet!"

"Hold it, mister!" The officer reached out to stop the man, but a heavily-tattooed arm shoved him back hard against the opposite wall.

Olivia heard a sickening thud as the officer's head banged against the door trim. The intruder ducked his head and sprinted for the exit.

"Don't let him get away!" Olivia shouted for more help.

But it was too late. No one else was in the hallway, and Officer James had slumped to the floor, dazed. Olivia rushed to him to be sure he was okay.

"Just stay still while I get someone to check you out," she said.

Rather than going back to the nurses' station, she went into Alyssa's room and pressed the call button. A nurse came on over the intercom. Olivia explained what had happened and asked to have someone come check on the dazed policeman.

"I'll be right there." It sounded like Angie's voice. She hoped it was. She trusted Angie, and she knew she would take the matter seriously.

"I called security," Angie said as she arrived, out of breath, outside Alyssa's room.

"Good. Maybe they'll catch him this time." Olivia pointed to Officer James, who'd managed to rise to his feet. "He took a nasty bump to his head," she said. "I think you'd better check him out."

Officer James insisted that he was okay, claiming that he was hardheaded and had endured worse. He expressed regret that he couldn't stop the intruder and asked if Olivia had any idea who he was.

Angie told him to hold still and let her check him over. She looked at his pupils with a small flashlight she took from her pocket. Then she checked the lump growing on the back of his head. She said his pupils looked fine but told him he would have a nasty bump for a while. "I'll get you an ice pack as soon as I've checked my patient."

"She's fine," Olivia said. "That guy never made it through the door." When Angie left to get the ice pack, Olivia looked at Officer James, who rubbed his sore head. "You may not have caught him, but you did keep him from getting to her. Thank you."

"Just doing my job," he said. "I really wish I'd caught him, though. Who knows what he'll try next time?"

"Do you think there'll be a next time?" Olivia hoped against hope there wouldn't be.

"He seems to be pretty persistent. Would you excuse me for a minute?" He reached for his cell phone. "I've gotta let Detective Sheldon know what happened."

"Be my guest," Olivia said. She was secretly pleased at the prospect of seeing the detective again.

"What's going on?" Alyssa had awakened and was looking at Olivia, her brows drawn together with concern.

"Nothing, Lissy. Nothing you need to worry about." She nodded her head toward the door, indicating that Officer James should call from somewhere else. He nodded, said he'd be right back, and left the room.

"How are you feeling this morning, Lissy?" Olivia reached over to plump the pillow for her a little.

"It's a little soon to tell, but I actually think my head feels better. My hips are still giving me some major pain, and it's hard not to be able to use either arm. Are you going to tell me today what happened? I think I deserve to know how I ended up in here."

"I'll see if the doctor thinks you're up to it yet. Meantime, let's let Nurse Angie do what she needs to do," Olivia said as Angie walked in carrying an ice pack and asking where Officer James was.

"He's gone to make a call," Olivia said. "He'll be right back."

"Who's Officer James?" Alyssa asked.

"We'll talk about that later," Olivia said. "I think your nurse wants to take care of some business first."

Olivia stepped aside as Angie turned to her patient. "Good morning, sunshine! How are you doing today? Let's get your vitals written down here, and then the doctor said if you're up to it, you can have a little bit to eat this morning." She busied herself checking Alyssa's vital signs.

"You're doing great," she said. "Now, do you think you're ready to try a little food?"

"I'm starving," said Alyssa. "What's in the bag, Livvy?"

"I brought a couple donuts."

"Nope. No, donuts for you yet," Angie said. "We'll start out with something a little lighter. How 'bout some Jell-O, a piece of toast, and a cup of herbal tea? If that stays down, we'll try a little more later on."

"I'll take whatever you will let me have," Alyssa said.

"Okay, then. I'll be back in a few minutes, and we'll get something in your stomach for you." She left to have a tray fixed for Alyssa.

"I'll be right back," Olivia said. "I just have to check something with Angie quick."

She caught up with the nurse a few yards down the hall. "Angie, she's been asking what happened to her. She wants to know what's going on. Is she strong enough to handle the truth yet? I hate keeping it from her."

"I think you can tell her. Just watch her reaction. If it looks like she's getting too upset, calm her down and change the subject."

Olivia returned to Alyssa's room and said, "I'm at your disposal. What would you like me to do for you?"

"I want some answers, please. What happened to me? How did I land in the hospital with two broken arms, a broken leg, a fractured pelvis, and a whopper of a headache?"

"What's the last thing you remember?"

"I remember you and I had supper together and then..." She thought for a moment, a frown creasing her face. "We must have been going to a movie. That's what we always do. But I don't remember seeing one."

"We didn't see one," Olivia said. "We were walking to the theater. We'd just stepped off the curb. A black Humvee came roaring around the corner from out of nowhere and hit you."

"Oh my gosh! But why can't I remember that?"

"You sustained a lot of trauma, including a pretty nasty bump on your head. I'm surprised you can remember anything at all about that evening, considering what you've been through."

Olivia's heart did a flip-flop when Detective Sheldon walked in, smiled at her, and said, "Good morning, ladies." He asked how the patient was this morning.

Olivia hoped her face wasn't as flushed as it felt when she answered him. "She's doing a lot better, I'm happy to say." She turned toward Alyssa and introduced her to the detective. She explained that he was in charge of her case and that he didn't think her being run over was an accident.

"You mean it was a deliberate hit-and-run?" Alyssa's eyes widened with fear.

"I'm afraid so," Shel said. He told her he had some questions for her when she felt up to answering them, but he made it clear that he didn't want to push her. "So you let me know when you're ready to talk to me, okay?"

"Actually, I'd like to talk to you now, if it's all right."

"If you're sure you're up to it, Mrs. Walton."

"Oh, please, call me Alyssa," she said.

"Okay, Alyssa it is." He got down to business. "I just have a few questions."

"I'll try to answer them if you don't mind if I have my breakfast while we talk. It's been a while since I've eaten, and I'm a little hungry this morning."

"Not a problem," he said. "Let's start with what you remember about the day you were run down."

"Okay. Well, the last thing I remember before waking up here is having dinner with Livvy. I don't remember anything else about that evening."

"Livvy—Olivia—told me you'd been edgy about something for a few days before that. Can you tell me what that was about?"

He held his pencil over his pocket-sized notebook, ready to write down whatever she told him, and waited for her to finish chewing.

"Yes." She related to Sheldon the same information she'd shared with Olivia, about setting up the surveillance camera near Lone Man's Road and meeting a strange man out there. She told him what the stranger had told her, adding that his story had seemed a little odd to her. It wasn't hunting season, it was still quite cold outside, and it could be difficult to get around in the forest when the snow was deep or when things started to thaw. "It just seemed like a strange time for five men to all be on vacation. Especially in our neck of the woods."

"Do you remember what day that was?"

"It was on March 1." Now that Alyssa had been talking about the incident for a few minutes, her head had begun to clear, and the details were easier for her to recall.

"And you said you didn't know the man?"

"No. I'd never seen him before."

"Did he offer any explanation for the long vacation?"

"He just said they were in the construction business, and the company they worked for went under, so they were laid off. They decided to take a little R and R."

"Hmm…Anything else you remember that might be helpful?"

She explained that she and Collin had gone up a few days later, since they were already in the area setting up more cameras, to see if the first camera had caught anything. She told him about finding several sets of footprints in the snow, which led back to a cabin. She described what she and Collin had seen when they watched the video—the five men, a couple of them looking pretty tough—who seemed to be checking out the camera. And she mentioned that they all did a pretty good job of keeping their faces hidden from the camera, as though they were shielding their eyes from the sun. "But we were pretty deep into the forest. The sun is never that bright there. The strange thing is I don't know why they'd be so interested in that camera."

She stopped as the nurse's aide fed her another few bites of Jell-O.

"I don't, either, yet," said Shel. "But I aim to find out. I think that's enough for today. I don't want to tire you out. I think I'll talk to your partner and see if he'd mind showing me where that cabin is. If you think of anything else that might be important, don't hesitate to call me anytime, day or night."

"That might be a little tricky," Alyssa said, indicating her two broken arms, "but I'll find a way if I need to. Thank you for your help."

"You're welcome. It's good to see you looking and feeling so much better. Keep doing what you're told, and you'll be out of here in no time."

He told her goodbye, and he and Olivia stepped outside and moved farther down the hall to keep their conversation from reaching Alyssa's ears.

"Was any of what she told you helpful?"

"Well, some of it was a little strange," Shel said, "but I'm not sure how helpful it was. Not yet anyway. But it does give me something to check into at least. I think I'll take a little jaunt up to Lone Man's Road tomorrow and do a little snooping around."

They walked a little farther and then he asked, "What happened here this morning?"

She told him exactly what had happened. His face reddened with anger.

When she finished, he asked, "Was it the same guy as before?"

"I think so, but I really can't be sure since I never got a good look at his face either time. He was wearing a surgical mask this morning. I guess I just assumed it was the same man. I did notice something else this time, too. He had a big tattoo on his arm and another on the back of his right hand. The man I saw messing with her IV the first time had a tattoo on his right hand."

"That could be very helpful. If we ever catch our suspect, it will go a long way toward identifying him," Shel said. "Did you get a good enough look at it to be able to tell what it was?"

"I'm not sure," Olivia said. "It looked like a circle—no, a double circle—with some kind of emblem inside it. But I really couldn't see it well enough to tell you anything more."

"That's okay. It's a good start. If you saw it again, you might be able to recognize it anyway." He changed gears. "So, how are you doing? Sorry I couldn't talk to you yesterday. I was up to my ears in this case and a couple others I've been following for a while."

"That's okay. I don't really expect you to call me every day, although I have to admit it might be nice," she said.

"It would be nice. I'd like to spend more time with you. It's just that right now time is one thing I don't have a lot of."

"When you do have a little time, how would you like to come to my place and let me fix you a home-cooked meal?"

"I'd like nothing better than that," he said. "Oh, before I go, I need to talk to Officer James." He took her elbow and turned her back toward Alyssa's room. "We'll step away from her door so she doesn't overhear us. However, I do think you should fill her in. The more she knows, the better she'll be able to protect herself."

"I guess you're right. I didn't want to alarm her, but maybe she should know. I'll tell her when we have some time alone."

As Shel started to turn away from her, Olivia took hold of his arm.

"Did you think of something else?"

"No, but I was wondering, do you think I could ride out there with you tomorrow? I've never been that far into the forest. Alyssa's always talking about how beautiful and serene it is. I thought I'd like to see it for myself and try to see what she sees."

"I'm not sure that's such a good idea. These are some pretty nasty guys we're dealing with."

"But we aren't even sure if these are the same guys. Besides, I'd be with you and Collin. I'm sure I'd be perfectly safe."

"Well…"

"Please, Shel. I promise I'll stay out of the way."

"Okay. But you have to promise to do as I say. If there's trouble, I don't want you in the middle of it."

"Thanks, Shel. I promise. What time do we leave?"

"I'll pick you up at your place about seven o'clock."

"I'll be ready."

The two parted company, Shel to speak to Officer James and Olivia to go back and fill Alyssa in on recent events. She wondered how she should tell Alyssa what had been going on then decided the simple truth, told straight out, would be best.

When the nurse's aide who'd been helping Alyssa with her breakfast was finished, she picked up the tray and said, "If you need anything else, just let us know. Have a good day!"

After she left, Alyssa looked at Olivia and said, "Now, I want to know what's going on. Why all the secrets and hushed voices?"

"Okay, I'll tell you. But I don't want you to get upset," Olivia said.

"Well, now you're scaring me."

"I don't mean to. I'm going to tell you this because Shel— Detective Sheldon—thinks the more you know, the safer you'll be." Olivia took a breath and continued, "Besides someone's trying to run you down in the Humvee, seemingly on purpose, someone has now made two attempts to get to you here in your room."

When Olivia saw the look of alarm on Alyssa's face, she hastened to reassure her.

"That's why there's a policeman standing guard outside your door day and night." She told her about the first time, when someone put cocaine in her IV, but assured her that none of it had made its way into her bloodstream. "I ran in here just in time to see him do it, so we were able to stop it before you got any of it. We gave the bag to the lab. They tested it and found the cocaine."

"Oh my gosh! Someone really did try to kill me?" Alyssa's voice was incredulous.

"It looks that way," Olivia said, and then she continued. She told Alyssa what had transpired just a short time ago outside her room. She ended her story with Officer James's hitting his head. "That's why Angie brought him the ice pack. He wasn't able to catch the guy, but he did stop him from getting to you."

Olivia saw tears well up in Alyssa's eyes as she tried to fathom why anyone would want to hurt her, or worse.

"I don't know what's going on, Lissy. The only thing that I can think of is that guy you ran into up by Lone Man's Road. You did say something seemed a little strange about him. Can you think of anything that would make you feel that way?"

"I don't know. It was just such a surprise to run into him out there to begin with. I mean, that's pretty far out of the way. There's no one around there for miles. The only cabin in the area is the one he said he and his friends were renting. And it's not the right season for hunters or vacationers."

"Did he do or say anything that might be construed as a threat? Was there something in his manner that struck you as threatening?"

Alyssa frowned, trying to recall the brief conversation she'd had with the man. "No. I don't think so. I told you everything he said to me. Nothing seemed threatening at the time, just weird."

"Okay. Let's put that guy and his buddies aside for a while," Olivia said. "Has anything else happened lately that seemed off to you? Has anyone said or done anything that didn't seem right to you?"

"Honestly, no. I just can't think of anything, Livvy." Alyssa was getting frustrated, and Olivia didn't want to upset her.

"Tell you what. Let's just stop thinking about it for now and talk about something else."

"Okay. Let's talk about you and your detective."

"He's not my detective."

"I'm really happy for you, Livvy. I can see it in your eyes."

"See what? I don't know what you're talking about."

"Every time his name comes up, I see that light in your eyes. And I saw how you reacted when he walked into the room. I haven't seen you look like that since the early days of your marriage. It's nice to see it again."

"What light? What look? Shel—Detective Sheldon—and I are friends, that's all. There's nothing going on between us."

"Maybe that's something we'll have to work on," a pleasant male voice said as Shel walked into Alyssa's room.

"Oh!" Olivia spun around, flustered. Never in a million years would she have wanted Shel to hear her discussing him with someone else. She felt her face flush with heat and turned away from him.

"I forgot to tell you, I'm free on Friday, if the offer still stands."

"What offer?" Olivia was hard-pressed to remember what they'd talked about just a few minutes ago.

"That home-cooked meal. You know, the one you promised to cook for me when I had some spare time," Shel said. He turned and winked at Alyssa. "Well, I'm off duty Friday evening, and I just happen to know I'll be wanting supper then. So if the offer still stands…"

Olivia laughed. "Sure. Of course. Why don't you come over around six?"

"Great! What can I bring?"

"Nothing," Olivia said. "I owe you for all your help with everything. Just bring yourself and your appetite. Did I mention I hate cooking for a man who won't eat?"

"No, you didn't mention that, but I don't think you'll ever have that problem with me. Unless"—Shel winked at Alyssa again—"you're a terrible cook?"

Before Olivia could answer, Alyssa interjected. "Livvy is a fantastic cook! You'll probably gain five pounds if you eat her cooking."

"Lissy..." Olivia said.

"Maybe I should stay home then. I can't afford to put on any more weight," Shel said.

"Huh!" Alyssa snorted.

"Lissy!" Olivia hissed.

Alyssa and Shel both chose to ignore her.

"Do you like spinach? Olivia makes this wonderful spinach casserole, almost like a quiche, but without a crust. It's fabulous. Actually, even if you don't like spinach, you'd love this. My boys both love—loved it..." Her voice faded away.

Olivia jumped in. "You aren't one of those 'real men don't eat quiche' guys, are you?"

"Heck, no," he said. "And it just so happens I do like both spinach and quiche. And now I know what I can bring. Do you like a light Zin wine?"

"Sounds perfect," Olivia said. "So I'll see you about six on Friday."

"It's a date."

Olivia told Alyssa she'd be right back and walked Shel partway down the hall. "Don't forget about tomorrow," she said.

"I have a feeling you won't let me," Shell said. "'Bye. See you in the morning."

* * * * *

"What do you mean you didn't get into the room? Why has this job been so hard for you?" Trent had just arrived back from Missoula and told Joe of his second failed attempt to get to Alyssa. Joe wasn't happy. When he gave someone a job to do, he expected it to be done and done right. So far Trent's track record with this job hadn't impressed him.

"They have a cop standing guard outside her room now, Joe. I don't know how the other woman figured out I don't work at the hospital, but she did, and she yelled at the cop to stop me."

"That woman is going to be trouble, I'm afraid," Joe said. "We might have to give her a little warning. Let me think about it for a while." He rubbed his hands over his eyes and waved Trent away. Trent sat down at the table across from Joe and lit a cigarette.

"I thought you gave those things up," Joe said.

"I did. But it gets so boring being stuck out here, and I get antsy. So I started up again. Where are the other guys?" He held the pack out to Joe.

"No, thanks. I never started that nasty habit, and I don't intend to now," Joe said, and then answered Trent's question. "I sent them into town for some supplies. They should be back in another hour or so." He coughed, gave Trent a dirty look, and said, "Take that thing outside. I can't stand the smell."

Grudgingly, Trent pushed away from the table and stomped outside with his cigarette. Joe knew Trent had a problem when it came to bowing to authority. He also knew that, of the four men he was with, Trent was the most dangerous. And he knew Trent would like to be in charge of this operation, and he didn't much like Joe.

Tough luck. I'm in charge, and I'm not here for them to like me. I'm here to see that the job gets done, no matter what it takes.

It was getting to be late in the afternoon and starting to cool down quite a bit. Through the window, Joe watched Trent take a few more puffs of his cigarette and drop it onto the ground. He saw the curl of the smoke as the glowing butt hit the wet snow.

When Trent stomped the snow off his boots and came back inside the cabin, Joe still sat at the table, deep in thought.

"I have an idea," he said. "We'll wait until that woman ranger— Ranger Walton— is out of the hospital. It'll be a lot easier to go after her at her own house. No point in taking any more chances of being caught at the hospital. Meantime, we might see what we can do about her busybody friend."

"Sounds good to me," Trent said. "I don't think there's any way we can get to her as long as she's there with a cop at her door twenty-four seven, not to mention the nurses and that other woman hanging around there all the time."

"My point exactly," Joe said. "So we wait. We watch and wait."

The construction of the compound was about a quarter of the way done. It had begun late the previous spring, when most of the snow was off the forest floor and the roads were passable. It was so deep into the forest they actually had to cut a few of their own roads.

The land had been purchased legally, so as not to have anyone coming after them with trespassing charges. It was probably the only legal aspect of the whole operation. Once the fence surrounding the area was up, with at least one locked gate on each side, for a hasty escape if needed, construction began on the buildings.

The first building they'd completed after the pole barn, which held the building supplies, was the headquarters for the operation. It housed not only four meeting rooms, but also a fully-equipped kitchen, six large bedrooms—each with its own bathroom, and a lounge with a huge flat-screen television built in above the wood-burning fireplace. There also were plans for to install a hot tub and sauna in the future, to compliment the already-in-place indoor swimming pool. This building was where business transactions between the heads of the drug cartels would be handled. Eventually, it would be fully staffed with a chef, waiters, and cleaning crew. The men at the top weren't willing to forego certain luxuries, even in this remote area in the Montana mountains.

It had taken all of seven months to build this first unit, with help from a crew of another twenty men supplied by the higher-ups. Now Joe and his crew were waiting once more for the snow to melt in order to start building the additional smaller units that would be put up. These would be little more than cottages, though nicely appointed, for those people who would be permanent residents. They'd be responsible for security and maintenance. Some also would act as chauffeurs and gofers when deemed necessary while others would handle the less pleasant tasks of dealing with such things as unwanted visitors, nosy forest rangers, and the like. As the overseer of all these people once the compound was up and running, Joe would be a more-or-less permanent resident and would have a slightly larger house with a few of the nicer amenities, like a dishwasher and a small private patio in back where he could relax alone or with a "friend." In addition, he would have the privilege of enjoying the luxuries of the main building when they weren't being used by the big bosses.

Joe's house and the smaller cottages would go up quickly during this coming summer. Once those were livable, they would house the construction crews who would work on the rest of the compound's buildings.

In addition to the large headquarters building and the living quarters, there would have to be a maintenance shed, two large multivehicle garages, and most importantly, the building that would house the "kitchen" where the drugs would be manufactured and the finished product would be stored. It was unfortunate that they didn't have longer periods of weather conducive to construction.

As it was, the compound was not expected to be completed for three or four years. In the meantime, the five men already here would make sure things stayed on an even keel. They periodically drove from their rented cabin up to where the compound was hidden, far away from any civilization, to check things out and be sure nothing had been disturbed.

Now, on top of the other responsibilities he had, Joe had a couple of women who, it seemed, were hell-bent on getting in the way. He settled on his plan to wait until the Walton woman was out of the hospital and back at her own home. It would be easy enough to take care of her then. And the other one, well, they knew where she lived already, and she unwittingly had set herself up for an ambush by buying a house with no close neighbors and forest on three sides.

Joe smiled. *I just might have to take care of her myself. It could prove to be a good outlet for some of my frustrations.*

CHAPTER 20

Thursday, March 19, 2015

Olivia opened the door to Shel's knock at 6:55 a.m. "Hope I'm not too early," he said.

"Nope. I'm ready. Just let me grab a couple things." She disappeared into the house.

Shel stepped inside and said, "I hope you realize you don't need to bring a lot of stuff with you. This is, after all, strictly business."

"We still need to eat, and I thought it would be nice to have some hot coffee along, too."

"Now that sounds like a good idea," Shel said. "Here, let me help you with that."

"You can take the cooler if you'd like, and I'll grab the thermos and the bag."

"What did you do, pack a feast?"

"No. I just made enough for three people. Collin will be with us, too," she said. "There are a couple snacks in there, too. It's going to be a long day."

"Okay. Are we set then? Got your coat and gloves? And a hat? It's going to be chilly out there."

"Yep. All set!"

"By the way," Shel said, "what excuse did you give Alyssa for your not being at the hospital with her today?"

"Oh, I just told her that if I was going to have company for dinner on Friday, I needed to get a few things done at home. I know, I'm a shameless liar. But I knew she'd just tell me to stay away from Lone Man's Road if I told her I was going with you."

JEANINE FRICKE

"Which is exactly what I should have done," Shell said.

"Too late," Olivia told him and headed out the front door, Shel in tow. She locked the door behind her and followed Shel out to his car. She waited as he opened the trunk and loaded the cooler and bag into it. Then he opened her door for her.

When they both had their seat belts fastened, he looked at her and said, "We're off!"

"But we're going anyway."

"What?"

"Oh, that's an old expression my mother used to say. 'We're off, but we're going anyway.' Haven't you ever heard it before?"

"Nope, can't say that I have." Shel chuckled and headed down Olivia's long driveway.

He drove in silence, navigating through the morning traffic. Missoula was awake and bustling. People were on their way to work or dropping children off at school. Olivia was quiet, letting him concentrate on his driving.

Then they were on the interstate until Shel came to the exit he needed to take them to Ranger Station Four.

Olivia suddenly felt a little self-conscious about being alone with Shel. *Maybe it's just because Lissy brought it up. I didn't know I was that obvious about my feelings.*

Shel broke the silence. "You seem awfully quiet all of a sudden. Is something wrong?"

"What? Oh, no, nothing's wrong. I guess I just don't have much to say for a change."

"You haven't said two words since we got in the car. Did I do something to upset you?"

"No. I just…Well, yesterday Lissy told me something about myself that I hadn't realized before, and it's got me a little flustered, I guess."

"Maybe I can help."

"Oh, I don't think so."

"Worth a try, isn't it? What was it? Did you put your shirt on backwards? Jeans on inside out? Was there lipstick on your teeth? Or was it that nasty habit you have of being so darn cheerful and positive all the time?"

"Okay." Olivia laughed at his words despite herself. "She told me there was a certain light in my eyes, and she said she thought..." She paused.

"She thought what? I promise I won't laugh or think badly of you."

"She thought it was because of you. Because of my feeling toward you." Olivia looked down at her hands in her lap.

"Well, now. What's so awful about that?" Shel smiled and reached over to take her hand. "I find that very flattering. But there is one thing I'd like to know."

"What's that?" she asked.

"I'd like to know just what your feelings toward me really are."

"I don't know if this is the right time or place to talk about it."

"What better time or place? There's no one else around right now. I think this is an excellent opportunity for a nice, friendly, honest conversation."

Olivia still looked hesitant.

"I'll tell you what. I'll tell you my feelings toward you, if you'll tell me yours," he said.

"You first," Olivia said.

"Okay, here goes." He kept hold of her hand while keeping his eyes on the road. "I think you're the most devoted friend a person could ever hope to have. The weeks you've spent up there, every single day and even some nights, were way above and beyond the duties of friendship. No, wait." He held up his hand when Olivia opened her mouth to speak. "Let me finish. I also think you have a very tender heart, while at the same time being a strong, tough lady. You're smart. You're educated. You have a sense of humor. In other words," he said, "I think you're pretty terrific, and I like you very much. In fact, I think that given just a little more time together, it could very probably turn into more than just liking you. Whew! Okay, now it's your turn," he said, but then added, "Oh, one more thing. I also think you're a very attractive woman. There. Now it's your turn."

"You don't pull any punches, do you? Okay, here I go. I like you, too. I think you are a hardworking man, who is dedicated to his job and to the people he cares about. I think you also are intelligent and educated. And I love your sense of humor." She paused for a moment. "This sounds an awful lot like what you said to me, but it's true. I also think you won't quit 'til you get your man. You're determined and you're honest." She looked down at her hands again and said, "And I find you very attractive, too."

"Well, thank you. So what, exactly, is the problem?"

"I just wonder if the timing is wrong. I mean, the only reason we even met was because of Alyssa's situation. We've only seen the good side of each other. You haven't seen me when I get up in the morning, with my hair a mess and no makeup. You haven't seen me get angry. And you haven't seen me when I'm feeling sorry for myself."

"I look forward to all of that someday," Shel said. "You wouldn't be a complete person if there weren't those aspects of you. Trust me, I'm no prince charming when I get up in the morning, unshaven, with my hair sticking out in all directions. And I think you've seen me get a little angry a couple of times, but I can pretty much guarantee you that when I catch the guys that hurt Alyssa, you're going to see me get a whole lot angrier." He took a moment. "As for feeling sorry for myself, I don't do that very often. I did enough of that when my wife died. But if you don't see fit to see me on a more-than-friends basis, well, then I will feel sorry for myself, and for you, too, because we'll both be missing out."

"So you're not worried that we're moving too fast? You know I haven't been divorced very long. I don't want you ever to feel like I turned to you on the rebound. You're special, Shel. I can tell you that much." Now she looked him in the eyes. "But you know, what? I really don't know much about you. For instance, until this moment I didn't even know you'd been married, much less widowed. Do you have kids? What's your favorite color? Do you like to read?"

"Fair enough. I was married, for almost eighteen years. My wife died of cancer almost five years ago."

"Oh, I'm sorry, Shel," Olivia said. "I didn't mean…"

"Don't worry about it. We had a good life together, but I guess it just wasn't meant to last forever. I've learned to live with it, and as much as I hate to admit it, there are even times when I can go two or three days without thinking about Sandy. I used to feel guilty about that, but I know she wouldn't want me to, so I've tried to get over it." He cleared his throat.

"Let's see…What else? Oh, kids. No, we never had any. We thought about it, but Sandy worried about my being a cop. She didn't want to end up a widow and a single mother if something ever happened to me. We were happy just being the two of us. Not that I wouldn't have loved to have a few little ones running around. When she died, I regretted not having had children with her, but I've learned to live with that aspect of my life, too."

He paused a moment before continuing. "As for my favorite color and anything else you want to know, why don't we save that conversation for over dinner tomorrow evening? Unless, that is, you really want to stop seeing me socially for a while?"

"I'll tell you what. We can keep seeing each other, just like we have been. But let's take it slowly. We don't have to rush anything. I would never want to lead you on and then end up hurting you, just because I wasn't really ready to get involved yet. How does that sound?"

"I think it sounds good," he said, "and I'll take whatever I can get." Then he realized how that sounded and rephrased his words. "I didn't mean that the way it sounded. I meant I'll be happy with whatever makes you comfortable."

"I knew what you meant," she said. "I never would have thought anything else of you."

"Good. Now that that's out in the open, can we continue with the easygoing camaraderie we've enjoyed up to now?"

"I think that sounds like a wonderful idea," Olivia said, as Shel pulled into the parking lot at Ranger Station Four.

He came around and opened her door.

"I guess I'm going to have to get used to that," she said.

"Get used to what?"

"Having you open my door for me. I'm just so used to hopping out on my own. Sometimes I even tend to get a bit impatient while waiting for a man to do the gentlemanly thing."

"I guess you'll have to get used to it then. At least, when you're with me." Shel took her arm and said, "Let's go see if we can find Collin."

"I never thought to ask you if you told him we'd be coming."

"Yep. I didn't want to drive all the way out here for nothing. He said he'd be here, and look. I bet that's him."

As he spoke, a younger man came out of the log-cabin office. The two men introduced themselves and shook hands. Then Collin shook Olivia's hand and said he was glad to finally meet her, having already heard so much about her from Alyssa.

"All good, I hope. I've looked forward to meeting you, too."

They discussed Alyssa's progress for a few minutes, and then Shel said, "Sorry to have to call this to a halt, but I think we should get moving."

"Right," said Olivia. "Are we taking your vehicle or Collin's?"

"I think, if you don't mind, we'd better take one of ours," Collin said. He explained that some of the roads weren't much more than wide game trails, and it was pretty easy to get stuck. He added that there might be some good-sized branches or rocks in the way, too. "I don't think you want to take your car over those. The Jeep will handle pretty much anything we might encounter."

While Collin checked the supplies that were always kept in the back of the Forest Service vehicles, Olivia and Shel transferred the things she'd prepared for their excursion from Shel's car to the Jeep.

After ducking back inside the office to let the dispatcher know where they would be, he reappeared, rubbing his hands together with anticipation. "Shall we go? I've been itching to get back up to Lone Man's Road ever since Alyssa and I found those tracks up there. And now, since her 'accident'"—he made air quotes with the first two fingers on each hand—"I feel the need more than ever to get up there and check things out."

Shel opened the Jeep's front passenger's door and motioned for Olivia to get in. She tried to decline. She thought he should sit in front so he and Collin could talk. She reminded him that was the reason for their coming all the way out here in the first place. But he insisted she take the front. "I'm sure it will be a little smoother ride over some of the trails we'll be on. You take it. I'll be fine in the back, and Collin and I'll have plenty of time to talk."

Olivia thanked him and climbed in. Shel followed suit, and when they were all fastened into their seat belts, Collin started the engine and backed out of his parking space.

"We're off!" he said.

"But we're going anyway!" Olivia and Shel said in unison. They grinned at each other, and then at Collin, who was pretty sure he'd just missed something.

Oliva was glad Shel had talked her into taking the front seat. His prediction proved to be right. The trails were quite rough in places. Every once in a while, when they hit a particularly big hump in the road, she heard Shel exclaim under his breath when his head met the ceiling with a dull thud.

"You're going to need an ice pack if there are many more of those," she said.

"You may be right," he said. "Or at least, some aspirin."

Finally, they reached the sign that directed them toward Lone Man's Road.

"Only a little farther now," Collin told them. "Less than a mile."

Shel noted how far into the forest they'd come. He expressed mild surprise that Alyssa would have come so far out alone. He asked Collin if they didn't usually work in pairs.

"Sometimes, but not always," Collin said. Putting out surveillance cameras was a pretty routine task. Usually there was no reason to expect trouble, especially at this time of year, when there were few people, and the bears were still in hibernation. "Mostly," he added.

"What do you mean, mostly?" Olivia's eyes widened and her face registered some slight unease. "Are we likely to run into any bears today?"

"No, not likely," Collin said, "though it's a remote possibility. Once in a while, a bear or two will wake up early and hungry, and come out looking for a meal. But it's rare."

"You're sure of that, are you?"

"Pretty sure, yes," he said. "But don't worry. I've got it covered if we do happen to see a bear or a mountain lion or a charging moose." Collin caught Shel's eye in the rearview mirror and winked. He turned to Olivia and made a point of patting the firearm strapped at his side.

"Mountain lion? Moose? Maybe I'll just wait in the Jeep," Olivia said. "I guess I'm not as brave as I thought I was."

"Nonsense." This came from Shel, who'd decided to play along with Collin a little. "If we see anything coming toward you, we'll toss you a gun before we run for the Jeep."

Now Olivia caught the looks on their faces and knew they'd been leading her on. "Oh! That's not nice, you two! Taking advantage of a poor, defenseless woman with all that talk about bears and mountains lions and charging moose." She turned in her seat, stretched her arm back, and gave Shel a playful slug on his arm.

"Ouch!" He feigned pain and rubbed his arm. "I'd hardly call you poor or defenseless," he said. "Not the way you slug, or the way you've been standing up for Alyssa the last couple of weeks."

Collin drove in to where he and Alyssa had parked two and a half weeks previously and announced that they'd arrived at their destination. He pointed to the tall, straight tree in which Alyssa had mounted the camera. Unfortunately, it had snowed since Collin and Alyssa were last in the area, so the tracks made by the five men were gone.

"But we can still watch the video, can't we?" Olivia didn't like the idea of having come all the way out here to see nothing.

"I think that would be a good idea," Shel said. He and Olivia waited while Collin took down the camera, brought it back, and set it on the hood of the Jeep. He hit the play button, and the three of them first saw Alyssa as she walked backwards, away from the camera, to be sure it was catching her image. Then they saw her give a thumbs-up sign, indicating that she was happy with the position of the camera.

The screen went blank for a moment and then, with just a little static between its off and on modes, it was filled with the images of five men, all seeming overly interested in the camera, all doing their best to hide their faces. Just as Alyssa had said, each man shielded his face as though trying to block the bright sun. But there was no bright sun this far into the forest.

"That's interesting," Olivia said. "It definitely seems like they're a little camera shy, doesn't it?"

"That's what it looks like to me," Shel said.

Olivia's brows drew together. Something on the tape had caught her eye. "Can we watch it again? One of those guys looked vaguely familiar to me."

"Sure," Collin said. He reached up to push play again.

The three of them watched for a moment and then Olivia said, "Stop! Stop it right there."

She pointed to one of the men on the screen. "This guy, right here. There's something about him. I wish I could see him better. Just let me look a bit longer. Maybe it'll come to me."

She studied the man who walked back and forth on the screen, looking up at the camera while keeping his hand over his eyes. Suddenly she saw what she'd been looking for. "There! See that on the back of his hand? It's the tattoo I told you about, Shel. And look, he's wearing cowboy boots, too."

"A lot of people around here wear cowboy boots," Collin said.

"Yes, but they don't all have tattoos like that on the backs of their hands," Shel said. "I think you may be on to something, Olivia."

"That's the guy who went after Lissy in her room!"

"I think you're right. I think we finally have our first real clue in this case," Shel said. He turned to Collin and asked if it would be possible to take this camera for a while and try to track the men down. "We may be able to use a facial recognition program we have in our database."

"Sure. We'll take it back with us and check it out with my boss, but I'm sure he's just as anxious to find the guys who went after

Alyssa as we all are. I have another camera in the Jeep. I'll put that one up, and the guys on the tape will never suspect that we've taken this one."

"Where is the cabin they're staying in?" Shel asked.

"I can show it to you if you're up for a little hike," Collin said. "I'm sure you've heard of Mike Sloan, haven't you?"

"Sure I have," said Shel. "What's he got to do with this?"

"It's his cabin those guys have been using."

"Does Sloan know they're there?"

"I assumed he did. But I don't think he checks it very often, so he might be completely unaware of them."

"We can check that out later, I guess," Shel said. He turned to Olivia. "How 'bout it, Olivia? Are you up to a hike?" Shel looked at Olivia, who was flushed with excitement at actually having come up with something that could prove helpful.

"You bet I'm up to it! Let's get moving."

"Wait a minute," Collin said. "Before we head out, let's get hats, gloves, and a weapon or two. Better to be prepared than not."

"Do you think we're going to need weapons?" Once again, Olivia had bears and mountain lions on her mind.

"You never know," Shel answered. "These guys have already proven how dangerous they can be. Collin is right. Better to be prepared."

"Oh. The men. I wasn't thinking of them. I was thinking of— oh, never mind." She turned back to the Jeep for her hat and gloves. She called over her shoulder, "Before we head out, does anyone want a quick cup of hot coffee?"

"You know, that sounds good," Collin said. Shel agreed. Both men accepted the cups Olivia held out to them.

"What else do you have back there?" Collin asked.

"I packed a lunch and a couple snacks for each of us. I figured it would be a long day and we'd need something. Nothing fancy, but it'll keep the hunger away. Do you want it now, or should we wait until afterward?"

"How 'bout just a snack to munch on while we're hiking up there?"

"Sure. I mixed up some trail mix and put it in individual baggies. Hope that appeals to both of you."

"Sounds good to me," Shel said, and Collin nodded in agreement.

Olivia passed out the bags of trail mix. They finished up their coffee, put the cups back in the Jeep, and set out on foot to see the cabin where the five men were staying.

None of them noticed the figure who'd been watching them from behind a huge granite boulder since they'd arrived. Now the man left his hiding place and, crouching low, moved quietly from tree to tree, back up the mountain, taking a different route so that his footprints wouldn't be seen.

* * * * *

"Joe! She's here! She's here!" Pete tore through the cabin door, forgetting to stomp the snow from his boots, and nearly slipping when his wet feet hit the wood floor.

"Damn it, pipe down, would you?" Joe glared at Pete for interrupting his reading. "Who's here? What the heck are you hollering about?"

"The nosy one. That ranger's snoopy friend. She's down by that surveillance camera and she's with two guys. One's a park ranger, but I don't know about the other guy."

"What were they doing?"

"Well, they took the camera down and were watching something on the screen. When I left they were finishing up a cup of coffee and were getting ready to hike out somewhere."

"Did you stay around to find out where they were going?" Joe asked. He suspected that would be asking too much.

"No, Joe," Pete said. "I wasn't close enough to be able to hear what they were sayin'. But it looked like they were maybe headed this way."

"You sure?"

"As sure as I could be. I didn't stick around to follow 'em. I ran back here as fast as I could to let you know what was goin' on."

"Okay, okay. So they may be looking for us. We need to look like we are what we said we were—five guys on vacation."

The other men had, by this time, gathered in the front room of the cabin to see what was going on.

"What do you wanna do, Joe?" Cal asked.

"Anyone up for a game of poker?"

"You wanna play games now?"

"Can you think of anything else, off the top of your empty head, that we could do to make us look like we're just here for some R and R?"

"Oh. No. Sure, I guess I can play some poker," Cal said, scowling at Joe's nasty remark.

The five men each pulled a chair out from the wooden table. Trent grabbed a deck of cards from the shelf on the wall behind him and started dealing.

* * * * *

"Whew! I'm out of breath. Can we stop for a minute or two?" Olivia bent over, hands on her knees, to slow her breathing.

Collin brushed the snow off a fallen log and motioned for Olivia to sit on it. He apologized for forgetting that she'd been a city girl until just recently.

"Are we planning to go all the way to the cabin? How much farther is it? And if we do, what do we do once we get there?" Alyssa shifted a bit on the log, trying to avoid the stub of a broken branch.

"It's still a bit of a hike from here. I'd say we're two-thirds of the way there by now," Collin said.

"I'm not sure we need to go all the way," Shel said. "I just want to get an idea how isolated it is and how hard it is to get to it. I may need to bring reinforcements up here one of these days to take these guys down, if we manage to get any proof of any wrongdoing on their part."

"You don't think running over Lissy and trying to kill her in her hospital bed is wrongdoing enough?" Olivia was almost ready to charge into that cabin and show those guys that they'd picked the wrong woman to mess with.

"We still don't have hard proof these were the guys who did it," Shel said. "We've still not seen that Humvee. Nor have we seen, clearly, any of the men staying up here. The only connection we've made so far is the tattoo on one guy's hand, and even that's not solid proof."

"And the cowboy boots," Olivia said.

"And the cowboy boots. But, like Collin said, lots of folks around here wear cowboy boots. The fact that this guy wears them *and* has a tattoo on his hand does seem to be more than coincidence, all right, but we can't rush in with only that much."

"Okay," Olivia sighed, and her shoulders drooped with frustration. "I guess I can see where you're coming from. It's just so maddening. I guess I'm not patient enough to be good at this detective stuff."

"I know it's hard," Shel said, "but we have to do this all in the right order. Even if we do get the proof we need, if we don't get it the right way, none of it will be of any use to us. We have to be sure of any evidence we find before we act on it."

"He's right, Olivia," Collin said. "I want the guys who hurt Alyssa as much as you do, but we have to go by the book on this."

"So what's next then?" Olivia was anxious to be doing something. Standing around and talking wasn't getting them anywhere. She suggested they hike up a little farther to see what they could see. The two men nodded, and they started their trek up the trail again. Around the next bend, about five hundred yards ahead, they spotted a cabin with plumes of smoke escaping from the chimney.

"That's Sloan's cabin, right there," Collin said, pointing to the north.

"Has anyone from the Forestry Department gone up to check things out?" Shel wondered if anyone else had noticed anything suspicious.

"No, not as far as I know. We've had no reason to suspect anything's wrong. We can't just go barging in on a hunch. I'm sure you're aware of that, Detective."

"Of course," said Shel. "But why can't we stop in just to be neighborly?"

"It doesn't look like there are any neighbors," Olivia said. "Won't we look a little suspicious to them?"

"Not if I tell them I came up to check out a report on a bear that decided to get up early and go hunting, and that I had a couple friends who wanted to come along for the ride," Collin said.

"So what do we do? Just walk up and knock on their door?"

"Why not? We have our weapons. I'm in uniform. Why should they doubt our story?"

"But what if the guy with the tattoo is there? What if he recognizes me?" Olivia wasn't crazy about the thought of running into the guy she'd tangled with at the hospital. She was relieved when Shel said she had a good point.

They discussed their options for a few minutes and decided that Collin would go up to the cabin alone. He would stick to his bear story but leave Olivia and Shel out of it. He would do his duty as a park ranger and warn them about early waking bears. If he could do so without seeming obvious, he'd try to talk to them a little and see what he could find out. Olivia and Shel would hang back where they were and wait for him.

"Okay. I'll give it a shot," Collin said.

"If you aren't back in fifteen minutes, or if we hear gunshots, I'm coming in after you. Just be careful. We don't want anyone else hurt by these guys."

"I'll be careful," Collin promised. He nodded his head and turned toward the cabin. Olivia and Shel watched as he trudged through a mix of snow, mud, and pine needles.

"I don't have a very good feeling about this, Shel," Olivia said. "I hope Collin finds out something that's worth the risk he's taking."

"That's all we can hope for at this point. Collin's smart. He won't take any unnecessary chances."

"I hope not. Can you still see him? I wish we could see the front door from here. I'd feel a lot better if we could keep him in our sight."

"I agree, but I'm sure he'll be fine." Shel gave Olivia's shoulder a squeeze. "Hopefully, this little investigation is going to turn up some information about Alyssa's would-be killer."

* * * * *

At the sound of a knock on the door Pete, Cal, Trent, and Sam first all looked at each other and then, in unison, at Joe.

"Well, don't just sit there. Pete, get up and answer the door," Joe said.

Pete rose from his place at the table and slowly strolled toward the door. Without asking who had knocked, he opened the door wide to allow entrance.

"Mornin'," Collin said. "How are you today?"

"I'm doin' fine. What can I do for you?" Pete asked.

"Oh, nothing. I was just up here checking out the game camera we put up a few weeks ago, and I saw your smoke. I wanted to warn you, we've had a report of one or two bears that have come out of hibernation early and are on the hunt for food." He smiled and said, "And we wouldn't want any of you to become their first meal of the spring. Beyond that, I just thought I'd check in and see how you're doing, and if there's anything you fellas need."

Joe's chair scraped the wooden floor as he rose from the table and joined the two men at the door. "Mornin', Ranger," Joe said. "No, I can't think of anything we need. Can any of you guys think of anything?" He turned to the three still at the table.

"No, can't think o' nothin', Joe," Sam answered while the others shook their heads. Joe feigned interest as Collin asked how their vacation was going and mentioned that his partner had said she'd run into one of them when she installed the camera. Collin said if they wanted peace and quiet, they'd come to the right place, with no one around to bother them at this time of the year. He looked around the cabin before asking what they did for entertainment so far out in the middle of nowhere. He noted that spring seemed to be coming a little early this year, and there wasn't much snow left for skiing or snowshoeing. He reminded them that it wasn't hunting season for any of the game in the area, but that there was always fishing, and suggested they stop at Station Four for some ideas on where they could find some good trout fishing.

"Thanks, but we already did that. We've been out a few times," Joe lied. "Mostly, though, we've just been taking it easy. You know, playing cards, reading, doing a little hiking. Just catching up on some down time before it's time to start looking for work again." He cleared his throat and tried to sound casual. "So that was your partner Pete met that day when he was out for a hike? Did I read something about a woman ranger in some kind of an accident a while back? Hope it wasn't your partner."

"As a matter of fact, it was," Collin said. He watched the men's faces when he told them that Alyssa was badly injured, and that it had been touch-and-go for a while. He didn't see any reaction at first. When Joe asked if the driver had been caught yet, Collin mentioned that Alyssa had no memory of the incident, so the police didn't have much to go on. He noticed that the men all looked at each other, somewhat furtively, except for Joe, who kept his eyes on Collin's face. Though Collin knew it wasn't true, he told them she was recovering slowly, and that her doctors still weren't saying if she'd ever be able to come back to work.

"So she doesn't know what happened?" Joe was fishing, hoping they'd be in the clear if Alyssa's memory didn't return.

"She does now, but only because she was told. She didn't remember anything when she woke up from the coma. The police are still trying to locate the vehicle that ran her down. You guys haven't seen a black Humvee with a dented front fender around here, have you?"

"No, none of us have seen anything like that. But then, we don't go out much. We're pretty much hanging around here. We'll be sure to let you know if we do see anything, though," Joe said, "but we probably won't be around here much longer. No more than a couple weeks or so."

"Well, enjoy yourselves." Collin extended his hand, which Joe shook amiably.

"We will," Joe said, "and thanks for stopping by, Ranger."

"Sure thing. See you around." Collin nodded at the other four men before turning for the door.

When they were sure he was gone and out of earshot, Joe said, "Well, maybe we don't have too much to worry about, if that woman ranger, Ranger Walton, can't remember anything. But then there's that nosy friend of hers. I'm afraid she still might present a problem."

"Yeah, and remember, Joe? Remember, I told you there was three of 'em? That snoopy woman and the other guy were with the ranger."

Joe cursed under his breath. "I remember," he said. "And I think it's about time we did something about that woman."

* * * * *

Olivia and Shel watched and waited. Now that they weren't moving, Olivia felt the cold more. She wrapped her arms around herself and stamped her feet. She wished she had the thermos of hot coffee with her. Shel noticed her shivering and stepped closer to her. He drew her into his arms, and she didn't hesitate to snuggle in closely. She let herself forget about everything else for just a moment and basked in the scent of his aftershave and the warmth of his body.

Oh, it would be nice to have this every day for the rest of my life.

She smiled to herself. Then she remembered where they were and what they were supposed to be doing. She brought her mind back to the task at hand.

When they saw Collin emerge from the far side of the cabin, Olivia sighed in relief. Her relief was short lived, however, when they saw him start toward them and then veer off into the trees to his left.

"Where's he going?"

"I'm not sure," Shel said. "We'll have to wait and see."

About ten minutes later, they heard something off to their right. They turned, hoping it wasn't any of their potential suspects. Once again Olivia was relieved to see Collin approaching.

"Thank goodness you're okay," she said. "We weren't sure what you were doing when you left the trail and went into the trees."

Collin told them he was fine, and while they walked, he explained that once he was out of view from the cabin, he'd doubled back, keeping out of sight behind the trees. He'd circled around the cabin to check things out. There were a red SUV and a blue Dodge Ram pickup parked behind the cabin, he told them. No black Humvee. "If it's theirs, they have it hidden somewhere else," he said.

Once they were all sitting in the Jeep, with the motor running and the heater turned on, Olivia and Shel listened intently while Collin told them what had transpired at the cabin. After hearing what the discussion at the cabin revealed, they felt more sure than ever that there was something strange going on. The fact that they seemed very curious about Alyssa's "accident" and tried to make Collin believe they knew nothing more than what the paper said, didn't ring true with any of them.

"They wanted to know if she remembered anything about it. I told them she only knew what she'd been told. I also let them think she may never be able to come back to work, even though I know she probably will."

"Anything else?"

"Not much. Just that five guys hanging around a cabin in the middle of nowhere for weeks on end doesn't add up."

"Yeah, I know what you mean," Shel said. "Well, let's try to keep an eye out for them. That red SUV you mentioned interests me."

"Me, too," Olivia said. "Do you think it could be the same one I've seen?"

"Could be," Shel said. "Collin, did you notice what make and model it was?"

"It was a late-model Ford. I couldn't see the license plate because it was covered with mud. But I'll keep my eyes open, and if I see it around again, I'll try to get a little more information for you."

"Good. Well, I think we've accomplished what we came her to do," Shel said. "Shall we head back?"

"Sounds good to me," Collin said.

"Sounds good to me, too," said Olivia. "Is anybody else hungry? I have lunch here."

"Let's find someplace else to eat it though," Shel said. "I don't want those five to catch us hanging around here."

Collin put the Jeep in gear and turned back the way they'd come.

CHAPTER 21

Friday, March 20, 2015

Olivia slept in the day after she, Shel, and Collin had trekked up to Lone Man's Road. She hadn't set her alarm clock when she went to bed on Thursday, figuring she didn't have to be anywhere by any specific time on Friday. When she finally woke up at 9:15, she couldn't believe she'd slept so long. She was normally a morning person and up by 6:30 at the latest.

Her day was pretty much mapped out for her: run a dustrag over the furniture, let her robotic vacuum (a fun little luxury she'd bought for herself at Christmas) make its way through the living and dining rooms while she worked a little on the manuscript she'd been wading through, pay a short visit to Alyssa in the hospital, and do a little grocery shopping to prepare for the dinner she'd promised Shel this evening.

While the hot water of the shower washed over her, she thought of Shel and the conversation they'd had on the way to the ranger station. And she remembered how good it had felt to be in his arms yesterday. She was glad they'd decided to take things slowly. She was very much interested in pursuing a relationship with him, and she was almost sure he felt the same. But she wanted to be sure she wasn't going after him on the rebound from her divorce.

We'll see each other as friends. We can enjoy each other's company without things getting too involved. Dinner, walks in the park, a movie now and then maybe. But at least until Alyssa is well on the mend and our lives are back to normal, whatever that is, that will have to do. It'll be a good opportunity to get to know each other better before jumping into anything serious. This is what she told herself. But deep down inside, she knew she really was hoping for much more.

She got out of the shower, toweled off, slipped into a lightweight robe, and sat down at the vanity to dry her hair and put on her makeup. It was already after noon, and she wanted to get to the hospital so she'd have some time to spend with Lissy before going shopping. She'd need to be back home by 4:00 or 4:30 to start dinner.

When Olivia got to the hospital, Alyssa turned off the soap opera she'd been watching.

"I've never gotten into the soaps before," she said. "Between Rob, my job, and the boys' activities, I never had the time. I'm beginning to see how they could be addictive for some people though. Some of the problems the people on those programs have make even mine seem small." She motioned for Olivia to pull the chair over and sit down.

Olivia laughed and said, "Better not get too absorbed in them. Remember you're still a working woman. Or you will be as soon as you're able anyway. You'll have to forget about the soaps when you're back on the job. Unless, of course, you want to record them every day and watch them at night."

"Good grief, no!" Alyssa said. "I don't want to be tied down to anything like that."

"Glad to hear it."

"So what's up with you today?"

"Remember? Shel's coming to dinner tonight. And, thanks to you, I'm stuck making spinach casserole. Not that that's a problem. It's probably the easiest thing I could have come up with myself."

"Oh, that's right. Tonight is your first date," Alyssa said, an impish grin on her face.

Olivia ignored the innuendo. "The reason I'm so late getting here is because first I slept in a lot later than I thought I would— 9:15, to be exact, and then I did a little light housekeeping. I took my shower before coming up here, and when I leave here, I have to go shopping for dinner this evening."

"No problem. I'm not going anywhere," Alyssa said, a slight frown on her face. "Oh, Livvy, I'm getting so tired of this place. I think I'll go stir-crazy before this is all over. If I couldn't live vicariously through you, I'd probably already be there."

"I know, Lissy. It's hard. But you've been through a lot, and you have a long road of recovery ahead of you. You're going to have to be patient and put up with people helping you and entertaining you. In the meantime, you can be helpful to Shel by trying to remember anything that might help him find who ran over you and then tried to get to you here."

"I've been trying," Alyssa said. "I just don't know why anyone would want to do this to me. I didn't think anyone hated me so much they'd try to kill me."

"Maybe it's not a matter of hating you," Olivia said. "Maybe you know something you shouldn't, something you don't even know you know."

"But what? And if I don't know I know it, how am I supposed to remember it? Oh, my head is starting to hurt thinking about all this."

"Okay. Then let's stop thinking about it and talk about something else," Olivia suggested.

"What do you think I should wear this evening?"

* * * * *

Joe scowled at Cal, who was at one end of the boat they'd rowed out to the middle of the lake a short while ago. The ice was still breaking up on the lake, so getting out there had been tricky. Joe wanted to fish in peace. He didn't want to have to listen to Cal exclaim over hooking a trout, as though he'd never caught a fish before in his life. "Keep it down, would you, Cal? You want to scare away the rest of the fish?

Joe didn't care that he'd doused Cal's pleasure at having caught the first fish. He watched as Cal struggled to hang on to the pole in his hands while trying to keep his balance in the rocking boat at the same time. He could have helped him land the fish, but at the moment, he found it more entertaining to watch him struggle.

Finally, Cal let go of his pole with one hand long enough to pick up the net at his feet. He scooped it under the large rainbow trout that was flopping around at the top of the water, trying desperately to rid itself of the hook in its mouth.

Joe missed the dirty look Cal shot his way. He grimaced when Sam, at the other end of the boat, said, "Nice catch, Cal. Hope there's a few more like that in this lake."

Just as he finished speaking, Sam felt a strong tug on his line. "Hey, I got one!" He grabbed his pole more tightly with his left hand and started reeling his line in with the other. Another good-sized trout flopped on his hook.

It annoyed Joe even more when Sam said, "Hey, Joe. Hand me the net, wouldja?" Joe snatched the net from Cal and nearly hit Sam in the face with it when he thrust it toward him impatiently.

Sam managed to get the fish in the net after three attempts. "A little help woulda been nice," he said.

Joe, simmering in his own annoyance, ignored him and kept his eyes focused on his bobber.

"A few more like these and we'll have enough for all five of us for supper," Sam said.

"Too bad the other guys didn't want to come along. What were Pete and Trent gonna do, Joe?"

Joe would have preferred to ignore Sam's question, but he knew that if he didn't answer him, Sam would just persist in asking until it drove Joe mad. "They said something about going into Missoula to catch a movie. Then they'll probably have some supper and hit a bar. I don't expect to see them 'til late tonight, or maybe even tomorrow sometime," Joe said. "I just hope they don't get rip-roaring drunk and do something stupid."

He was quiet for a few minutes. The other two men knew from past experience that when Joe stopped talking and started thinking, it was best to leave him alone. For the last couple of days, ever since that ranger had shown up at the cabin, Joe had been in a foul mood. Neither one of them wanted to be at the receiving end of Joe's temper.

The three of them fished in silence for another ten minutes, and then Joe said, "I'm still thinking about Ranger Walton's nosy friend. I wonder if I shouldn't try to dig up some information on her. She keeps getting in our way. Right now, I think she's more apt to give us trouble than the ranger."

"You want us to go into town and see what we can find out?" Cal was getting tired of being stuck in the boondocks.

"No. This is something I want to do," Joe said. "That woman is getting to be a bigger problem by the day, and I want the satisfaction of handling that problem myself." The wicked smile on his face made Sam and Cal glad they weren't in Olivia's place.

"Okay if I just tag along with you then?" Cal was oblivious to the look Joe gave him. He just wanted to get away from the forest and do something.

"We'll see," Joe said. "Like I told you, I'm still thinking about what I want to do. I'll let you know if I want company."

* * * * *

When Shel knocked on Olivia's front door at precisely six o'clock, Olivia was ready. The casserole was being kept warm in the oven. A crisp Caesar salad was ready in the refrigerator, and a loaf of garlicky French bread was wrapped in aluminum foil so it would stay hot. The table was set for two. Candles and flowers from the grocery store added a soft touch.

She opened the door to find Shel standing on her porch with a bottle of wine in one hand and a book in the other. In khaki slacks and a navy polo shirt open at the throat, he looked relaxed and, Olivia thought, very handsome.

"Hi." He held out the wine and said, "A white Zin to go with dinner and a book of poetry I thought you might enjoy."

"Poetry? Emily Dickinson? T. S. Eliot?"

"Nope. None of those old standbys. It's Shel Silverstein. I'm sure you've heard of him, seeing as how you're an editor."

Olivia laughed. "Shel Silverstein! I love his work. And I think it might be just what the doctor ordered."

"That's what I thought," Shel said. "Somehow, reading a few of his poems can lighten your mood, no matter what kind of day you're having. I hope you enjoy it."

Olivia read the title of the collection of poems.

"This is the only one of his books that I haven't yet taken time to read. I'm sure I'll enjoy it. Thank you so much." She gave Shel a hug and ushered him to a stool at the breakfast bar.

"Dinner is ready. I just have to get it on the table. Would you like to open the wine?"

She indicated two stemmed glasses sitting on the bar, a corkscrew beside them.

"Sure thing," Shel said and got busy coaxing the stubborn cork out of the bottle. He poured two glasses of wine and handed one to Olivia.

"A toast," he said. "To old friends and new ones. And to very special ones with the potential to become more than friends."

They each took a sip and Olivia said, "That's a nice toast, Shel, but I still think maybe we should take things slowly."

"I know, that's what we agreed to do. I won't rush you. But I can hope, can't I?"

Olivia changed the subject. "Dinner is on. Shall we eat?"

Throughout dinner they kept the conversation light. She learned that his favorite colors were blue and green. She told him hers were blue and yellow. They talked about books they'd both read or wanted to read. They discovered they had similar tastes in music.

"Do you play that beautiful piano over there, or is it just for looks?" he asked.

"I play," she said. "I minored in piano in college. At one point I toyed with the idea of changing it to a major and becoming a concert pianist."

"What kept you from doing that?"

"Concert pianists lead demanding lives with very little time for family or anything else. I decided I didn't want to have to give all of that up."

"That's understandable," Shel said. He changed the conversation to enlighten her on some of the places in Missoula he thought she might enjoy seeing. He told her about the university there and said he'd had the opportunity to teach a class on criminology. He mentioned the museums, of which there were a few, and suggested they visit them together soon.

"That would be great. I've heard that the art museum is especially nice," Olivia said.

"It's one of my favorites. Let's plan to see that one first. Have you ever heard of the painter, Charlie Russel? When I was a kid, he was my favorite artist. He painted true-to-life pictures of the Wild West. There is a good representation of his works there."

They were silent for a few minutes while they each finished their meals.

"Would you like more?" Olivia asked.

"No, thanks. I'm full to bursting already."

"Oh, does that mean you won't want dessert then?"

"Now, I didn't say that. I just might have to wait for a bit to let my supper settle so there's room for dessert. Meanwhile, I was wondering if I you'd give me a tour of your home. I like what I've seen so far. You have good taste. I like your style."

"Thank you. Of course, I'll give you a tour. Let's start with my office."

She led him down the hall to the third bedroom, which she'd furnished with simple rustic pieces. The style of the room, which fit in with the chic rustic mountain theme she'd tried to capture throughout the house, belied the fact that she had completely up-to-date equipment that she used in her work, including a fax machine, as well as her laptop and a desktop computer.

The furniture was made of hickory wood, finished with a natural stain and clear varnish, to bring out the beautiful grain. She'd chosen a soft tan for the walls in this room, the only one she'd painted so far. The window treatments consisted of wood-grained blinds flanked by light blue curtains with comical scenes of frolicsome bear cubs on them. On the hardwood floor was a large braided rug in earth tone colors with touches of blue, green, and red. Scattered around the room were playful figurines of bears, deer, and moose.

"I like this room. It shows at least three sides of your personality," Shel said.

"And what would those three sides be?"

"Well, there's the designer in you, first of all. As I said, you have good taste. You've managed to play off a theme in here without going overboard. It's fun while still conveying that it's a place to get some work done. Then there's the serious side. The furniture is sturdy and functional. It suggests that when you sit down to work in here it's a place where you'll get a lot accomplished."

"And what's the third side?"

"The third side is the little bit of a young girl who wanted to have something fun to look at when she wasn't looking at her work. Hence, the curtains and the knickknacks around the room. I think this is my favorite side."

"Hmm…All that, huh? No wonder you became a detective. Do you want to see what you can deduce from the rest of the house?"

"Sure. How 'bout your room?"

"Shel…"

"No, I don't mean anything by that. But I think that room will tell me a lot more about you than even this one does."

"I'm not so sure about that," Olivia replied. "That's the last room to be finished, and I haven't done much in there yet. Right now it's pretty much just a place to sleep and dress. I've been so busy and preoccupied lately, I haven't given much thought to finishing it. But I'll show it to you if you still want to see it."

"Sure, why not?"

Shel followed her to the largest of the three bedrooms. Like her, the part that impressed him most was the master bathroom with the intricate mosaic scene in the shower. He whistled with appreciation when he saw the beautiful view of her backyard with its backdrop of the forest.

"I think I see what drew you to this place," he said.

"Yes, the views from all sides are wonderful. I love soaking in the tub, when I have time, and looking out on the gardens. The previous owners did a beautiful job of landscaping. Now it's up to me to keep it looking good."

"Seems like a lot of work for one person."

"It is, but it's relaxing, too. When I'm puttering among the flowers, I don't have to think about anything. Or I can think with a clear mind. It feels good to get out and get my hands dirty a couple times a week."

"That's something I miss at my place," Shel said. "I keep my yard mowed and the hedges trimmed, and I try to keep the weeds under control and pick up the leaves. But since Sandy died, I haven't had much interest in gardening. She loved puttering in her flower beds and vegetable garden, too. I was usually too busy to be able to help her much. Now I wish I'd just made the time." He looked into Olivia's eyes and said, "If I ever have the chance again, I'll do things a lot differently."

Olivia averted her eyes, not wanting him to see the feelings they must surely be revealing.

"Well, the only room left is the guest room."

"Let's see it," Shel said, "and then I think I'd like another glass of wine while you play something for me on the piano."

"Oh, I don't know, Shel. I haven't had much time to practice lately," Olivia said.

"It doesn't have to be anything complicated. Just play something you like, and I'm sure I'll like it, too."

"Well, all right," she said.

He followed her into the guest room. "Alyssa should be comfortable in here when she comes to stay with you. The decor is soothing. I particularly like the photos of Montana's scenery and wildlife."

"I'm finding more and more that I love about this state," Olivia said. "Alyssa has always been more of the outdoor type than I, but I'm definitely beginning to understand her feelings for the great outdoors in Montana. Every time I come home, I appreciate even more the spectacular view of the mountains I have from my front porch. I wanted to bring that into this room so that whoever stays here will have the same feeling of serenity that I feel when I look at the mountains."

"Well, I think you've succeeded. It's very restful. Those photos were taken by one of my favorite photographers," Shel said, taking her hand. "Now, how 'bout that wine and song you promised me?"

They walked hand in hand back to the kitchen. Shel poured himself a glass of wine while Olivia went into the living room and sat down at the piano.

He listened as she played the first few measures of Debussy's "Clair de Lune." He thought, *she's good.* Then as she got further into the piece, he began to feel the music, and for the first time, he thought he was beginning to understand what their music meant to the musicians who really loved it and took it seriously.

When she played the final notes of the piece, Olivia sat with her hands in her lap and her head bowed for a few moments. Shel was so moved by the music he didn't say anything at first. Then he applauded her performance and said, "Bravo! Bravo!"

Olivia felt herself blush at his words of praise.

"That was beautiful, Olivia," Shel said. "I had no idea you could play like that. I almost feel sorry for the rest of the world who won't get to hear your talent."

"Thanks, Shel. I'm glad you enjoyed it. Debussy is my favorite composer. His music contains such rich, full harmonies. It's easy for me to get lost in it. This piece is one that I played for my college juries."

"It must have earned you an excellent score."

"My piano professor said I passed with flying colors." Then she changed the subject. "Okay, I think I'm ready for another glass of wine, and then why don't we go sit outside with it?"

"Aah, I could get used to this." Shel sank down into one of the comfortable Adirondack chairs on the front porch. He breathed deeply of the crisp spring air and took a sip of his wine. "What a great place to unwind after a long day at work."

"Yes, it is," Olivia agreed. "I come out here quite often. When I'm home, that is. It seems like it's been a lot longer than a couple weeks since I've had a chance to sit here and relax. Not that I'm complaining," she added hastily. "I wouldn't want to be anywhere but with Lissy while she's in the hospital. I know she'd do the same for me if the tables were turned."

"I think the two of you are more like sisters than friends," Shel said.

"Yes, you're right. Of course, neither of us had any siblings, and we grew up right next door to each other most of our lives. If Lissy hadn't pulled through this, I really don't know what I would have done. I moved to Missoula to be close to her."

"I'm glad you did," Shel said, raising his glass. "Here's to destiny—Alyssa's, yours, and mine. May we all find exactly what we're looking for."

"To destiny," Olivia said, taking a sip of wine.

"Do you want to talk about the case at all?"

"If you don't mind, I'd rather not. Just for tonight. I'd like to keep the evening relaxed and comfortable, the way it has been so far."

Shel shifted his glass to his other hand. He reached over and took Olivia's free hand in his. They sat together that way and watched the lights come on in the city spread out below them until a sudden cool breeze made Olivia shiver.

"Brr! I should have brought a sweater out with me."

"Let's go inside," Shel suggested. "I think I remember being promised dessert."

"You remember correctly. Hope you like cherry cheesecake."

"It's one of my favorites," he said and held the door open for her. "I guess almost any dessert is my favorite at the time I'm eating it."

They chuckled at that, and Olivia dished up the dessert.

"Shall we take it in the living room?"

"Lead the way," Shel said.

When they sat down side by side on the deep, comfortable sofa, Shel leaned forward to pick up the TV remote control.

"Oh, is this what your idea of an evening in is?" Olivia raised her right eyebrow at him and teasingly nudged him lightly with her shoulder.

"Not always, but there is a program on Friday evenings that I try to catch when I'm not on duty. It's a program featuring mountain men in different parts of the United States. I find it interesting to see how they live their lives in isolated areas, doing things the old-fashioned way. I thought you might enjoy it, too, but maybe you'd rather not watch TV at all?"

"As a matter of fact, believe it or not, I watch that one, too, when I get the chance. My favorite mountain man of all of them is the older guy from up north of here. He's a tough old guy, but he seems to have a heart of gold at the same time. Kind of grandfatherly, if you know what I mean."

"You're talking about Tom," Shel said. "I like him, too."

"The show makes me think back to how life must have been when the pioneers first settled out here," Olivia said. "Of course, today's mountain men have it somewhat easier, with snowmobiles, cell phones, power chain saws, etc. But still, they live their lives much closer to nature than most of us do. I admire that."

They settled back on the couch to watch the show. Olivia didn't object when Shel's arm found its way around her shoulders.

When the program was over, Shel stretched his arms and long legs and said, "I guess it's about time I headed home. I have to be up early tomorrow morning."

"You're right. I was having such a nice evening, I wasn't even paying attention to the time."

"Since you enjoyed yourself so much, maybe you'd like to do it again? Only this time I want to take you out so you don't have to do all the work."

"That would be nice sometime."

"How does tomorrow sound to you? I work until five. I could pick you up by six."

"Oh, tomorrow's too soon, don't you think? I mean, I..."

"I know. You think we're going too fast. But you have to eat, and if I know you, you'll spend the entire day up at the hospital. Dinner doesn't have to mean anything else. We'll just talk, like we did this evening. And if we feel like it, maybe we'll take in a movie after dinner. We can play it by ear."

"All right." Olivia gave in. "I'm planning to spend the day with Alyssa, so I'll cut my visit a little shorter tomorrow. Do you want to pick me up at the hospital? If I know Lissy, she'll want to see what I'm wearing."

Shel kissed her lightly and said, "It's a date then. See you tomorrow."

"Good night," Olivia said. She wished he didn't have to go at all and hoped her voice didn't betray her feelings.

When she went to bed thirty minutes later, she couldn't sleep. Her mind kept replaying the kiss and the feel of his arm around her shoulder.

CHAPTER 22

Saturday, March 21, 2015

The day dawned with weather a that's a little more typical for an early spring morning. The sky was overcast, and the forecast was for rain, possibly turning to sleet or snow later. Olivia exchanged the short-sleeved shirt she'd laid out the night before for a lightweight sweater instead.

She'd called Alyssa early this morning to say that she needed to stay home for a while to get some things done. She promised she'd be at the hospital later to keep her company for a few hours. Alyssa had protested, saying Olivia needed to take time for herself and catch up on things after having spent every day of the last couple weeks by Alyssa's bedside.

"What? Are you trying to get rid of me? I just need to do a little laundry and pick out something to wear tonight," Olivia said.

"Oh? Something I don't know about going on tonight? Something special?"

When Olivia didn't answer her immediately, Alyssa pushed on. "Out with it. I want to know everything."

"There really isn't all that much to tell," Olivia said. "I'm just going out for the evening with Shel, that's all. He asked me when he was over for dinner last night." She knew what Alyssa would be thinking and told her not to get too excited. "It's just dinner, and maybe a movie afterward."

"So I was right about you two, wasn't I?"

"What do you mean?"

"You know very well what I mean. I mean..." Alyssa said.

163

"I know what you mean. We're just friends for now, okay? We had quite a long talk about it—about the two of us—the other day."

"You mean there's an 'us' between you two?" If Olivia could have seen her over the phone, she would have seen a woman who looked like the cat that ate the canary.

"Only in so far as that we're good friends. We agreed we'd see each other, just the way we have been, an occasional lunch or supper…"

"Or dinner and a movie," Alyssa said.

"But nothing too serious for now," Olivia said. She spelled out for her friend exactly what she and Shel had decided. "I'm not saying nothing will ever come of it, but for now, we're taking things slowly.

"Okay. I'll accept that. For now. But when I'm out of this hospital, and out of your way and back in my own home, there will be no excuses for you two to not spend time exploring the possibility of a more permanent relationship."

Olivia laughed at her. "Oh, Lissy. You're still a hopeless romantic. Like I said, I like Shel. I'm looking forward to seeing more of him. But we agreed to take it slowly, and that's just what we're going to do."

With Olivia's promise to be at the hospital soon, they ended their conversation so Olivia could finish her chores.

Now, while she folded a load of laundry and put it away, Olivia found herself looking forward to another evening with Shel.

Remember, we're taking things slowly. There's plenty of time, she thought. *Yes, but I can still enjoy being with him and fantasize about him a little.*

She put another load of laundry into the washer. Then she walked back through the house and picked up the rug by the front door to shake. As she stepped out onto her front porch, she glanced at the road below. Was that the same red SUV she'd noticed before? No, probably not. There were probably a hundred or more red SUVs in Missoula, she reminded herself for the umpteenth time.

But why is it just sitting there? Oh, I'm getting paranoid. It's probably just someone enjoying the view. It's pretty spectacular from there. Still, she shivered, and she wasn't sure it was because of the chill in the air.

She shrugged off her slight sense of unease and gave the rug one more good shake. Then she turned and went back inside.

When she'd finished the last of the laundry, watered her plants, and taken out the trash, she went back to her huge closet and eyed the clothes hanging there. *What to wear? I wish I knew where Shel plans to take me this evening.*

Finally, after pulling out several outfits and laying them across her bed, she settled on a pair of black leggings, a sapphire satin tunic, and black ballerina slipper-styled shoes. She knew the leggings emphasized the length and shapeliness of her legs, and the color of the tunic set off her long blond hair and brought out the blue of her eyes. The flat shoes were easier to walk in and more comfortable for a long evening.

There. This outfit should fit in with just about any place Shel wants to go. Just need to change purses and I'm set.

She hung the leggings and tunic on a hook on the back of the bathroom door, and set the shoes and purse on the bench at the foot of her bed. After hanging up the other clothes she'd pulled out of the closet, she decided to take a shower.

She let the hot water run on her back for a while, stepped out, and toweled herself off.

She pulled on clean blue jeans, a raspberry red paisley shirt, and her cowboy boots. She glanced at the clock and saw that it was already close to noon. Deciding she really didn't want cafeteria food again, she took a can of soup out of the cupboard and heated it on the stove. She pulled the fixings for a sandwich out of the refrigerator and poured herself a diet soft drink. She sat on a stool at the breakfast bar and looked out the kitchen window while she ate.

She still couldn't believe how fortunate she'd been to find this place and be able to afford it. She loved the privacy and the views she had from every window in the house. She finished her meal, drank the rest of her pop, and loaded her few dishes into the dishwasher.

Then she grabbed her jacket and was off, locking the door behind her as she left.

When she pulled onto the road below, she noticed that the red SUV was no longer there.

Yep, just as I thought. I was being paranoid. Nothing to worry about.

She turned her attention to the road ahead and was on her way. What she didn't see was the red SUV moving farther up the hill behind her and out of sight. Now it made a U-turn in a wide spot in the road and slowly made its way to the bottom of her driveway and then up to her front yard.

* * * * *

When Olivia got to the hospital twenty-five minutes later, Alyssa was sitting in a chair next to the window. Her empty lunch tray was on the rolling bedside table, which was off to the side. She was clumsily holding a plastic glass with a lid and a straw between her hands, her broken arms making it a difficult task.

"Look at you!" Olivia said. "It's good to see you out of that bed"

"Yes, but it would be even better if I could feed myself. With these casts on both arms, I still can't do that, or anything else, for that matter. The nurse's aides have to feed me every meal. And as you can see, I can barely hold this glass between my hands. But I still can't get it close enough to my face to be able to take a drink. I think if the table were over my lap, I could just bend down to take a sip when I want one."

"Okay. Well, let's just give that a try, shall we?"

Olivia moved the lunch tray to the foot of the bed. Then she rolled the table over, locked the wheels, and lowered it to the right height. She put the glass on the table and turned it so the straw was pointed in the right direction.

Alyssa leaned forward and managed to take a long sip of the liquid in the glass.

"What are you drinking, anyway?"

"Chocolate shake," Alyssa said, licking her lips.

"Yum! No wonder you wanted to be able to get to it. What else did you have for lunch?"

"Grilled chicken breast sandwich, tossed salad, and cherry pie. You know, the food here isn't bad for a hospital," Alyssa said and went back to her shake.

"And to think, I had canned soup, a salami sandwich, and a can of Diet Coke for lunch. Guess I should've had the cafeteria food after all."

They laughed and then Alyssa said, "But you are going out for a wonderful dinner this evening, don't forget."

"Oh, I haven't forgotten," Olivia said. "In fact, that's what took me so long to get up here today. I did a little laundry, picked out my outfit for tonight, and showered. It took me a while, because I don't know where we're going, so I had to find something that would be appropriate wherever we go."

"What did you settle on?"

"Black leggings, sapphire blue tunic, and those little black ballerina slippers I got when you were with me a few months ago." She looked at her friend for her approval.

Alyssa nodded. "I wish I could see you in it before you go out."

"You will," Olivia said. "Shel's picking me up here. So I'll go home a little earlier today, change clothes, and then come back up here. You can give me your opinion then."

"Sounds good, even though it would be too late to do anything about it if I don't approve. Oh, I wish I could get out of here and go back to a 'normal life.'" She made air quotes with the second and third fingers on each hand.

"Ha! What's a normal life? I don't think either one of us has had what other people would consider a normal life for quite a while now."

"You're right. But I'd sure like to get out of here and give it a try again." She paused and then said, "I've had a lot of time with nothing to do but think, and I've made a decision."

Olivia waited for Alyssa to continue.

"I'm going to sell the house. It just doesn't feel like home to me anymore. It's too big and too empty. I need a new start somewhere else."

"By somewhere else, you don't mean a different town, do you?"

"Oh, no! I love it here. And I'm going to keep my job. Oh, I forgot to tell you. Right after you left last night, Collin stopped by for a short visit. It took some convincing on my part, but Angie finally got him a visitor's pass. He said they're all waiting for me to get my rear in gear and get back to work. Too much work for the rest of them when I'm gone, he said." She laughed and Olivia was glad to hear the enthusiasm in Alyssa's voice.

"Have you thought about where you want to move? Another house? Or maybe a condo in one of those gated communities? You know, that's not a bad idea. Especially since you live alone. It would be safer, more secure. Plus, you'd have the added benefit of not having to take care of the yard all by yourself."

"I haven't really decided yet. I thought when I'm up to it, you and I could do some looking around. I don't know if I'm ready to give up the privacy of a house though. You live alone, too. Would you be willing to give up your house? No, I'm pretty sure I want another house. Just a different one."

"Maybe there's something up in my neighborhood that you'd like. Wouldn't it be great if we could be neighbors again?"

"It would," Alyssa answered. "How would you like to do me a favor and do a little checking around for me?"

"I can do you one better," Olivia told her. "When I come up tomorrow, I'll bring my laptop, and we'll go online and see what real estate is available here. I was quite happy with my realtor. We can check with her and see what she has to show us, too."

"That would be fun. It would give me something to do besides stare at the TV or out the window, and I'd feel like I was accomplishing something. Let's do it!"

"Okay. In the meantime, what would you like to do this afternoon? Or are you tired? Do you need to rest?"

"Good grief, no! I'm so sick of being in that bed. Let's play a game," Alyssa said.

"Alright. Any preferences?"

"Well, if I had my choice, I'd always choose *Scrabble*," Alyssa said. "But it's kind of hard to do that with no hands. What can we do that requires no hands?"

"Hmm...I'm thinking." Olivia scratched her head. "Oh, I know! How 'bout Mad Gab? We can take turns, and I can change the cards for you when it's my turn to guess."

"Sounds good, but where are we going to get it?"

"Just so happens that when I was in the gift shop downstairs, I noticed they had a few games there. I'm pretty sure that was one of them. I'll run down and get it, and I'll be back in a flash. Don't go anywhere!"

"Ha, ha. You are so funny." Alyssa stuck her tongue out at Olivia as she ducked out the door.

Ten minutes later, Olivia was back, game in hand. She situated her chair across the table from Alyssa and opened the box. For the next half hour, they entertained themselves trying to decipher the nonsensical phrases. Every once in a while, they had to shush themselves when they started laughing too hard.

"That felt good," Alyssa said when they'd had enough of the game. "I needed that."

"Me, too. And I thought of something else you might enjoy. On the game channel there are several fun game shows that you can play along with. I can find that channel for you if you want me to."

"That'd be great. But I don't have to watch it right now. Let's talk a bit."

"Okay. What shall we talk about?"

* * * * *

"Hopefully, that will keep that nosy woman from snooping around and getting in the way from now on." Joe had just returned from his solo trip to Missoula and was telling the four men playing poker around the kitchen table what had transpired. "I let her know I meant business. There wasn't a spot in that house I didn't trash. I found out some information about her, too," he said.

"Her name is Olivia Clayton. She's divorced, lives there alone. No kids, no pets. Just herself for company. I got a look at some of the stuff in her office, too. It looked like she has something to do with some publishing company back east. From what I could tell, she works at home. The house is secluded, which I could pretty much tell from the road below. If she gives us any more trouble, it won't be a problem to surprise her with another little visit. Only next time, it'll be while she's at home. And we'll do more than just scare her."

"Sounds like you put a real good scare into her today, Joe," Cal said. "Sure wish I coulda gone along with ya. Did ya take anything from the house? Jewelry, cash, computer, anything?"

"No. I didn't want to take anything that could be traced. Besides, I'm not a thief, and I went there to scare her, not steal from her." It didn't occur to Joe that his sense of honor was a little warped.

"So what's next, Joe? I could try for that ranger again." Trent was a little more bloodthirsty than Joe preferred, but he could be useful if the moment called for drastic measures.

"I don't know yet. They'll be expecting us to try again and will be more on their guard. Let me think about what our next move should be."

"Whatever you say, Joe," Trent said, disappointment in his voice.

Joe poured himself a cup of strong coffee from the pot on the stove. He wanted some time to think, so he went into the room he'd claimed as his own and shut the door.

He sat down in the old, but comfortable armchair, with its red-and-black buffalo plaid upholstery, and kicked off his boots. He crossed one stockinged foot over his knee, resting his cup of coffee on the arm of the chair. Things were going to start up at the compound again soon now that the weather was warming up. They were going to be busy trying to get as much finished as they could in the few months before fall and winter came around again.

He'd exaggerated when he'd told that ranger they'd be out of the cabin in a couple weeks or so, but hopefully, a few of the cottages would be finished soon so they could move out. He was afraid it would be dangerous to hang around here much longer.

I have a sneaking suspicion that ranger already thinks it's odd for the five of us to be on vacation.

The four men in the other room were getting antsy. Sitting idle for a few weeks had been okay, but now they were ready to get moving again. Joe was worried that the longer they sat around, the more potential there was for trouble. No telling what they'd do if they got bored enough.

I think it's time for all of us to go to town for a good time. If I'm there, I can keep them under control. Maybe I'll treat them all to a good steak dinner and a couple drinks. That should make them happy for a while, at least.

He finished his coffee, wedged his feet back into his boots, and went back to the other room where Pete and Trent were just starting to argue over Pete's last play in the card game. He spoke up before things between the two had a chance to get too heated.

"You guys get cleaned up and ready to go. We're all going to Missoula for a steak dinner, my treat."

The four men just looked at Joe. He'd never leaned toward such generosity before. Then, as though they were afraid he might change his mind, they all rose together and headed off to get ready. Within twenty minutes, they were all set.

"We'll take the SUV. You drive," Joe said, tossing the keys to Trent, who caught them and got in behind the wheel.

"Where are we going?" Trent asked.

"I spotted a steak house this afternoon that looked pretty good, if the number of cars in the parking lot was any indication. It's called Danny's. Thought we might give it a try. Just drive, and when we get to town, I'll tell you where to go."

Joe settled back in his seat and closed his eyes. For the next half hour or so, he intended to block all sights and sounds out of his mind. The other four carried on some inane conversation, accentuated occasionally by raucous laughter, that he really didn't care to follow.

His self-imposed time-out was interrupted twenty minutes later when Trent suddenly stomped on the brakes. Joe's eyes flew open in time to see a huge whitetail buck run onto the shoulder of the road and into the forest.

"Watch it, will you! We don't need another banged up vehicle."

"I am watching it," Trent said. "If I wasn't, I woulda hit the damn thing." He shot Joe a dirty look, but luckily for him, Joe was still looking out the window to his right.

For the rest of their drive, Joe kept his eyes on the road while still trying to block out the ridiculous conversation amongst the others.

* * * * *

When Angie came in to check Alyssa's vitals and get her settled back in her bed shortly after four, Olivia declared that it was time she went home and got ready for her date with Shel.

She hugged Alyssa and told her she'd be back in a couple hours.

"Don't forget to put on some of the perfume I gave you last Christmas," Alyssa said. "You want to smell pretty for him." She winked at Angie and told her, "Livvy has a hot date with our favorite policeman, Detective Sheldon."

"Ooh! He's a real catch," Angie said.

"I know. I can't wait 'til they set the date."

"Enough! I'm leaving now," Olivia said and walked out the door.

On her drive home, Olivia was barely aware of where she was going. *I have to admit that I'm am looking forward to this evening.* She smiled to herself and stepped on the gas when the light turned green again.

When she pulled into her driveway, she used the remote door opener and drove into the garage. When she got out of the car, her steps were light. *I'm actually feeling a little giddy*, she thought. She turned the key in the door that opened into the kitchen.

Her giddiness was short-lived. She stepped into the kitchen and was stopped short by what confronted her. Her home was a shambles. Chairs were tipped over, pictures were off their hooks and lying on the floor, a couple of them damaged, probably beyond repair. Cupboard doors and drawers had been left open and looked like someone had thoroughly rummaged through them. A few of the dishes had shattered when they hit the floor. The refrigerator door was left hanging open, and some of the food had been tossed out. Even a carton of milk and a bottle of orange juice had been opened and dumped all over the floor.

Olivia stifled a scream. She hesitated only a split second before turning and running back out to the garage. She got in her car, locked the doors, and dug her cell phone out of her purse.

Rather than calling 911, she opted for dialing the police station directly. Fortunately, she was good at remembering numbers and had committed this one to memory after calling it the first time. She asked for Detective Sheldon, who came on the line almost immediately.

"I hope you're not planning to break our date," he said. "I've already made reservations for the hottest restaurant in town."

"I'm afraid I'm going to have to," Olivia told him. "I need you to come to my place as quickly as you can."

He heard the urgency in her voice and asked her, "What's wrong? Are you okay?"

"I'm okay. Just a little shaken up. Someone broke into my house while I was at the hospital."

"What? I'll be right there. Give me ten minutes. In the meantime, where are you now?"

"I'm in my car, in the garage, with the doors locked."

"Good. Stay there. Don't go back into the house until I get there."

"No problem," she said. "I didn't go beyond the kitchen to see if there was still anyone in there or not. And I don't want to find out the hard way."

She hung up. She was starting to feel slightly claustrophobic, so she started her car and backed out of the garage. She turned the engine off and sat waiting for Shel. Her eyes darted nervously from the front door to the garage, to the corners of the house, and back to the front door again. She desperately hoped she wouldn't see anyone coming from any of those locations.

She was immensely relieved when, true to his word, ten minutes later she saw Shel's car, strobe lights flashing, pull in at the bottom of her driveway. She waited until he'd parked and walked over to her car before opening the door and getting out.

He pulled her to him and wrapped his arms around her in a bear hug. Finally, she was able to relax just a little bit.

"You sure you're okay?"

"Yes. I'm fine. I've actually gone from being terrified to being furious. How dare someone invade my privacy like this?"

"You said you didn't go beyond the kitchen?" Shel guided her toward the porch by her elbow as he spoke.

"That's right," she said.

"Well, I'm going to check out the rest of the house. I want you to wait here on the porch until I tell you it's safe to come in."

"Okay," she said and handed him the key to the front door. She took a seat in one of the Adirondack rockers on the porch.

Shel drew his gun and cautiously opened the door. Before moving farther into the house, he looked around the living room and kitchen. He let out a soft whistle.

Quickly, gun hand leading him down the hall and through doors, he checked out all the other rooms, finding that they'd all been ransacked. But he found no one still lurking in a closet or behind a door anywhere. When he was sure it was safe, he holstered his weapon and made his way back to the front porch.

"No one's in there," he said. "It's safe for you to come in now. I have to warn you, though, whoever was here did a pretty thorough job of trashing the place. Be prepared."

Olivia stood and walked past Shel through the door. She put her hand to her mouth as she took a longer look at the mess that had been made.

"Come with me and take a look at the other rooms," Shel said. "I need you to tell me if anything's missing. Just be careful not to touch anything." As they moved toward the hall, he pulled out his cell phone and called the sheriff's office. He explained the situation and asked for a forensics team to meet him, along with the sheriff, at the scene. He pocketed his phone and looked at Olivia.

"I'm sorry, but your privacy is about to be invaded even more."

"I didn't even think about calling the sheriff," Olivia said. "I guess I'm not used to living outside of city limits. And I just automatically thought of you, I guess, because you've been handling Lissy's case, and for some reason, I tend to think this and that are related."

"That's okay," Shel said. "But we do have to get the sheriff involved now. His name is Ken Harrison. You'll like him. He's been sheriff here for almost fifteen years. He's a good man."

As they inventoried the mess in each room, hot tears of anger and fear sprang to Olivia's eyes. Beds had been stripped. Clothes were strewn all over the floors. The medicine cabinet had been emptied, its contents spilled into the sink and onto the floor. In her office the manuscript she'd been reading was scattered from one end of the room to the other. Her laptop was open and turned on, as was the desktop computer. Fortunately, though, she'd been careful to create a very strong password, so the perpetrator hadn't been able to access any of her files.

"Do you notice anything missing?"

"No. I don't think so. But whoever it was, he sure didn't leave anything untouched, did he?" Olivia swiped at a tear as it rolled down her cheek.

"No, he didn't," Shel agreed. "You're sure, though, that nothing is missing? Jewelry, cash, anything else of value?"

"I don't really have anything a burglar would want, except maybe my TV and sound system, and he didn't take those, he just smashed them. He made a mess of my jewelry, what little I have, but it doesn't look like he took any of it. Why would someone break in just to mess up my house and not take anything?"

"I hate to say this, but I think the intention was to intimidate you," Shel said. "And maybe to see what he could find out about you. He may intend to return soon."

This last statement got Olivia's undivided attention. She hugged her arms to herself and gave Shel a look of quiet panic that told him she didn't want to be alone here tonight. As they walked back to the living room, leaving everything just as they'd found it, the forensics team arrived in a sheriff's van and started bringing in their equipment. Shel introduced Olivia to Sheriff Harrison, who'd arrived in a separate car. He extended his hand to her and offered his sympathy.

"I'm really sorry you have to go through this, Ms. Clayton. We'll try to finish up here as quickly as we can. And I promise you, we won't stop looking for whoever did this until we find him, or them."

"Thank you, Sheriff. I appreciate that," Olivia said.

Olivia and Shel took up positions in the two Adirondack chairs on the porch.

"Some date, huh?" Shel said. "Or do you feel like you still want to go out? You do need to eat, and the team will be busy in here for quite a while."

"I don't know," Olivia said. Then she changed her mind. "You know, I am a little hungry, and you're right. I'd just be in the way if I hung around here. Do you think it would be a problem if I went in and changed clothes, at least? I would like to wear something a little more presentable."

"You look just fine in what you have on, and I don't think the forensic team would be too happy to have you contaminating their crime scene."

Together, they walked back into the house, and Shel had a few quiet words with the team leader, who nodded a few times at what Shel said to him.

"Okay, we're all set." Shel nodded to Olivia and motioned toward the front door with a sweep of his hand.

"Oh, Lissy!" Olivia's hand flew to her mouth. "I told her I'd be back in a couple hours to show her what I was wearing. She has to be wondering where I am by now."

Just as she spoke, her cell phone rang. She pulled it from her purse, looked at the screen, pushed the receive key, and said, "Hi, Lissy... Yes, I know. I'm sorry. I'm running a little late."

She listened for a moment and then said, "No, I didn't chicken out. In fact, Shel is right here with me now. We were just leaving to come up and see you."

After telling Alyssa she'd explain the reason for her tardiness when they got there, Olivia hung up and put her phone back in her purse.

"Ready to go now?" Shel asked.

"Ready. Let's get out of here for a couple hours, please."

"Hope you don't mind riding in my patrol car again," Shel said. "I'd planned to go home and change clothes, too, and pick up my personal car. In fact, why don't we do that after we stop and see Alyssa? There's something else I need to do at home, too, if you don't mind?"

"Fine with me," Olivia said, "if you think they'll hold our reservations for us."

"No problem there," he told her. "They know me at Danny's, and they know things come up that make me late every so often. Not," he added quickly, "that I go there with that many dates, but the owner is a friend of mine."

After making sure Olivia's car doors were all locked, Shel went around to the passenger side of his car and held the door open for her. Then he climbed behind the wheel, turned the car around, and headed down the driveway. Twenty minutes later, he pulled up in front of the hospital.

They proceeded to Alyssa's room. Alyssa, who'd been half-heartedly watching a rerun of an old sitcom, slid her cast-encased left arm across the bed and switched off the TV with the button on the bed rail.

"It's about time you got here," Alyssa said. Then she noticed the stress on Olivia's face, as well as the fact that she still wore the clothes she'd had on earlier that afternoon. "What's going on? That's not what you said you were going to wear tonight."

"There was…" Olivia searched for the correct word. "…an incident."

"What kind of incident?"

Shel spoke up. "Someone broke into Olivia's house and ransacked the whole place."

"Oh my gosh, no!" Alyssa's eyes grew huge. "Were you hurt, Livvy? Please tell me you weren't hurt!"

"No, no. I wasn't even home. It happened while I was up here this afternoon."

"Did they take anything?"

"No, I don't think so. A few things were broken, and my TV and sound system were smashed, but mostly the house is completely torn apart. I think I'll be able to salvage most of the rest of it."

"Still, that had to be frightening."

"I was terrified at first," Olivia said. "Now I'm furious. How dare anyone do this to me? I feel like I've been violated, not just my home."

"I wish I were out of here so I could help you clean up," Alyssa said.

"No problem there," Shel said. "I'll be over tomorrow to help her get started on it. The two of us should be able to get it done in a couple days, I think. I have a few weeks of vacation I haven't used, and if I don't use it, I lose it."

"But, Shel, you don't want to waste your vacation on this," Olivia protested.

"Who said it would be a waste?"

"Livvy, take the help while it's being offered," Alyssa said. Then she gave Olivia a sideways nod of her head, indicating that she wanted her to step closer. When Olivia did, Alyssa said in a stage whisper, "Besides, this will give you two a great opportunity to get to know each other better."

"Lissy, I told you Shel and I are just good friends. Don't make more of this than it is."

"Lissy," Shel whispered loudly and winked at her. "You feel free to—let's say, urge her toward more."

"I thought we agreed to keep things as they were for a while," Olivia gave Shel a questioning look.

"You're right. We did. Sorry." Shel looked contrite. "I'll just have to be happy with our friendship for now."

"Are you still planning to go out this evening? You do have to eat, right?" Alyssa said.

"Yes, so Shel informed me. We'll go to dinner, but I don't know about anything after that. I'm starting to feel the effects of the day. But I am getting hungry."

"I think we should get going," Shel said. "I doubt they'll hold our reservations forever,"

"Oh, just one more question. Where are you staying tonight? You can't stay at your house," Alyssa said.

"I haven't thought about that yet," Olivia said. "But I will, I promise."

"Okay. Well, you two go enjoy your dinner. And I'll want to hear all about it soon."

Olivia gave Alyssa a hug, and Shel carefully took her hand and said, "It's good to see you doing so much better. See you later."

Fifteen minutes later, he pulled up in front of a modest, but attractive, Craftsman-style house. "Here we are. Home sweet home," he said.

He went around and opened Olivia's door for her. "Come on inside for a few minutes. I promise to be a gentleman, and I won't take too long."

She smiled at him and said, "I'm not worried." She walked with him up three steps to a cozy front porch. "I like it already. It's charming."

"I try," Shel said. "Just because I live alone, it doesn't mean I have to live like a slob."

He opened the door and escorted her inside.

She stopped just inside the door, taking in the polished wood trim, the beamed ceilings, and the many built-in bookshelves, lined with more books than she'd ever seen in someone's home.

"Wow! Do you like to read, Shel, or are all those books there just to make you look smart?" She grinned at him and said, "No, I think it's great. As you may have guessed from my job, I love to read, too. I may have to borrow a few books from you from time to time, if that's okay."

"I do love to read," he told her. "My grandma once told me a person could do anything and go anywhere, if he knew how to read. She got me my first library card when I was only six years old."

"She sounds like a wonderful lady."

"She was a very special person," Shel told her.

Olivia turned when she heard an unfamiliar clicking sound behind her. A huge German shepherd walked slowly toward her, his toenails tap-tapping on the hardwood floor, and his tail wagging a mile a minute.

"He won't hurt you," Shel said, "as long as he knows you're with me. He may lick you to death, but I promise that will be painless. You wouldn't want to be a burglar breaking in here, though." He reached down to scratch behind the dog's ears.

"What's his name?"

"Columbo," Shel said. Then, to the dog he said, "Columbo, this is Olivia. Tell her hello."

Columbo sat down in front of Olivia, held up his right paw, and said, "Woof!"

"Well, hello, Columbo. I see you like to shake hands." Olivia bent down, took the dog's huge paw in her hand, and gave it a gentle shake. "Oh, you're a nice boy, aren't you?"

Columbo gave her another happy wag of his tail and then went over to his bed in front of one of the over-loaded bookcases. After turning a few circles, he lay down and pretended to sleep, while keeping one eye open so he could watch what his master and his guest were doing.

"He is a good dog." Shel told her that Columbo was just over a year old, and he was in the process of training him to be a search and rescue dog. He'd been training him since he was about two months old, and he was almost ready to go to work. Usually, he said, the dogs were ready when they were a year to eighteen months old. "I've been thinking about taking him out in the field with me one day soon."

"He's a beautiful dog," Olivia said. "I love German shepherds. I always wanted one when I was married, but my ex didn't like dogs."

"That's too bad. I think how people relate to animals tells a lot about them. I'm glad you like dogs. Somehow, I knew you would. That's what I came home to do, by the way—feed him and let him out."

He patted his thigh and said, "C'mon, Columbo. Let's get your supper, and then I'll let you outside while I change my clothes."

Columbo jumped up eagerly and ran toward the kitchen where Olivia assumed his food dish would be.

Shel followed the dog, and Olivia followed Shel. She watched as he opened a large tote and scooped out a generous helping of food. Then he took the dog's water dish to the sink, rinsed it, and filled it with fresh cold water. He set the water dish down and waited a few minutes for Columbo to finish eating and take a quick drink.

"Who takes care of him when you can't get home to do it?"

"There's a little old lady next door who loves Columbo. He loves her, too. If I can't get home to take care of him, I call Emma, and she comes over to feed him and let him out."

Shel saw that Columbo was finished eating and opened the back door. "Want to see the backyard?"

Columbo bounded down the steps, ran three or four laps around the fenced-in yard, and finally chose a tree in a corner at the back where he did his business. Then he came racing back to Shel and Olivia, who stood on the steps laughing at his antics.

Shel picked up a ball from the back porch and tossed it to the far end of the yard.

Columbo ran headlong toward the back fence, managing to stop just in time to snatch up the ball in his mouth before hitting the fence. He turned and raced back to Shel, who took the ball and threw it again.

After a few more tosses, Shel said, "Okay, boy. That's enough for now. You stay out here and entertain yourself for a while. I need to get ready to take this pretty lady to dinner."

Olivia smiled at him, impressed with how gentle and patient he was with the dog. She turned and followed Shel back into the house.

"Have a seat in the living room. I'll be about ten minutes," he said.

Instead of sitting, Olivia walked over and started perusing the titles of the books Shel owned. A few of them were the old classics: *The Grapes of Wrath, War and Peace, A Tale of Two Cities, Gone with the Wind*, and a few others. A few were nonfiction, some about Montana history, a few about the lifestyles and cultures of the different Indian tribes in the state, and some were about geology and prehistoric times. She was amazed to find that Shel's interests paralleled hers in so many areas. Many of the other books were what looked like murder mysteries and detective stories, which didn't surprise her. Then she noticed that he had several books by one of her favorite authors, some of which she'd not yet read.

I'll have to be sure to ask him if I can borrow some of these.

A few minutes later, Shel appeared in the living room door, clean-shaven and dressed in an attractive tan-and-turquoise sweater and slim-fitting jeans. Olivia couldn't keep herself from thinking, *He looks gorgeous!* And then she felt her face flush when she realized she'd been staring at him.

"I'm ready. Just have to let Columbo back in and lock up, and we can take off." Shel headed for the back door.

He opened it and Columbo came running. When the dog reached the back steps, he stopped, calmly walked up them and through the door, and then sat beside Shel, who reached down to scratch behind his ears and told him what a good dog he was.

"I don't think I've ever seen such a well-behaved dog," Olivia said. "If I ever do get a dog, would you consider training him for me? You've done an amazing job with Columbo."

"I might consider that, but it would mean the dog would have to live with me for a while. Training is an ongoing thing. It doesn't just include teaching the dog to sit and heel and come and all that stuff. It also involves his learning how to behave in the house and in public, how to greet people, when to be or not be aggressive. Also, the dog's owner needs to be trained."

"Be aggressive? You've taught him that, too?"

"I want him to be a good guard dog here at home, as well as a good search and rescue dog and pet, though I tend to think of him as more like family. Columbo is a smart animal, and I think he's learned his lessons well. But it's taken hours and hours of training, discipline, and patience. I've had to develop a well-rounded rapport with him."

"It looks like it's really paid off," Olivia said. She reached down to scratch Columbo's rump. "Oh, you like that, don't you?" She got down on her knees and put her arms around the dog's neck. He accepted her hug, wagging his tail happily.

"I think you've made a friend for life," Shel said. Then to the dog, he said, "Okay, pal, it's time for us to go. You lie down. Keep an eye on things while I'm gone." He gave the dog one last pat on his head before he guided Olivia to the door.

"Bye, Columbo. It was nice meeting you," she said.

Columbo looked up at her, woofed again, and put his head back down on his front paws, his tail swishing back and forth as if inviting her to come again.

* * * * *

"This looks like a popular place," Olivia said, as Shel pulled into one of only a few parking spaces left.

"Danny's took off right from the start," Shel said. "Danny is the friend I was talking about. He and I graduated together. We were on the football and track teams together, and we've been good buddies ever since."

"An ex-jock restaurateur?"

"Don't knock it 'til you've tasted his steak," Shel said. "I'm not exaggerating when I say it will melt in your mouth. And the mushroom and onion sauce he puts on it is the best I've ever had. But I guess I should just shut up and let you judge for yourself."

He got out of the car and went around to open Olivia's door for her. As she stepped out, she glanced over his shoulder in time to see an SUV carrying five men pull into the parking lot.

"Boy, red must be a popular color for SUVs," she said.

"Why's that?"

"Well, it just seems I've been seeing an awful lot of them lately."

"Let's get inside, and then you can tell me about it,"

They went in and were immediately greeted by a tall, blond, good-looking man who shook hands with Shel and waited for him to introduce his date.

"Danny, how's it going?"

Without waiting for an answer, Shel turned to Olivia and said, "Olivia Clayton, I'd like you to meet Danny Bridger, Missoula's most eligible bachelor. Danny, this is Olivia."

Olivia started to extended her hand but, instead, suddenly found herself wrapped in a welcoming hug.

"I'm very happy to meet you, Ms. Clayton. Shel has told me absolutely nothing about you!" He gave Shel a friendly punch on his shoulder.

Olivia laughed and said, "Please, call me Olivia, and I guess I have the advantage. At least, I know that you grill the best steaks this side of the Continental Divide, according to Shel."

"Welcome to Danny's, and ignore the eligible bachelor stuff. Please allow me to choose your meal for you, on the house." He looked at Shel, winked, and said, "You can pay for your own!"

The three of them laughed, and as Danny showed them to a cozy table for two near the large fireplace, he said, "Just kidding, buddy. Both meals are on me tonight. I hope you enjoy them."

Shel said, "I told you he was a great friend. Thanks, Danny. Appreciate it."

When they were seated, Danny was off to the kitchen to oversee the preparation of their steak dinners. While they waited, Shel asked, "So what's this about red SUVs?"

"Oh, it's probably nothing. It just seems…" Olivia's voice trailed off as she glanced toward the front of the restaurant. "Those are the men from the one in the parking lot, aren't they?"

Shel turned just enough in his seat to be able to see the men. "Yes, I think they are. Do you know them?"

"No. I don't think I've ever met any of them before. But something does seem a little familiar about one of them." She looked puzzled for a moment and then shook her head and said, "No. I'm sure I don't know any of them. My imagination is running away with me."

"Back to the subject," Shel urged. "Tell me about this red SUV you say you've seen so many times."

"Well, to be honest with you, I'm not sure it's always been the same one. Really, I don't see how it could be." She told Shel about the first one she'd noticed, the one parked across the street from Alyssa's house last Halloween. She said that, in the end, they'd decided it was probably just parents waiting for their trick-or-treaters and dismissed it. She told him it was well after 9:30, and too dark to see much of anything, so they couldn't see who was in it.

"Come to think of it, Alyssa did mention that she'd seen one like it parked in her neighborhood several times before that. She wondered if someone in the neighborhood may have gotten it recently, and she just hadn't noticed or heard anything about it. I kind of think that's more likely the case. It was months before Alyssa was run down, and she hadn't mentioned anything else suspicious at that time."

Shel asked her what other times she'd seen the SUV.

"Well, like I said, I don't know if it was the same one. I never thought to look at the license plate." She told him about the other times she'd seen a red SUV and simply chalked it up to being a popular color. She mentioned just glimpsing one in the Kwik Shop parking lot, as well as the one that was in the park across from the hospital. "That one could have been red or brown. It was evening, and those yellow streetlights were shining on it, which made it hard to see what color it actually was."

"It's a bit of a coincidence," Shel said. "Is that it?"

"Yes—no! Wait!" She told Shel about the SUV sitting on the road below her place that morning. When she saw Shel's eyebrows arch, she explained that she hadn't thought anything of it—simply that someone had stopped there to enjoy the view. "It is a gorgeous view, after all. And when I left for the hospital, it was gone."

"Just this morning? Before your house was ransacked," Shel said.

"Do you seriously think that SUV has something to do with that?"

"Too soon to tell yet, but we can't rule it out. I want you to do me a favor. Next time you notice a red SUV—any red SUV—in your vicinity, jot down the license number, okay? Meantime, I'm going to make a quick call, if you'll excuse me for a couple minutes."

"Of course," Olivia said.

"I'll be right back. Sit tight." He rose and walked toward the sign that said "RESTROOMS."

He took his cell phone from his pocket and called the police station.

"Yeah, this is Shel. Listen, I need you to do something for me…"

Across the dining room of Danny's, the five men were seated at a large round booth. They each nursed a predinner drink while looking over the menu. But Joe had something else on his mind at the moment.

"Trent, take a look at the woman sitting alone by the fireplace over there." He nodded his head in Olivia's direction. "Does she look familiar to you?"

Trent turned his head to look where Joe had indicated. "Yeah, she does."

Joe found it interesting that she'd be out on a date the same day her house was trashed.

"Let us in on it, will ya," Sam said. "Who is she?"

"That, boys, is our snoopy friend from the hospital. The one who got in Trent's way in the Walton woman's room twice."

"Hey, that's the same woman I saw with the ranger and the other guy the other day!" Pete said.

Joe motioned for him to keep his voice down.

"That's her?" Cal said. "She's somethin' to look at, Joe."

"She's something to contend with, is what she is," Joe said. "I wonder what she's doing here now. Wouldn't you think she'd be at home after finding her house turned upside down?"

As they watched, a tall, dark-haired man came from the direction of the men's room and joined Olivia at the table. He reached across and took her hand.

"Wonder who he is," Sam said. "Boyfriend, maybe?"

"I don't know, but I think we'd better try to find out," Joe said.

The waitress came over to take their orders, and they had to cut their conversation short.

After the waitress left, Pete leaned in toward Joe and said, "Hey, Joe, that guy with her, that's the one that was with her and the ranger the other day."

"Are you sure about that?"

"Yeah, I'm sure. I'm good with faces. You know that. That's the guy I saw checking out that camera before the ranger came to the cabin."

"I think it would behoove us to find out who he is, too." At the blank look on Pete's face, Joe said, "Be good, be to our advantage." He shook his head and wondered how Pete had ever made it through high school.

Danny reappeared at Olivia and Shel's table with two steaming bowls of French onion soup, loaded with melted cheese and croutons, and set them on the table.

"Where'd you take off to a few minutes ago?" he asked Shel.

"I had to make a phone call."

"Some date he is, huh? If I had someone like you to look at across the table, I sure wouldn't be off making phone calls, believe me," Danny said to Olivia.

"Well, I think I can forgive him because I think this call is on my behalf," she said.

"Oh?" He raised an eyebrow but was too polite to ask what the problem might be.

"Someone broke into my house and pretty much trashed the whole thing this afternoon. That's why we were late keeping our reservation," she said.

"You're kidding! You weren't hurt, were you?"

"Oh, no. I wasn't even home at the time, thank goodness. But it was enough to put a good scare into me. Shel and I already had this dinner planned, and we were just in the way of the forensics team at my house, so we decided to come here, anyway."

"Well, I'm very glad you did, although I wish it had been under happier circumstances."

"Thank you. I'm glad we came, too. I needed to get away and be able to relax for a while."

"Enjoy your soup. The rest of your dinner is being prepared as we speak." Danny gave her shoulder a quick squeeze. "I hope everything else turns out okay, too." He turned and left for the kitchen again.

Olivia watched him walk across the room and then turned to Shel.

"May I ask what the call was all about? I'm assuming it had something to do with those five men and the red SUV in the parking lot."

"It did. I called the station to get someone over here to check it out. Hopefully, they'll be able to get a name to go with the license plate. We should have an answer pretty soon."

They went to work on their soup and were quiet for a few minutes.

Then Shel cleared his throat and said, "Olivia, I don't want you staying in your house alone tonight."

"Do you think he'll be back? He didn't take anything this time, so he obviously wasn't after anything. I mean, he could have taken any number of things, but he didn't even bother. All he did was smash several things to pieces."

"Exactly," Shel said. "If whoever did this wasn't after any of your possessions, what did he want? I think it was a warning."

"A warning? About what?" She thought she already had a pretty good idea.

"You've interrupted their attempts to get to Alyssa twice already. Three times, actually, if they were the ones in the Humvee, too. I think they're more than a little miffed at you."

"Okay, so now you've scared me."

"I'm not trying to scare you, though if that's what it takes to keep you out of your house for a few days, then so be it. Do you know anyone you could stay with?"

"Not really. I haven't been here all that long, and I really haven't had much opportunity to meet people. I suppose I could stay in Lissy's room for a few nights. That cot and I were starting to get pretty well acquainted."

"I'd offer you my hospitality," Shel said, "but I don't want you to feel like I'm taking advantage of the situation."

"No, that's fine. I'm okay with staying at the hospital. That way I can keep an eye on Lissy, too." In fact, she was already feeling better at the thought of being around lots of people, especially with a policeman standing guard outside the door. "Would you mind taking me home first, though, so I can pick up a few things?"

"Not at all. The team should be finished by the time we're through here. I'll come in with you while you get what you need. Do you mind not seeing a movie tonight?"

"I was going to ask you the same thing," she said. "For some reason, I'm just not in the mood for a movie now."

"Understandable," Shel said. "After I get you settled with Alyssa, I'm going to go back to the station for a while to see what they came up with on the SUV."

"Do you ever sleep? Can't you let it wait until tomorrow morning?"

Danny brought their steaks, accompanied by a steaming serving of rice pilaf seasoned with fresh mushrooms, garlic, sage, and parsley, and asparagus broiled with butter, garlic, slivered roasted almonds, and fresh ginger. There were also plenty of freshly baked rolls, so light that Olivia was envious of the baker's skills.

Danny waited until they'd tried their steaks.

"Delicious," Olivia said. "This is done to perfection. You can cook for me any time."

"I'm glad you like it," Danny said. "Please don't wait too long to visit us again. You don't have to wait for him to bring you either." He nudged Shel's shoulder. "I'll leave you two alone. Enjoy your dinners."

Olivia fell silent while they ate, thinking of all that had happened over the last few weeks.

She was grateful that Shel didn't try to make small talk. It was nice to be with someone and not feel like she had to always have something witty to say. The term "awkward silence" didn't apply to the lulls in their conversation.

When they were finished, Danny came back over to ask if they wanted dessert.

"Oh, thanks, but I really couldn't," Olivia said. "I'm not sure I'll even be able to walk out of here, I'm so full. But it really was wonderful, Danny. Thank you so much."

"My pleasure. It's a real treat for me to see someone truly enjoy my cooking."

"Who wouldn't?" Olivia couldn't imagine anyone not appreciating cooking like his. "I came in here not sure if I'd be able to eat anything at all. Obviously, it wasn't a problem."

The two men chuckled at her comment.

"He's been at this for a long time," Shel said. "It was a hobby of his when we were in high school. The guys on the football team used to rib him about wearing an apron. Until he shut them up by cooking for the whole team once."

"You cooked for the whole team?" Olivia was incredulous.

"I told them if we won our homecoming game, I'd cook a spaghetti dinner for them. We won. I cooked. But it was worth it. They didn't give me any more grief about my cooking after that."

Olivia laughed. "That's quite a story. I'm sure glad you didn't let them goad you into giving it up. I wouldn't have wanted to miss this meal for anything."

They said their goodbyes to Danny and headed toward the front of the restaurant. Olivia deliberately averted her eyes from the five men seated in the booth. She held on to Shel's arm and pretended that she wasn't aware of their stares.

On the drive to Olivia's house, Shel asked, "Are you sure you're okay with staying at the hospital?"

"I'll be fine, as long as it's okay with the hospital staff. Honestly, Shel, I'm actually kind of looking forward to it. It'll give Lissy and me a chance to have a good chat. I know the days and nights get really long for her."

When they reached Olivia's house, she handed her key to Shel, who opened the front door and went into the house ahead of her. Nothing had changed. The forensics team had left things just as they'd found them. Olivia moved slowly through the living room, picking things up here and there, and putting them where they belonged. She noticed a black powder on several areas, and she deduced that it was what the team had used to see if they could lift any fingerprints.

"Don't worry about this tonight," Shel said. "I'll be over tomorrow to help you get things back in order."

"Oh, you really don't have to do that. It surely isn't part of your job description."

"No, but it does come under the description of friendship. You didn't think I was going to let you deal with all of this on your own, did you?"

"Thanks, Shel." Olivia felt herself starting to tear up. *Oh, no! Don't do this now! Don't cry in front of him again.* But she couldn't stop herself. The dam burst, and the tears she hadn't realized were there finally came.

Shel was relieved to see her break down at last. She'd had a very long, very trying day, and she'd been holding back her emotions ever since she'd discovered the break-in at her home.

He stepped forward and put his arms around her. Gratefully, she laid her head against his chest and let the tears come.

Shel didn't say anything but just held her. After a few minutes, Olivia pulled away, swiping at her eyes and sniffling. "I'm sorry," she said. "I'm not usually a crier."

"I wondered when you were finally going to let go," Shel said. "You've done an amazing job of keeping it all together for this long." He looked into her eyes. "And if you feel the need for a shoulder to cry on again, you know I'll be right here for you."

"Thanks, Shel," she said, "but I've learned that in most cases, crying doesn't really do much good. It certainly isn't going to change the fact that my house and my privacy were invaded and some of my personal treasures, some of them irreplaceable, were destroyed. I just have to buck up and get busy putting my home and my life back together."

"Is that how you handled yourself when you got your divorce?"

"Pretty much. I mean, yes, I cried. A significant part of my life was over. I loved my husband at the beginning, and for a while, we had a good life together. But then things changed. We both changed. It was sad to see our relationship dying right before our eyes. So, yes, I cried.

"But not for long. There were things to do. I had to find a job, sell my house, find a new home. I was so busy I didn't have time to dwell on it. Then I thought about what Lissy had been through, losing her husband and both sons, and I realized that her problems were much bigger, and much more final than mine."

She paused and was deep in thought for a moment before continuing. "That's the way we've always been, I guess. Always there for each other, through thick and thin. Having to care for her has been good for me. It's made me feel like I do have some worth, after all."

"Don't tell me there was ever a time when you felt you didn't," Shel said. "I don't think I've ever known anyone like you. Not many people have such a devoted friend."

"But isn't that just what friends do for one another?"

"I guess it is," Shel said. "In which case, I'm glad I can call you my friend, and I hope you feel the same."

In response, Olivia stepped forward and into the warmth of his arms again.

"We'll tackle this together tomorrow then," Shel said. "Meantime, let's get what you need and get you over to the hospital."

Olivia gingerly stepped around the things strewn over the living room floor and made her way to her bedroom. She put an overnight bag on the bed and put enough clothes in it for a few days. Then she gathered her toiletries, adding them to the things in the bag.

"I suppose I should take that manuscript, what's left of it, and see if I can get it put back together."

"Is that your only copy of it?"

"No. I have it on my computer, too. It was sent to my company over the Internet and then forwarded to me. I like to have something in my hand to read, so I always print out whatever I'm working on. Sometimes I think it's easier, for me, anyway, to make notes in the margins the old-fashioned way. It's easier on my eyes, too. Guess I'm just set in my ways."

They went into her office and began picking up pages of the manuscript. They straightened them the best they could and put them in her briefcase, along with her laptop. Then they went back through the house and double-checked all the windows and doors to be sure they were locked before leaving the house.

"Shel, I think I should take my car in. I don't like the idea of being stranded at the hospital without my own transportation."

"Okay, but you have to promise me you'll be extra vigilant if you go anywhere on your own. And I don't want you coming back here by yourself either."

"I won't. Cross my heart," she said.

Shel loaded her things into the backseat of her car and held her door for her. "I'll see you at the hospital," he said.

"You don't really need to come up there."

"Yes, I do. In the first place, it's dark outside now, and parking lots are notoriously dangerous places, especially after dark. In the second place, I want to be sure it's okay for you to stay there, now that Alyssa's out of the woods. If it's not, you'll either come home with me, or we'll find you a motel room and place a guard outside the door for you."

"Do you think that's all necessary? You don't expect them to come back tonight, do you?"

"Not really, no. But I don't want to take any chances. I'll follow you there." Not giving her any time to argue, he closed her door and went to his own car.

He waited for her to turn her car around and then followed suit. The drive to the hospital took about twenty minutes. Both of them were deep into their own thoughts, though they were pretty much along the same line.

Olivia pulled into a parking spot as close to the front doors of the hospital as she could.

Shel found a place a few cars down from hers. He met Olivia at her car and got her overnight bag and briefcase out of the backseat. Olivia grabbed her purse and pushed the remote lock twice, hearing the reassuring *honk honk* of her horn that told her the car was locked.

Shel carried her things, and they went inside and over to the bank of elevators. When the doors opened, they stepped in, and Olivia pressed 4. Neither of them said anything on the short ride up.

They stopped at the nurses' station before heading for Alyssa's room. Shel explained Olivia's situation to Angie who, Olivia was happy to see, was on duty this evening. Angie was appalled to hear of Olivia's misfortune.

"But they didn't take anything, and you weren't hurt? We can all be very thankful for that," she said.

"I was wondering if it would be a problem for me to sleep on the cot in Alyssa's room again for a few nights," Olivia said. "It'll take a little time to get my house put back together, and truth be told, I really don't think I want to stay there alone just yet."

"I don't blame you. No, it's no problem at all," Angie said. "I'll get the room ready for you. I'm about 99.99 percent sure that Alyssa will be glad to have you close again, too."

She hustled off to get the room ready to accommodate Olivia. Olivia and Shel followed her down the hall.

"Remind me to stop and order a nice big bouquet for the nurses up here. They've been so good to me and taken such good care of Alyssa, I feel like I need to do something for them." She smiled a small smile and said, "I'm actually a little surprised they're not charging me hotel rates for all the nights I've stayed here."

Alyssa was still awake and was staring out the window, looking at the night sky with a wistful look on her face.

"Penny for your thoughts," Olivia said, as she walked into the room.

"Make it a quarter," Alyssa said. "A penny doesn't get you much these days."

"Neither does a quarter," Olivia said. "Seriously, though, Lissy, you looked deep in thought when we came in."

"I was just trying to think back and figure out some of this mess. I feel like it's my fault you house was ransacked."

"Nonsense! Just how is that your fault?" Olivia gave her friend a look that said she thought that statement was absurd.

"Well, I'm up here, and from what I hear, lucky to be alive. Someone obviously wanted to hurt or kill me. They've made two more attempts on my life right here in the hospital, which you have thwarted." She held up her hand to stop Olivia from interrupting. "And now your house is trashed, and you're afraid to sleep in your own home." She looked at Shel and asked, "Don't you agree with me?"

"Yes, I agree with you, to a point," Shel said. "To the point that all of these incidents seem to be connected somehow. But in no way do I think it's your fault."

"There now, you see? You don't have to worry about me. I'll be fine," Olivia said. "All you have to do is behave yourself while you're in here and get better."

"I think…" Alyssa said.

"Nope! Not tonight. No more thinking," Olivia said.

"I was going to say, before I was so rudely interrupted, that I think it's time to forget about all of it for now and try to relax for a change."

"Good idea," Shel said. He nodded his head. "And on that note, I'm going to leave now and let the two of you talk about me while I'm gone."

The two friends looked at him and laughed.

"We just might have something better to talk about than you," Olivia said with a grin.

"But we sure can't think of what it would be," Alyssa finished for her.

Shel gave Olivia a hug and a light kiss on her forehead, told Alyssa to keep her eyes on Olivia, said he would see them in the morning, and left.

When he was out of earshot, Alyssa looked at Olivia and said, "Now spill!"

CHAPTER 23

Sunday, March 22, 2015

After a restless night on her cot, Olivia was feeling stiff and slightly agitated. She was up and in the shower before Alyssa was awake. After toweling off, drying her hair, and putting on her makeup, she dressed in blue jeans and a sweatshirt, knowing she was going to be working in her house most of the day.

She was sitting in the chair by the window, tying her sneakers, when she heard Alyssa say, "Good morning, sunshine!"

"Huh!" Olivia snorted.

"Oh, it's one of those days, is it?"

"Sorry, Lissy. I didn't sleep well last night. I guess I'm more upset about things than I thought. I didn't mean to take it out on you."

"You're forgiven. Was the cot uncomfortable, or was it more than that that kept you awake? Maybe you should get a motel room where you'd be more comfortable."

"I think a little of both. I thought I'd gotten used to the cot, but a few days back in my own bed reminded me how uncomfortable it really is. But I don't need to check into a motel. I think it was more to do with my things being rummaged through by some stranger. I'll tell you one thing, I'm going to put dead bolt locks on every door, and get one of those bars for the sliding patio doors. In fact, I think I'll get a home security system."

"That's a good idea. I think I'll follow suit once I'm into my new place."

"Oh, Lissy! I forgot we were going to look at real estate listings today."

"No problem. You have work to do, and I'll have therapy later on today. If we're both up to it, maybe we can look at a few places this evening. Why don't you just leave your laptop here along with your other things? No point in your having to drag it back and forth all the time."

"That's what I thought I'd do." Olivia changed the subject. "I'm hungry. I think I'll go down to the cafeteria and see what they have for breakfast today. Yours will probably be up here by the time I get back."

"Sounds good. There are a couple personal matters I need to attend to that you'd probably rather not be here to witness." Alyssa pushed the call button for her nurse.

"Okay. I'll be back up in a few minutes. Have fun!" Olivia winked at Alyssa as Jen walked into the room.

"Good morning!" Jen said. "How can I help you this morning?"

Alyssa told her what she needed, and Jen set about helping her get ready to face the day.

After helping her take care of nature's call, Jen gave her a quick sponge bath and combed her hair for her. "Do you want me to brush your teeth now or wait until after you have your breakfast?" she asked.

"After would be fine," said Olivia, who'd just returned from her visit to the cafeteria. "I saw the cart in the hall with the breakfast trays on it, and I have mine here, so if you can do it after we eat, that would be great."

"Can do," Jen said. Then she turned to Alyssa. "Do you want to try to sit in your chair to eat or stay in bed?"

"The chair would be wonderful. I'm so tired of this bed I want to scream sometimes."

"Okay. Let me call an aide to help me move you over."

Olivia wanted to start learning how to help Alyssa with her needs. She watched closely when Jen and the aide helped Alyssa into a chair. "She'll be going home with me when she gets out of here, and it would be good for me to know how to do these things."

"Good idea," Jen said. "We can't let you do it here because of insurance. But when she gets home, she'll need some help for a while."

She told Olivia exactly what she needed to do as they got Alyssa situated, more or less comfortably, in the vinyl-clad recliner that was standard in each room. Jen pulled the rolling table over, adjusted the height, and set the brake. Olivia pulled her chair up to the table and set her breakfast on it.

"I'd like to try feeding her, if it's okay."

"Sure," Jen said.

An aide came in carrying Alyssa's breakfast tray. She set it down on the table and started removing covers.

"Well, look at that. We have the same breakfasts this morning," Olivia said. "French toast, Canadian bacon, tomato juice, milk—I don't have the milk—and coffee. Looks great, doesn't it?"

Alyssa didn't answer. She looked at Olivia and then looked away again, her eyes suddenly filling with tears.

"Lissy, what's wrong?"

Alyssa waited for the aide to leave the room before answering. "Oh, Livvy, it's just so…so…humiliating!" Tears rolled down her cheeks.

"What are you talking about?" Olivia asked though she thought she already knew the answer. She grabbed a tissue and dabbed at Lissy's wet cheeks.

"You can't imagine what it's like to have someone else do everything—and I mean *everything*—for you. I can't dress myself, brush my own hair, clean my teeth, wash my face, put makeup on, or even…" She let the end of the thought fade away.

"So? Aren't you glad you have someone who's willing and able to do those things for you? I know it's frustrating for you but, Lissy, for heaven's sake, you almost died. I'm so grateful to have you here for me to be able to help! And you know that if the roles were reversed, you'd be doing the same things for me. Come on, now. Let's not think about this anymore. Let's think of how great it's going to be when you finally get out of here and are able to come home with me. And in the meantime, let's enjoy this yummy breakfast while it's still hot."

Alyssa sniffed once or twice and gave Olivia a small smile.

"That's better," Olivia said. "Now, open wide!"

Their conversation during breakfast consisted of what things Alyssa would be looking for in her new home. She'd decided on a house, not an apartment or condo. She wanted to be able to do whatever she pleased and not have to adhere to some home owners' association's rules. She also wanted a yard and a view, and a place where she could have a dog, and maybe even a cat.

"A dog and a cat? Think you're getting a little carried away?"

"No. They'll keep each other company while I'm at work. And they both have different things to offer. Dogs are loyal and faithful and protective. They'll walk with you and play fetch and greet you with a wagging tail when you come home. Cats will cuddle, under their own conditions, of course, and they'll curl up on your lap and purr and knead their paws. They'll play with you, too, when it suits them, and they're so soft."

"Okay, okay! I get it. Speaking of dogs, did I tell you about Shel's?"

"No. When did you meet Shel's dog?"

"Last night. After we left here and before we went to dinner, we stopped by Shel's place so he could feed Columbo."

"Interesting name," Alyssa said.

"He's training him to be a search and rescue dog. Hence, the name. You know, after the detective on TV. Anyway, he's the best dog I've ever met. Shel has spent the dog's whole life teaching him how to behave. He doesn't just sit, stay, and roll over. He's very calm when he meets you. He sat in front of me, gave me his paw to shake, and said, 'Hello.' I mean, 'Woof.' I could tell how much he loves Shel, and vice versa." She explained that Shel had said Columbo wouldn't hurt her as long as he knew her, but if someone ever tried to break into his house or hurt Shel, he wouldn't want to be in his shoes. "I wouldn't either. He's a huge dog!"

"What kind of dog is he?"

"A German shepherd, and he's absolutely beautiful."

"Well," a deep voice said. "I thank you, and Columbo thanks you. He was quite taken with you last night, too." Shel came in and planted a small kiss on Olivia's cheek. "How is everyone this morning?"

"I guess I'm better than I thought I'd be, considering how little I slept last night, and what I have to look forward to today," Olivia said.

"You get to look forward to spending the whole day with me," Shel told her. "So I'd say you should be feeling pretty great," he said. "Anyway, I am."

"Did you learn anything about the SUV we saw last night?"

"It's owned by a Joseph Little Hawk. Nothing on our database about him. No arrests, not even a parking ticket. If this is our guy, he's either very careful or very lucky. It was interesting to me, though, that his first name is Joseph. Collin said the man at the cabin who seemed to be the leader went by Joe." Shel looked at Olivia. "Remember, you're going to keep an eye out for any red SUVs in your vicinity. If you can get the license plate number, we can check it against the one from last night."

"Yes, I remember. I'll be more observant from now on."

"Well, are you ready to dig into that mess today?"

"I am, but, Shel, I really hate for you to spend your days off helping me."

"I told you I was going to help you, and I meant it," Shel said. "Besides, maybe some new clues will turn up when we go through your things. You never know."

"Well, when you put it like that…"

Shel turned from Olivia to Alyssa and asked, "How are you doing this morning?"

"Much better, thanks. I have my dearest friend with me to help me and to keep my mind off the negative and on the positive. And I'm feeling better, too. The pain level has gone down considerably, and it's so nice to be able to get out of that bed for a while. I only wish I were able to be at Livvy's to help you two."

"I wish you could too, Lissy, but all I want you to do now is get better. Oh, and I want you to give Maggy, my realtor, a call. I'm sure she'd be happy to come up here and show you what she has available now. Can't hurt to get a little bit of a head start on it."

"That sounds like a great idea," Alyssa said. "When Jen comes in next time, I'll ask her if she'll help me make the call or send someone who can."

"Good. Great. Then I guess you're all set and I'm all set, so I may as well quit putting it off and get home and start in on that mess." Olivia bent over to give Alyssa a hug. "I'll see you later on. Maybe in time to have supper with you."

"Okay. Be careful. And remember, whoever did this to your house is still out there."

"That's why I have Shel," Olivia said.

"I'll keep an eagle eye on her. She'll be safe with me. I promise," Shel said.

The two of them left Alyssa gazing out the window, after handing her the TV remote and the nurses' call button.

As they rode down in the elevator, Shel said, "Let's take my car. No point in both of us driving up there."

"Fine with me," Olivia said. "I'll need to get gas in my car before I drive it much farther, anyway."

When they reached Olivia's house, Shel looked at her and said, "Are you ready to get started now?"

"I think so. I guess I have to be, don't I?"

But when she stepped into the living room, she felt a surge of anger well up in her again.

Why would someone do this to me? I've never done anything to anyone to deserve this.

Shel noticed her trembling hands and the look on her face, and he knew she was struggling with her emotions. He led her over to the sofa and made her sit down beside him. He turned her to face him and put his hands on her shoulders.

"Livvy, I know this is hard. I know you feel violated, betrayed, angry, and hurt, all at the same time. It's okay that you feel all those things. What's not okay is your keeping it all bottled up inside. Go ahead and cry if you need to. Or scream or punch something. If you don't let it out, it's just going to eat at you and make you sick or crazy."

"I know," Olivia said. "But I didn't want you to see me lose it. I'm afraid you'd never want to see me again."

"You can't scare me off that easily," he told her. "Go ahead. Try it."

"Oh, I don't know, Shel. I mean, why did this happen to me? I never did anything to deserve it. It just makes me so angry to think of someone coming into my home, throwing my things around, breaking some of my most prized possessions." Her voice rose higher and got louder with each phrase.

Without realizing what she was doing, she picked up a throw pillow and punched it as hard as she could, over and over again, tears spilling down her cheeks, until finally she was so spent she couldn't punch it anymore. Finally, she threw the pillow down onto the couch, dropped her head into her hands, and sobbed.

"Okay, Livvy. It's okay now." Shel pulled her close and held her, whispering words of reassurance to her. He let her cry until she finally planted her hands on his chest and pushed away from him.

"Oh, boy. I really didn't know all of that was in me," Olivia said. "I'm so sorry, Shel. I didn't mean to do that in front of you."

"I'm glad you did. Otherwise, I may have found myself with a crazy woman on my hands at some point down the road. Do you feel better now?"

She nodded.

"Shall we get to work then?"

She nodded again and let Shel pull her to her feet. She dried her eyes on the cuff of her sweatshirt.

Shel turned in a circle in the middle of the room. "Where do you want to start?"

"Might as well start right here, I guess."

She bent over to pick up a lamp that had been tipped over onto the floor. Fortunately, it hadn't broken, she saw, and was glad, because it was one of a pair she'd bought just for this room. They were made of real driftwood. She'd found them in a specialty shop in the mall and had fallen in love with their uniqueness the instant she saw them. The wood was twisted and gnarled and had been polished to a high sheen. She'd known they would fit the house and its surroundings immediately upon spotting them. The other lamp still stood on its table.

As they put things back in their proper places, Olivia and Shel found that most of the items in the living room had suffered no damage. Only the TV and sound system had been smashed, but insurance would cover those. Mostly, it was a matter of picking things up and putting them where they belonged.

When they went into the kitchen, however, it was a different matter. Dishes had been swept out of the cupboards onto the floor, and several had shattered. The teapot she'd inherited from her mother was in several pieces in the kitchen sink, and her grandmother's large turkey platter had been dropped on the floor and smashed.

Olivia was heartbroken when she saw those last two items. These were things that were irreplaceable. Shel took the whisk broom and dustpan from her and told her to tend to something else. He quietly swept up the broken pieces and dumped them into the trash.

They worked for about two hours, not saying much besides Olivia's telling Shel where things went. Then Olivia wiped her hands on her jeans and declared that she was ready for a break.

"How 'bout a cup of coffee? I think there may still even be some cookies left. The cookie jar seems to be one thing that was left alone."

"I could go for a cup of coffee and a couple cookies," Shel said.

Olivia set her single-cup coffee maker upright on the counter and pushed the on button to see if it still worked. It did, so she went about making a cup for each of them. She put several chocolate chip cookies on a plate, got a couple napkins, and put them all on the breakfast bar.

Shel took a sip of coffee and said, "This hits the spot."

He looked around the room. Olivia had managed to put the valances back up over the windows, and most of the things that had survived the rampage were back in cupboards and drawers where they belonged. "This room is coming along pretty well," he said.

"I guess so," Olivia said. "I never cared much for this set of dishes, anyway. Now I have a good excuse to buy some new ones. It's just the things that can't be replaced that hurt. My mom had that teapot for as far back as I can remember. And the platter was a wedding present to my grandparents. I promised I would take care of it and pass it down if I had children of my own someday. And now..." Her voice trailed off, and her gaze went to the spruce trees at the edge of the backyard.

"I'm sorry, Livvy. I know it's hard to lose things that have so much sentimental value. But I want you to remember one very important thing, the good part about all of this."

"What would that be?" Olivia had a hard time finding any good in the situation.

"You weren't here when it happened. Had you been, you may have been hurt, or worse."

He looked her in the eyes and added, "I, for one, am glad you're still in one piece. And I know Alyssa is, too."

"You're right. I'll try to keep that in perspective. I promise." She gave him a half-hearted smile and finished her coffee. "Well, I guess it's back to work, huh?"

They worked for another half hour in the kitchen. Olivia was grateful that, fortunately, the appliances hadn't been damaged. Nor had the countertops or cabinets. She washed the countertops, swept the floor, and declared the kitchen finished.

As they were picking things up in Olivia's office, Shel's cell phone rang.

"Detective Sheldon," he said. He listened for a minute and then said, "Thanks," and hung up. He pocketed his phone again and told Olivia, "The forensics team wasn't able to get any fingerprints or any other solid leads. Whoever did this wore gloves and was careful not to leave any clues behind. And the gravel in the driveway makes it impossible to get tire tracks. Don't give up, though." He noted that Olivia looked let down at the news and tried to reassure her. "Something else will come up. We'll get the guy or guys who did this. Didn't Ken Harrison promise you that? He keeps his promises. And so do I."

"I'm really lucky to have met you," Olivia said. "In the short time we've known each other, I feel like I've made a very special friend. Hopefully for life."

"I guarantee it," Shel said.

CHAPTER 24

Monday, April 27, 2015

A month had passed since the incident at Olivia's house. She had long since moved back home and, having had dead bolt locks and an alarm system installed, she felt much more secure about being there alone.

Now, after it's being so quiet for so long, Olivia was tempted to believe whoever had ransacked her home had nothing to do with Alyssa's situation and had only done it for a one-time thrill.

She was tempted, but she wasn't convinced. She still heeded Shel's advice, kept an eye on everything going on around her, and was careful to be sure no one followed her, especially when she was headed for home.

This afternoon she was at the hospital where she'd been every day but one since the day in March when someone in a black Humvee had run down her best friend. March 7, Alyssa's birthday.

"I'm sorry I didn't get here sooner. I was finishing up that new manuscript I've been working on. I think we may have a best seller in the works with this one."

She stopped talking long enough to look at Alyssa who, she'd just realized, was minus some hardware. "Wow! Look at you!" Olivia bent down and gave Alyssa a hug. "No more brace! This is a sight for sore eyes," she said.

Alyssa looked much more comfortable with the unwieldly brace no longer holding her in the rigid position she'd endured for so long.

Olivia said, "I bet you thought you were going to spend the rest of your life in that thing."

"It was beginning to feel that way," Alyssa said. "And there's more news, too. They're going to take me for an MRI later this afternoon. If everything looks good, I'll be starting my physical and occupational therapy."

"Lissy, that's great news! Did they say anything about how much longer you'll have to be in the hospital?"

"Well, the therapists will come here to my room to do my therapy for a few days. If it looks like I'm going to be able to tolerate it, they'll move me to the rehab center for a couple weeks. After that I guess I'll be able to go home." She smiled at Olivia. "Oh, I can't wait to get out of here!"

"I'm still hoping you'll come home with me for at least a couple weeks, and let me take care of you," Olivia said. "I don't like the idea of your being home all alone right away. Especially with the stairs in your house."

"Oh, but Livvy, I can't put you out like that. You have work to do. You've already spent so much time here that I feel guilty."

"That's a crock, and you know it. I wouldn't have been here if I didn't want to be. You needed me, and I was glad to be here for you."

"Well, yes, but—"

"No buts," Olivia said. "You'll come stay with me for as long as you need to. We'll have a great time. I can learn how to help you with your exercises. We can have movie nights and game nights. We can eat all of our favorite foods. We can talk all night if we want to. And as for work, I do that at home anyway. So end of discussion. Period."

"Okay, ma'am. Whatever you say," Alyssa said. "It does sound like it could be fun, if being crippled can be fun. And maybe you're right. I probably shouldn't be alone for a little while, at least." Alyssa didn't want to voice her feelings out loud, but every time she thought of someone deliberately running her down and then trying to get to her at the hospital, her blood ran cold. Just the thought of being alone in her big empty house terrified her. So when Olivia insisted that she stay with her, relief flooded through her, in spite of the twinge of guilt she felt for taking up so much of Olivia's time.

"Good! That's settled. Now we just have to wait for the results of your MRI. And I'm sure those will be excellent," Olivia said.

"Good afternoon, ladies!" said Jen, the nurse who'd come on duty at the shift change. She breezed into the room and looked at her patient, who was sitting in a chair by the window. "Hmm…There's something different about you today."

"Isn't it great?" Olivia looked like a proud mother as she gestured toward Alyssa.

"It certainly is," Jen said. She looked at Alyssa's chart. "And I see here you're going to have an MRI this afternoon." She spoke as she moved about, taking Alyssa's vitals, fixing her bed covers, pouring a fresh pitcher of water, and straightening the room. As she left, she said she'd be back later to take Alyssa down for her MRI.

Olivia stood beside Alyssa and looked at the view through the window. "Just look at that big sky. Won't it be wonderful when you can get out in the fresh air again?"

"I can't wait. I can hardly wait to go back to work."

"Let's not get ahead of ourselves now," Olivia said. "You know that it's going to take several weeks of therapy before you're ready for the real world again, don't you?"

"Yes, I know. But I can dream, can't I?"

"And just what are you dreaming about now?"

The two women turned their heads to see Collin walk into the room with a pretty girl on his arm.

"Collin! It's great to see you! Actually, I was just thinking about going back to work. Bet you're glad to hear that, aren't you?"

"I am, but I think you're jumping the gun a bit. Don't you think it would be good to be able to walk and drive and do a few other things on your own first?" He winked and flashed a grin at her. "It will be great to have you back whenever you can get there, though."

Olivia gave Alyssa an "I told you so" look and said, "Thanks, Collin. I just told her the same thing." She nodded toward the young woman with him and said, "So tell us, who is this lovely person?"

"Oh, sorry. Alyssa, Olivia, this is Ginny. She works at the 7-Eleven on the west side of town. We met about a year and a half ago when I stopped to pick up something. I had to do some fast talking to get a pass for her to come in here."

"Hi," Ginny said. She reached out to shake Olivia's hand and nodded in Alyssa's direction.

"It's nice to meet you at last. I've been hearing a lot about the heroine who works with Collin. I was starting to wonder what kind of competition I was up against."

Alyssa laughed. "I'm no heroine, and I'm certainly no competition. I'm far too old for Collin. We're just partners at work and good friends." Alyssa looked inquiringly at Collin. "If you met so long ago, what took you so long to introduce us?"

"Well, I didn't actually ask her out until just a couple weeks ago. I thought she was way too young for me."

"He thought I was only seventeen or eighteen years old," Ginny told them. "I'm actually twenty-three. He just never asked, so I finally just had to come right out and ask him why he never asked me out. He seemed to like me. We talked all the time when he came in, which he did more and more over the last several months. When he told me I was too young for him, I asked him how old he thought I was. Would you believe he made me show him my driver's license to prove I was old enough to date him?"

"Oh, that's funny! Collin, did you really do that?" Alyssa respected Collin as a partner and as a very capable ranger, but that didn't stop her from giving him a hard time.

"Yes, I really did that. I didn't want to be accused of robbing the cradle. These days you can't be too careful. But I'm sure glad she had the nerve to finally ask me what was up." He put his arm around Ginny's waist.

"Anyway, it's good to meet you. Both of you," Ginny said, including Olivia in the conversation. She looked at Alyssa again and said, "It looks like you're doing pretty well, considering what Collin told me you've been through."

"I am. Thanks. I got the casts off my arms a couple weeks ago, and I got the brace off my hip just this morning. And in a little while, I'll have an MRI to see if I'm ready to start physical therapy."

"That's great," Collin said. "When do you get to go home?"

She filled them in on what the doctor had said.

"And then," Olivia said, "she's coming home with me for as long as it takes to get her on her feet again. Fortunately, I work from home, so I can be there with her whenever she needs me."

"I tried to tell her that was asking too much," Alyssa said, "but she insists that I'm staying with her."

"I think that's a great idea," Collin said. "You need to do what you need to do. We'll keep your job for you. Of course," he teased with another wink, "that means so much more work for me until you're back."

"Oh, you!" Ginny laughed and pushed him aside. "You are incorrigible. Let the poor woman be. You know you've been missing her, and not just because you have more work to do with her gone, either."

"She's right. I do miss you, Alyssa. And truth be told, this time of year the workload isn't too heavy yet, as you know. Sure would like to have you back by hunting season though!" He smiled and then turned when he heard someone else come into the room.

Olivia caught the familiar scent of Shel's aftershave as he stepped up beside her and asked, "Why wasn't I invited to this party?"

"Hi, Shel," Olivia said. She instantly felt like her day had improved just with his appearance. "You're always welcome. You know that." Then she turned toward Collin and Ginny. She introduced Ginny and Shel and mentioned that Shel was the detective working on Alyssa's case.

Shel and Ginny shook hands. Then Shel turned to Collin with a more serious look on his face. "Collin, when Olivia, you, and I were up at Lone Man's Road last month, didn't you tell us there was a red SUV and a late-model blue Dodge Ram pickup parked behind that cabin?"

"Wait a minute!" Alyssa glared at Olivia. "When were you up at Lone Man's Road?"

"The three of us went up there the middle of last month. Shel was going up to talk to Collin, and I went along for the ride."

"Livvy, what were you thinking? I thought you said you were going to stay away from those guys."

"I didn't go anywhere near them, and besides, I was with Shel and Collin, who both had guns. I was perfectly safe."

"I tried to talk her out of coming along," Shel said, "but you know how hard she is to persuade when she's made up her mind."

"I didn't tell you because I didn't want you to get stressed out about it. You had enough to worry about already." She gave Alyssa a look that said she didn't want to discuss it anymore and turned back to Shel. "Now what were you saying about a blue pickup?"

"I asked Collin if he'd seen one at the cabin that day."

"Yeah, I do remember telling you that. Why?"

"There's a blue Ram parked in front of the hospital right now."

A look of alarm crossed Olivia's face. "What? Do you think it's the same one?"

"Having never seen it myself, I can't answer that. I was hoping Collin would be able to take a look at it and tell me."

"A blue Dodge Ram?" Ginny looked thoughtful. "A couple of years ago five guys in a blue Dodge Ram came to the store. I remember it because they seemed a little off to me. I had a really creepy feeling about them the whole time they were in the store. They were no one I'd ever seen around here before. One of them had a long, jagged scar on his face. I'm sure I'd know him if I saw him again. I even wrote down their license plate number just in case."

"Five guys? Do you remember what any of them looked like?" Shel figured it was a long shot, but it never hurt to ask.

"Well, actually, I only got a good look at three of them. The other two stayed outside by their truck." She stopped to think a moment and then continued. "I seem to remember one of them calling the one guy—the leader, I think—John. Or Josh. No! It was Joe. I'm sure now. It was Joe. He had dark hair and eyes, a wide mouth, and high cheekbones. He looked to me like he was part Native American. He was dressed nicely, but the other two were kind of sloppy. They seemed less concerned about their appearance all around."

"Joe? Collin, you said that was the name of the one who did most of the talking when you hiked up to Sloan's cabin last month," Shel said. "It has to be the same five guys." He looked at Ginny and said, "That's one heck of a good memory you have."

"Well, like I said, something just didn't seem right about them. They were...hmm...furtive, I guess is the word. They seemed nervous about something, and the two outside kept looking up and down the road, like they were watching for something or someone."

"If it is the same five guys, they're sure having one heck of an extended vacation," Olivia said. "They've been here for at least a year and a half already."

"They have to be up to something," Shel said. Turning to Ginny, he asked, "Do you think you might still have that license number somewhere? We could run it and see if we can turn up anything on our guys." Then he had another thought. "Ginny, how long do you keep the tapes from your security cameras?

"We usually keep the tapes for a couple years. I've been meaning to get around to sorting them out so we can record over them, but I haven't gotten to it yet. So we should still have the one from that day."

"Do you remember the day and date, by any chance?"

"No, I don't remember the exact date, but I'm pretty sure it was in late October, about a year and a half ago. I remember that because it was the beginning of hunting season. That's what seemed odd to me. They didn't look or act like the hunters I'm used to seeing around here. They weren't dressed like hunters. No camouflage, no orange vests. You know, none of the things we're used to seeing on hunters. Also, the stuff they bought wasn't food they were getting for just a day in the woods. And I think it was a Saturday or Sunday. It wouldn't take much to figure that out. We'd only have to watch the tapes from the last week or so of October.

"And as for the license plate number, when we find the tape, we'll know what date to look for on the receipts. That's what I wrote the number on. We keep copies of the receipts for five years. I'm not sure why, but that's what my boss wants, so that's what we do. I think it may be for tax purposes. Anyway, do you want me to go to the store and start looking?"

"No, I'll go with you," Shel said. "Collin, let's go down now and you can take a look at that pickup parked out front. Then we'll head out to Ginny's 7-Eleven."

"Shel, if you don't mind," Olivia said, "I think I'll stay here with Lissy this time. It hardly seems fair that she's being left out of all the excitement."

"I was going to suggest you stay here, anyway, because if that is the same pickup down there, it could be our guys are back in action."

"You mean they've come back to take another shot at Lissy?" She looked at Alyssa and said, "Sorry, Lissy, poor choice of words."

"That's exactly what I mean," Shel said. "Or you. And that's why I don't want you to leave this building until I get back here. Understand?"

"Yes, sir!" Olivia snapped to attention and saluted Shel.

"Sorry, I didn't mean to sound like I was giving you an order. But I really do want you to stay here and stay inside. If any of those guys are lurking around here, don't give them an opportunity to get to you or Alyssa."

"I won't, I promise," Olivia said.

"Let's see," Shel said, consulting his watch. "It's about five minutes to three now. We should be able to get there and back by quarter to four easily, provided you can find what we're looking for right away, Ginny." He turned toward Olivia. "Then I'll take you to supper, Olivia, and after that we'll have a look at those tapes."

The guard that had been outside Alyssa's room for a few weeks, since the first attempt to get to her, had been dismissed when it seemed her attacker had given up. Now Shel was on his phone requesting a uniformed officer be sent to the hospital immediately, in addition to four plainclothes officers.

"There will be an officer here in a few minutes. I'm going to talk to the nurses and ask them to keep an eye on anyone who tries to come into this room. If they don't recognize someone as an employee or someone they're used to seeing here, they'll alert the officer right away. I'm having two plainclothes officers placed in the lobbies, and two more by the exit downstairs that the door at the end of this hall leads to. If someone tries to leave in a big hurry, or even looks a little bit suspicious, they'll stop him and detain him until I get back here."

"Do you really think all that is necessary?" Olivia wondered if Shel was getting a little carried away since nothing out of line had happened for so long.

"As much as I hate to say it, it is. If these are the same guys who ran you down and who trashed your house, they mean business. And putting that cocaine in Alyssa's IV was more than just a warning. It was a serious attempt to kill her," Shel said, "not to mention running her down in the first place."

"Now you're scaring me," Alyssa said. Olivia moved to take her hand.

"Good," Shel said. "I hope you're both scared because it'll keep you on the alert."

"Shel," Olivia said, "Lissy's scheduled to have an MRI this afternoon. That means she'll have to be taken from her room, and the people from radiation will be coming to get her. I don't know them the way I know the people on this floor. What if one of these guys tries to pass himself off as someone from there?"

"We shouldn't be gone too long. We'll just grab the tapes and receipts from the time period we're looking at, and we'll head right back here. If I'm not back here before it's time for Alyssa's MRI, I'll call and have one of her guards escort her down to it."

Shel nodded at Alyssa and gave Olivia a quick hug. "Let's go," he said to Collin and Ginny.

* * * * *

"They know about the pickup and the SUV." Joe listened to Trent, who'd called to fill him in. "I was in the hallway near her hospital room. I had scrubs on over my clothes and made like I was busy with a cart full of medical charts. I could hear everything they said. You know the guy we saw with that Clayton woman at the steak house the day you trashed her house? He's a cop. Detective Sheldon. He's been looking for the person that ran the lady ranger down."

"Stop calling her the lady ranger. Her name is Walton, Ranger Alyssa Walton," Joe said.

"Yeah, okay, Ranger Walton. Anyway, it sounds like the detective is getting real close to figuring out that everything is connected: the Humvee, the SUV, the Ram, trashing Clayton's house, and trying to get to the ranger in the hospital."

"But he doesn't know anything for sure yet, right?" Joe was thoughtful. "And as far as we know, they don't have a clue about the compound."

"I guess not. But they went to the 7-Eleven on the west end of town. I thought that girl looked kind of familiar when I saw her walk in with the ranger. She's the one who works at that 7-Eleven. I remember cuz I thought she was kinda hot." Trent looked as though he were afraid Joe was going to come down on him for looking at the clerk, but Joe wasn't thinking about Trent's libido.

"Did they all go?"

"No. Clayton stayed at the hospital. The detective gave her strict orders to stay here. And he's posted extra security at the doors and by the lady ranger's—I mean Ranger Walton's–room. I don't think there's any way we're going to get to her now," Trent said.

"No, I don't think so either," said Joe. "For the moment, at least."

"What do you want us to do next?"

"Where's Sam?"

"He made a beer run. There's a liquor store just a couple blocks from here, so he walked down there. He should be back here any time now."

"When he gets back, move the truck. Get it away from the hospital. Then get back to the hospital and watch. See if the Clayton woman follows orders well. If she leaves, have Sam follow her. You hang back and see if you can get a chance at Walton. I want those two out of our way once and for all. I don't think they know anything about the compound yet, but they sure have complicated things for us. Now there's a cop who knows more than he should, but maybe not as much as he thinks. If we can eliminate the two women and then disappear to the compound, we should be safe."

"What do you want me to tell Sam to do?"

"Just what I said—follow the Clayton woman and call me. But I don't want him doing anything on his own. Tell him to just keep an eye on her and wait for me. That woman has been a headache for me, and I want to take care of her myself. Oh, and keep him out of the beer."

"You coming in to town, Joe?"

"Yes. I'm on my way right now. In the meantime, I'm going to call Pete and Cal and have them start packing things up. I think it's time we left the cabin."

* * * * *

Olivia went to the window in Alyssa's room and looked down at the vehicles parked in front of the hospital She wasn't a car buff, by any means, and wouldn't know a Dodge Ram from a Ford Ranger or a Chevy Silverado, but she did spot a blue pickup parked near the north end of the hospital.

As she watched, a familiar-looking figure stepped out of the truck, holding a cell phone to his ear. He spoke a few more words, ended his call, and put his phone in his jacket pocket.

"Lissy, can you see that man down there? No, the other way, toward the other end of the hospital, by the blue truck. I think that's the man I've caught trying to get to you here."

"Are you sure?" Alyssa's features tightened with alarm.

"I'm pretty sure. I can't see his face from here, but then I never saw his face when he was up here either. He always had a hood pulled over it as far as possible, and he kept his face turned down. But just his stance…there's something about him."

"Livvy, what should we do?"

"First, don't panic. Second, I'm going to go talk to the officer outside your door. He can alert the plainclothes men. Third, I'm going to call Shel." She patted Alyssa's shoulder. "I'll be right back."

Olivia spoke with Officer James, who'd been assigned to watch Alyssa again because Olivia was familiar with him. He came into the room with her and looked out the window toward where she indicated.

"Okay, I see him. I'll let the plainclothes guys know who to look for. While I'm doing that, do you want to call Detective Sheldon?"

"Yes, I'll do that. Thank you."

Olivia dug her cell phone out of her purse and called Shel's number. He answered after the second ring.

"Oh, Shel, I'm so glad I got you. I was looking out the window and found the blue pickup you were talking about. As I watched, a man got out of it, talking on a cell phone. When he quit talking, he leaned back, lit a cigarette, and I could swear he was staring up at Lissy's window."

"Did you recognize him?"

"I'm 99 percent sure he's the same man I've caught up here twice before. Shel, I'm worried."

"Have you told Officer James about him?"

"Yes. He came in, and I pointed out the man to him. He's alerting the plainclothes men now, but he asked me if I could call you while he's doing that."

"Okay. We're not very far from 7-Eleven now. Ginny says she knows exactly where the tapes and receipts are. I'll have her run in and grab them as quickly as possible, and we'll leave right away for the hospital. Meantime, I think you're safe with Officer James and the other four officers I have posted there. Just don't leave the room."

"Alright. I'll stay put until you get here."

"We should be back there within twenty minutes."

"Please try to hurry."

She hung up and turned to Alyssa. "Okay, Lissy, Officer James and the other four officers are all on the alert, and Shel said he'd be back here within twenty minutes. Meantime, we just stay here in this room, and we'll be fine."

Olivia walked over to the window again, just in time to see a second man join the one by the pickup. He was carrying a large brown paper bag, which he put in the back seat of the extended-cab truck.

Olivia watched as the two men exchanged a few words. They both got into the pickup, the newcomer climbing in behind the wheel. As she watched, the truck backed out of its parking space and drove south and out of her range of vision.

"Maybe we don't have anything to worry about after all," she said. "The truck just drove off with two men in it."

"Two men? I thought there was just one."

"A second guy just came. Evidently, he'd done some shopping. He had a large paper bag in his arms. They spoke to each other briefly, and then they got in and drove away."

"Should we let Shel know?" Alyssa asked.

"I will, but I'll talk to Officer James first," Olivia said.

"Okay," the officer said when she told him what she'd seen. "I'll let the others know, but we'll still keep our eyes open in case they come back. If you notice anything else fishy, tell me."

"I will," Olivia said, "and thank you. I do feel better knowing you're here. I'm not so worried about myself, but Alyssa is pretty much helpless in there."

"We're glad to be here for you," he said. "And we'll get this guy, sooner or later."

"I'm sure you will. Again, thanks."

She rejoined Alyssa and said, "Okay. I'll call Shel next."

When she spoke to Shel, he told her they were on their way back and should be at the hospital in about fifteen minutes. Relieved that the situation seemed to be resolving itself, Olivia felt some of the tension in her neck and shoulders start to ease up.

"Well, what shall we do until they get here?" she asked Alyssa.

"We could look at real estate."

"That would be a great idea, if I'd remembered to bring my laptop with me. Tell you what. I think the danger has passed. I'll run home and get it. I should be back here shortly after Shel and the others get back."

"Oh, Livvy, do you think that's a good idea? Maybe you should just wait for Shel. It won't be that long." Alyssa's brows drew together with apprehension.

"It'll be okay, Lissy. Officer James is here, as well as the other four downstairs. You'll be fine. And I promise to keep my eyes open at all times. If I see anything suspicious, I'll head straight for the police station, or I'll give Shel a call if I'm already home."

"Are you sure? Oh, I wish I hadn't said anything about looking for a house."

"I'll be fine. Sit tight." She gave Alyssa a quick hug and was gone.

When Officer James asked where she was going, she said she'd be back in a few minutes. She was pretty sure if she'd told him she was going home to get something, he wouldn't have let her leave.

Which means I probably shouldn't be doing this. But I'm sure it'll be okay. I'll hurry and I'll be careful.

As she left the hospital, she nodded to the two officers at the front door. They didn't know her, so they did nothing to try to stop her. She looked up and down the block and saw no sign of a blue pickup anywhere. She couldn't see the parking ramp at the back of the hospital from where she was, but since she'd seen the truck drive south, away from the hospital, she didn't think twice about getting in her car and heading for home.

Keeping a close watch on traffic, Olivia pulled onto Highway 10, which was the fastest route to her neighborhood. Instantly, she was in traffic. As she drove, she thought about the promise she'd made to Shel.

He's not going to be happy that I left the hospital. But the pickup left, with two men in it. I'm sure I'll be fine. And I'll apologize to Shel about breaking my promise next time I see him.

When she reached her driveway, Olivia breathed more easily, relieved to have arrived safely at home. She pulled up in front of her garage without driving inside. She wouldn't be home that long, so she figured she'd go in the front door.

She used her key to unlock the dead bolt and disarmed the alarm system when she stepped inside. She didn't bother locking the door behind her because she planned to pick up her laptop and leave again right away, going out the same way she'd just come in.

Glancing around at her house, she didn't see anything out of the ordinary. She went to her office and picked up her laptop. She paused, wondering if there was anything else she'd forgotten. She decided there wasn't and went back to the living room.

As she stepped from the hallway into the living room, she heard the crunch of gravel in the driveway. Had Shel found out she'd left the hospital and come after her?

I hope he's not going to be too angry with me.

Heart racing, she ran to the window and cautiously peeked out. A red SUV was parked behind her car. Panic threatened to overcome reason. Olivia fought to stay calm and think about what she should do. She put the laptop on the breakfast bar next to her purse and glanced toward the front door again. There was no way she could go out the way she came in now, and even if she could, she wouldn't be able to get her car out of the driveway. Her only options were the garage door or the patio door in the kitchen. He surely would look in the garage. So that left the patio door, but then what?

I'll think of it while I'm running!

She was out the back door, down the deck stairs, and starting across her backyard to the edge of the forest as the front door opened. She could hear the man calling her name as he went from room to room looking for her. Without looking back, she plunged toward the shelter of the forest.

"I know you're here somewhere," Joe called, as he calmly searched each room. "I'll find you, and when I do, you'll wish you'd never stuck your nose into my business to begin with. Why don't you just come out so we can get this over with quickly?"

Olivia shivered as he spoke the last words. Then she realized she'd left the sliding door open. It was the only way she'd be able to hear him. It was also a giant clue telling him that she'd left the house through it. Her very next thought was that she'd left her purse on the breakfast bar—with her gun in it. Shel had insisted on buying her a gun a few weeks before and teaching her how to use it. Now she kicked herself mentally for not remembering it and kept running, not sure where she was going.

"I'm coming for you." She heard Joe yell from the back deck.

Olivia kept running. She stumbled over a tree root, went down on her knees, and gasped when a sharp rock cut through her pant leg into her skin. She couldn't take time to worry about it though. She got up and started running again.

She could hear someone crashing through the brush behind her. *Oh, God, please help me.*

Suddenly, she remembered the deer trail she and Lissy had found the first time they'd hiked back here, right after she moved in. And the cave.

They'd talked about coming back and stocking the cave with emergency supplies in case she should ever get stuck out here in a sudden storm. They'd never once thought she might need to hide from a deadly pursuer there. Unfortunately, they hadn't made it back up here yet to do anything. Now Olivia just hoped she'd be able to find the cave by herself.

She remembered that the trees had gotten thicker and the climb a little steeper before they'd found the deer trail, but she knew it wasn't very far into the woods. She paused briefly to get her bearings. *Did we go left or right here?*

Not wanting to take time to think about it, she veered to the left, into the dark forest. She ran several yards before pausing to listen.

When she didn't hear anything, she waited a moment. If the man chasing her had stopped to listen at the same time, she didn't want to make a sound. Fortunately, the leaves and needles beneath her feet were damp and soft, which quieted her footsteps. Unfortunately, that made them slippery and treacherous on the steep path.

As she started off again, her feet went out from under her, and she slid about fifteen feet back down the slope, arms flailing, trying to grasp hold of anything she could to stop her descent.

The noise she made as she slid sounded deafening to her, and she knew her pursuer probably heard it, too.

Suddenly, she heard the loud report of a gun, and at almost the same time, the *thwack* of a bullet hitting a tree not five feet to her right.

She didn't hesitate any longer. She was off again. *Thwack! Thwack!* Her eyes had finally adjusted to the semidarkness of the forest. After running a couple more minutes, she thought she heard the splashing of creek water over rocks.

I don't remember hearing running water when Lissy and I were here last fall.

She stopped for a moment and looked around. None of her surroundings looked at all familiar to her.

Oh, no! I'm going the wrong way! In spite of herself, she started to panic.

Suddenly she heard the man's voice calling out. "Okay, Ms. Clayton, let's stop this now. I'll tell you what. We're both tired. Let's stop running and just talk this over. I'm a reasonable man. I'm sure we can work something out."

Fat chance, she thought. From the sound of his voice, Olivia knew he wasn't far behind her. *I have to move. I have to find that cave!*

Since it seemed left had been the wrong direction, she turned to her right and started running. If she could move up and to the right and stay in the shelter of the trees, she thought she might be able to lose him. Hopefully, he'd keep going in the general direction they'd been heading up until now.

Panting hard and trying to ignore the pain in her side, she kept running. Suddenly, her feet were no longer beneath her. She tumbled down a long, rocky slope.

When she finally was able to stop herself by grabbing at a broken tree stump, she was afraid to move for fear of having broken something. Everything hurt. Cautiously, she moved one leg and then the other, one arm and the other. Reassured that she was bruised and bleeding, but had no broken bones, she got to her feet and looked up to the top of the scree, half expecting to see him standing there. But to her immense relief, there was no one in sight.

How she'd managed not to scream when she went down she had no idea, but she was grateful that, at least, she hadn't given up her location that way. Hopefully, he hadn't heard the racket of the tumbling rocks that went down under her.

Now she had to figure out how to get back up there and back on track to finding the cave.

As she looked at her surroundings, she noticed that about twenty feet to her right, the scree ended, and there was what looked almost like a natural set of steps heading part of the way up to where she'd been.

Carefully, she made her way across the loose rocks. Looking behind her and then up, she still saw no sign of anyone following her. She stood still to listen and heard nothing but the quiet sounds of the forest. She seemed to have lost her pursuer for now, but she knew he'd figure out sooner or later that he hadn't been following her for a while and change his direction to come after her.

She reached the natural stairway and started up. The climb wasn't as easy as it looked to be from farther away. The steps were jagged and had sharp edges. They weren't level but tended to slant downward. That, combined with the moisture from melting snow and ice, made it a perilous undertaking.

Doggedly, Olivia worked her way upward, digging her toes into the side of the mountain when the steps ended. She discovered that the going was easier if she worked her way sideways and up, rather than trying to go straight up.

Finally, she reached the top. Exhausted, she slumped against a pine tree to catch her breath. She looked at her hands and discovered she'd ripped skin off both palms and several fingertips. Her elbows stung and her knees, which were torn and bloody, throbbed; but she knew she had to get going again.

She slowed her pace a little, figuring she'd managed to get far enough ahead of him to make it safe. She kept close to the trees and skirted around any open areas she came to. When she'd been moving for about fifteen minutes, watching the ground ahead of her, she came upon what looked like a game trail.

Oh, please let this be it, God, she prayed.

She followed it, not sure if it was the right one, but figuring she didn't have anything to lose. When, about five minutes later, she saw the change in color on the side of the mountain, she sobbed with relief. This had to be the cave.

She continued to move as quickly and as quietly as she could, watching for branches, roots, and rocks that could trip her up again, and hoping that the trees around her were thick enough, and the forest dark enough, that he wouldn't spot her again before she reached the cave.

Oh, thank you, God, she breathed when she finally made her way to the brush that mostly hid the dark opening. She pushed her way through, hoping against hope that the cave was still empty of anything else that might have wanted a cozy shelter. When she and Alyssa had been up here before, it had been in September. The bears hadn't gone into hibernation yet. Now, in early spring, they'd be coming out of hibernation, but would probably still be using their dens, particularly if they had cubs to protect.

Please, please, please, don't let there be a bear in here! Or a mountain lion. Or anything else.

It was pitch-dark in the cave, and cold and damp. Olivia, in her tattered short-sleeved cotton T-shirt, shivered. If she were forced to hide out in here for very long, it would all probably be for nothing. She'd eventually die of hypothermia or dehydration, or both. But for now, it was better than facing whatever the man hunting her had in mind.

She pushed farther back into the cave. Cautiously, she slid her feet in front of her to keep from tripping on anything poking up from the floor. As Alyssa had said last fall, it wasn't very deep. Olivia soon felt the cold, rough wall at the back as she groped through the darkness. She'd have given anything for a flashlight, but then, she figured, she wouldn't be able to turn it on, anyway. Feeling her way along the wall, she stubbed her toe against a hard surface. She ran both hands over it and deduced that it was a huge boulder. There was just enough space between it and the cave wall to provide her some cover if her cave were discovered.

She crouched down behind the large rock and hugged her arms to herself, trying to control the shivering that had taken over her body. She didn't dare cough or sneeze, or even breathe hard.

If she could just stay strong enough, long enough to outlast the man outside…

* * * * *

"What do you mean she's not here?" Officer James cringed when Shel nearly bellowed at the news that he hadn't seen Olivia for at least fifteen minutes.

Shel, Collin, and Ginny had just returned from retrieving the tapes and receipts from 7-Eleven. He'd fully expected Olivia and Alyssa to be engaged in a girly conversation or watching something on TV. He had not expected Olivia to go back on her promise and leave Alyssa's room.

"Well, where did she go?"

"She didn't say, sir," the chagrined officer said. "She only said she'd be back in a few minutes. I guess I thought she was going down to the cafeteria or the restroom." He looked at Shel and apologized. "I'm really sorry, sir. I just didn't know."

"It's your job to know. What good does it do for you to be here, if you don't know?" Shel gave him one last scathing look and went into Alyssa's room.

"Don't be so hard on him," said Alyssa, who couldn't help but hear Shel's harsh remarks to Officer James. "It's not his fault. Olivia decided to go home and get her laptop. I tried to talk her out of it, but she swore she'd be okay since the two guys in the blue pickup drove off."

"Just because she saw them drive off doesn't mean they're not here. It also doesn't mean they aren't following her."

"She promised to be careful. She's smart, Shel. She can take care of herself."

"Maybe under normal circumstances she can. But these are not normal circumstances. These guys are playing for real. They're dangerous. They've proven that."

"What are you going to do?"

"I'm going after her. Was she only going home, no place else?"

"As far as I know, yes. She just wanted to get her laptop."

"She didn't say anything about working up here today."

"Not to work." Alyssa was near tears as she said, "She went to get it so we could look at real estate. For me. I'm so sorry, Shel! It's my fault."

Shel refrained from saying what he wanted to say. Instead, he put a hand on Alyssa's shoulder and said, "No, it's not your fault. It's mine. I should have known she was too independent to take orders from me."

"Please find her, Shel. Don't let anything happen to her. I'd never be able to forgive myself if something happened to her."

"I'll find her. I promise."

Shel squeezed her shoulder and promised to call her as soon as he knew anything.

On his way out, he stopped to talk to Officer James. "Sorry I came down on you so hard. I tend to overreact sometimes. But, that said, I want you to be on your toes from now on. I'm going after Olivia. She went home to get something. Don't take your eyes off Mrs. Walton. No one goes in or out that you don't recognize." He started to leave but then turned back. "Oh, Mrs. Walton is scheduled for an MRI this afternoon. I want you with her every step of the way down to radiation and back again."

The officer was relieved that Shel hadn't threatened to write him up for his mistake. He assured him that he wouldn't let anyone who wasn't supposed be there get near Alyssa.

Downstairs, Shel apprised the plainclothes officers of the situation. "If you see a blue Dodge Ram or a red SUV pull up here, you question anyone who gets out of them before you let them in this building. Understand?"

"Yes, sir," they both said.

Shel got back in his car, turned on the red beacon light in his front window, and sped down the street. There was one stop he wanted to make before going to Olivia's.

He pulled into his driveway about six minutes later and ran to his front door. He fumbled with the keys, reminded himself to slow down a little, and managed to get the door open on the second try.

"Columbo! Come here, boy!" He had no way of knowing if Olivia was in trouble, or if she was only doing what Alyssa had said she went home to do. But just in case, he thought it might be a good idea to take Columbo with him.

The dog came running as soon as he heard his master's voice. His tail wagged wildly, but he was careful not to jump up on Shel.

"Good boy," Shel said. "I may have work for you to do, Columbo. You may get a chance to show just how good you are at search and rescue. Come on, let's get you into your harness."

Two minutes later, Shel and his dog were in the car and on their way to Olivia's house. He planned to take the same route Olivia had taken, along Highway 10. He knew it would get him to her place faster.

He made it in ten minutes, thanks to the judicious use of his lights and siren. When he pulled into her driveway and saw the red SUV blocking her car, his heart leapt into his throat.

He flung open his car door, commanded Columbo to come with him, and tore up the walk to the front porch. He took the porch stairs three at a time and went through the open door, gun in his right hand, the dog's leash in his left.

He gave Columbo the command to stay and quickly, but thoroughly, searched the house. In Olivia's bedroom, he grabbed one of her shoes and took it with him. When he didn't find anyone in the house, he went back to the living room and glanced around quickly. No signs of a struggle. No bullet holes that he could see. Then he noticed the patio door, which was standing wide open.

"Come on, boy," he said to the dog and went out onto the deck. He scanned the backyard and didn't see anything unusual there. The sound of a gunshot jolted him into action. He headed down the deck steps and ran for the forest, Columbo ahead of him, tugging at his leash.

When he reached the edge of the trees, he stopped, knelt down in front of the dog, and held Olivia's shoe in front of his nose. "Find, Columbo," he commanded. The dog excitedly sniffed at the shoe, and Shel repeated, "Find."

At that, Columbo took off. Shel let him have his nose and followed hastily, careful not to let go of the leash. If he had, the dog would have been off, and Shel wouldn't have been able to keep up with him.

* * * * *

The musical alarm tone of her cell phone startled Olivia so much that she knocked her head into the cave wall behind her. She'd completely forgotten that she'd set the alarm earlier to remind her that she'd promised to call her boss at 3:45. Frantically, she dug it out of her jeans pocket and turned the alarm off.

Please, please, I hope he didn't hear that!

She didn't dare turn her phone off now, because if she did, she was sure he'd hear the sound of the chimes when it powered off.

Outside, Joe stopped in his tracks when he heard the unmistakable tone of a cell phone. He listened intently to see if he could hear it again. He wasn't sure from which direction the sound had come, but it seemed like it was up ahead on the game trail a short distance.

When the sound didn't come again, he started his hike back up the trail. It frustrated him that he hadn't gotten the woman with his first shot. Normally, he was a crack shot.

Must've been the upward angle. I should've known better, he thought.

He walked a few more yards and then stopped once more. He thought he'd heard something behind him, but he didn't hear it again.

Must've been a deer or something.

He continued up the trail, and stopped when he thought he saw something different about the landscape.

Was that a cave up ahead, or was it just a change in the coloration of the rocky mountainside? He drew closer, his eyes straining to make out what he was looking at. It was a cave, and it would be a good place for someone on the run to hide.

"Are you in there, Ms. Clayton? You know I'm going to find you, don't you? Why don't you just make it easier on us both and come on out now?" Joe waited a moment and then continued. "Dammit, I'm beginning to lose my patience! It'll go a lot easier on you if I don't have to come in there after you."

Inside the cave, Olivia pressed herself back against the cave wall as though she were trying to become part of the rock. Terrified, she held her breath, tried to stop the noisy chattering of her teeth and prayed her cell phone wouldn't ring again.

Oh, why didn't I do as Shel said and stay put with Alyssa? It's not like a house is going to sell right out from under our noses if we don't look today. Please, God, get me out of this, and I promise I'll listen to good advice from now on.

She heard the cold, cruel voice again. This time it echoed, as though it were coming from just inside the mouth of the cave. "Come on, Ms. Clayton. I don't want to have to come in there. I hate caves. But I will come in, and I'll drag you out by your hair if I have to."

Suddenly, Olivia heard another voice and then a loud commotion.

It was Shel's voice. "I don't think so, Joe. That is your name, isn't it? Joe Little Hawk?" Then he turned to the huge German shepherd and said, "Hold, Columbo!"

Columbo leaped on Joe, knocking him to the ground. Joe's gun went off as he fell. The bullet ricocheted off a nearby boulder. When his arm hit a rock protruding from the forest floor, he lost his hold on the gun, and it flew several feet behind him. Columbo stood over Joe, teeth bared right above his face, waiting to be told what to do next.

Inside the cave, Olivia heard the report of the gun.

Oh, no! Shel! Please be alright, Shel!

She was terrified that Joe had shot him, but she knew she didn't dare leave the safety of the cave to find out.

"Olivia! Livvy, are you in there?"

Olivia, sobbing with relief at the sound of Shel's voice, couldn't answer.

When he didn't hear a reply, Shel took his handcuffs out of their case, slapped one onto Joe's right hand, yanked him up, and pulled him to a nearby tree. He told Joe to hug the tree and closed the other cuff over Joe's left hand. Once he was secure, Shel called Columbo to him.

Shel pulled Olivia's shoe from the waistband of his pants, and once again, he held the shoe for the dog to smell. Columbo responded with a wag of his tail and a yelp and took off, nose to the ground, right for the cave. Shel followed him, slowing in order to make his way through the thick brush.

"Olivia, it's Shel. You're safe now. He can't hurt you."

When Olivia first felt the warm, furry body that rushed into the cave and came straight at her, she almost fainted. She was sure a wild animal of some kind had returned home and wanted her gone. But when a wet tongue started licking her face, she reached out and felt the harness over the dog's neck and back. "Columbo! Oh, I'm so glad to see you!"

Outside the cave, Shel let out the breath he'd been holding when he finally heard her voice. "Livvy, you can come out now. I promise you're safe. Just take hold of Columbo's harness, and he'll lead you out."

A few seconds later, Shel was rewarded with the sight of Columbo guiding Olivia to the mouth of the cave. When she saw Shel, she released her hold on the dog and ran toward him. He opened his arms and took her into them. She buried her face in his shoulder.

"Oh, Shel. I'm so sorry! I should have done as you said and stayed put. Lissy tried to warn me, but I wouldn't listen. I thought I'd be okay. I'm sorry. Will you forgive me?"

"Do you know how close you came to not making it out of here alive?" He sounded angry and relieved at the same time. "If we'd gotten here one minute later, it would have been too late."

"I know. I really am sorry, Shel," Olivia said. "I guess I just didn't think. I should have known better, but I thought I'd be fine. I watched the traffic around me all the way home. I never saw anything until I looked out at my driveway and the red SUV was behind my car."

"Someone who knows what he's doing gets pretty good at following without being spotted. I'd guess these guys have had some experience, both at following and being followed."

He nodded toward Joe, whose hands were still safely cuffed around the tree.

Only then did Olivia see him. "That's him? He doesn't look so tough," she said.

Shel laughed. "Not now, he doesn't, but you were about to find out just how tough he is." He hugged her closer and said, "Oh, Livvy, I don't know what I'd have done if something had happened to you. I don't want to lose you now that I've finally found you."

"You mean now that Columbo found me. I think he's earned his stripes, don't you?"

"Yes, I do. Come here, Columbo," he said and knelt down to praise the dog. He scratched behind his ears and pet his back. "You're a good boy. Good dog, Columbo! I think you're ready to go to work with me."

Shel rose to his feet and released Joe from his tree hug. Then he cuffed his hands again, behind his back.

Giving Olivia a thorough once-over, he saw the bloody wounds she'd inflicted upon herself in her wild run through the forest. Instantly, his demeanor toward her softened.

"Are you okay? You look pretty beat up."

"I'll be fine. It might take me a little longer to make it back down this mountain though." She limped a couple steps away from him.

"Hold on to Columbo's harness," Shel said. "He'll guide you and give you some support. Take your time so you don't hurt yourself more. I'll take our friend down, and I'll call for Ken Harrison to pick him up."

He yanked on the cuffs, holding Joe's hands behind his back, making sure they were securely locked. "Let's go," he said and shoved him, none too gently, down the game trail ahead of him, making sure Joe knew the gun was pointed at him the whole time.

Olivia and Columbo followed behind them at a much slower pace. When they finally were within sight of Olivia's house again, she nearly fainted with relief. Her legs went out from under her, and she sank down to the grass. Columbo sat beside her nuzzling her with his nose and licking her face. She wrapped her arms around his neck and sobbed into his furry coat.

When Shel was sure she was okay, he took Joe around to the front yard. He told him he was under arrest for two counts of attempted murder and whatever else he could find against him and make stick. Then he read him his rights, opened the back door of his car, and pushed him inside. Once he'd made sure the safety locks were on and Joe couldn't get out of the car, Shel left him there and called for the sheriff. Then he went to rejoin Olivia.

When he got to the backyard, she wasn't there. "Olivia!" He almost panicked until he heard her call his name from the deck.

"Shel, we're in here. Come on in."

He climbed the steps up to the deck and went into the kitchen where he saw Columbo eagerly devouring a piece of meat Olivia had taken from the refrigerator.

"I thought he deserved a reward," she said. "I hope you don't mind."

CHAPTER 25

Monday, May 18, 2015

"That does it," Olivia said and wiped her hands on her jeans.

Shel, Ginny, and Collin had just moved the last of Alyssa's things into Olivia's guest room. Alyssa had stayed true to her promise and moved in with Olivia when her therapists deemed her ready to leave the rehab center.

"Thanks, guys," Olivia said. "Anybody for a cold beer?"

"I think I could manage to drink one," Shel said. "How 'bout you, Collin?"

Collin agreed that it sounded good, and the two men sat down on the living room sofa, with Ginny seated between them, and accepted the cold bottles Olivia held out to them. Olivia offered Ginny a beer or a glass of wine, but she declined, and said she'd rather have a glass of cold water. Olivia would have liked a glass of wine, but since Ginny didn't want one, and Alyssa couldn't have one because of the meds she was taking, she opted for a glass of water, too.

Alyssa was sitting in the chair opposite the sofa, and Olivia took her favorite oversized armchair and sat with her legs curled up under her.

"So tell us what you found out now, Shel," Olivia said.

"Well, turns out we didn't need those tapes and receipts, although they did help us nail down the date Joe and his men turned up here. Olivia managed to get them out in the open without our having to track them down the hard way."

"You don't think my way was the hard way?" Olivia laughed, rubbing her knees, which had finally healed from the beating they'd taken on her run through the forest.

"You can laugh now," Shel said, "but you do know how close you came to being killed, don't you?"

"Yes, I do," she said, at once becoming serious. "And I promise I won't pull anything like that ever again."

"I hope you never have reason to," Alyssa said. "I know I don't want to have to go through anything like this again."

"You had the worst of it, Lissy. You really did come close to death."

"Do you want to know what we found out now, or do you want to compare your near-death experiences?" Shel looked from Olivia to Alyssa and back to Olivia again.

"We want to know what you found out," Olivia said.

"Well, it turns out Joe was the head of the construction crew putting up a large compound. They had a privately-owned, twenty-five-acre plot of land that butts up against national forest. They planned to manufacture, store, and distribute drugs from there. It was quite an elaborate plan. They already had their main building done. That's the one where the bigshots would meet and stay. It has all the luxuries you can think of, including an indoor pool and a media room. And the plans I saw called for a number of other buildings, including several cottages for permanent or semipermanent residents to live in, a machine shed, storage shed, and of course, the building where the drugs would be manufactured."

"Wow!" Collin's eyebrows shot up. "They really were serious, weren't they? And the whole time I was thinking they were small-time crooks with really nasty tempers."

"Now we know why they ran down Lissy to begin with," Olivia said. "When they saw her putting up the camera, they were afraid she'd somehow figured out what they were up to, or at least, that they were up to no good. They thought they had to stop her."

"The irony of it all," Shel said, "is that if they'd never run over her, they probably wouldn't have been found out. At least, not for quite a while."

"And I was just doing my job," Alyssa said. "The bears I was checking on seem almost harmless compared to those guys. In fact, I think I'd rather run into a big old black bear than one of those men again."

"You might be safer, at that," Shel said. He filled them in on the five men and their backgrounds. Joseph Little Hawk, the man in charge of the crew and the construction of the compound, had had several brushes with the law; but somehow, he'd always managed to avoid being convicted of anything. He'd grown up on the Flathead Reservation and left to attend the University of Montana in Missoula. He had a degree in business administration. "He actually could've gone on to make something of himself," Shel said, "but he has a bad streak in him a mile wide. He uses his education for ill gain rather than for good."

Cal Diggs had been a troublemaker since junior high school. He'd graduated from high school by the skin of his teeth and had gone on to trade school to become an electrician. He was fairly intelligent but didn't care enough to make good grades. After trade school, he moved from job to job, never holding on to any of them for longer than a few months. He'd been arrested and tried for rape but had gotten off on a technicality. However, he'd still managed to land in jail a few times for burglary and for selling drugs to high school kids.

Pete Kessler, too, had chosen trade school. He was a decent carpenter and knew his way around a blueprint. But Pete had a mean streak and loved a good fight. A broken beer bottle in a barroom brawl had etched the long scar on his face. He'd served time for assault and battery, as well as armed robbery. "Pete has a nasty disposition to go along with his looks," Shel said.

Sam Ahlers was a high school dropout, the product of a dysfunctional family. His father, who'd had a fearsome temper, had beaten Sam and his mother mercilessly, until one day Sam couldn't take any more and left home. He lived on the street from the age of seventeen, checking in on his mother whenever he could when his father wasn't at home. He stopped going back to his parents' house the day he learned his father had finally beaten his mother so severely she'd landed in the hospital in a coma. She died, and Sam's father was sentenced to life in prison. That was the end of any connection Sam had with his family. Unfortunately, Sam had learned well what his father had taught him and had become very adept at torture. "He hasn't killed anyone yet," Shel said, "but if he hadn't been caught along with the rest of them, that day would've come eventually, I'm sure."

Trent Roach was the most dangerous of the five. At the very young age of seven, he tortured and killed the neighbor's puppy. He found that he enjoyed inflicting pain on helpless animals, and eventually, he moved on to tormenting his schoolmates. He landed in reform school but was released when he reached age eighteen. Rather than being reformed, he'd learned more advanced means of torture. His first tattoo, of the multitude covering his body, was of a cockroach, huge and grotesque, on his left bicep. Trent was bloodthirsty and was the man to call if you wanted someone eliminated. "I'm not sure how you managed to escape him twice, Alyssa," Shel said. "He doesn't often miss his mark."

The group in Olivia's living room all looked at Alyssa whose face had turned white when Shel spoke of Trent's talents. She looked at Shel and said, "I'm not sure I need to know all of that, but I'm so grateful that Livvy was with me. I know Trent was the one who tried to get to me in the hospital, but was he the one in the Humvee to begin with?"

"No," Shel said. "Actually, that was Sam. When he bungled that job, Joe handed it over to Trent, who he thought would be able to finish you off with no problem. But Olivia came to your rescue both times at the hospital. This"—he gestured toward Olivia—"is one strong woman. I wouldn't want to be on the wrong side of her."

"What happens next?" Olivia brushed aside the compliment.

"They'll have their day in court, of course, but with all the evidence we have against them, as well as the testimony of several reliable witnesses," he said, indicating Olivia, Collin, and Ginny, "I guarantee they'll all be spending several years in prison. By the time they get out, they'll be too old to swing a hammer, much less build an entire compound."

"What happens to the compound now?" Collin asked. "It'd be a shame to just abandon all those brand-new, fancy buildings and let them go to ruin."

"The land and everything that's been built on it have been confiscated," Shel told them.

"When all of this mess is cleared up, it'll go up for auction. I think someone might like to buy it and turn it into a nice little resort. It could do quite well there with the right people running it. It could run all year 'round, too. Fishing, hiking, and boating in the summer and hunting, skiing, snowshoeing, and snowmobiling in the winter."

Ginny looked up, interested in Shel's last comment. "That sounds great," she said. "You know, I've been saving up for several years now, and I earned my degree in business administration at the university—something I'm not proud to have in common with Joe Little Hawk—with the hope of starting my own business eventually. I mean, who wants to be stuck behind the counter of a 7-Eleven forever? Do you think I'd have a chance of getting that land, Shel?"

"I don't see why not," he said. "You have just as much right as anyone else to bid on it when it goes up for auction. I think it'd be a great venture for you."

"I do, too," Collin said. "You have a good head on your shoulders, Ginny, and with the right people to help you run and maintain the place, I think you could make a real success of it. I think you should go for it."

"I think so, too," Olivia said, and Alyssa nodded her agreement.

"Okay, then. It's settled!" Ginny said. "I'm going to do some research and see how much it could all be worth. I want to be able to enter into the bidding at least somewhat educated on the subject."

That settled, Shel rose from the couch, took Olivia's hands in his, and pulled her out of her chair. He looked at her questioningly and cleared his throat.

"Oh, go ahead," she said. "I know you're dying to tell them."

"Tell us what?" Alyssa was pretty sure she knew what, and she clasped her hands together in anticipation.

"Well..." Shel began.

"Shel asked me to marry him," Olivia said.

"And she said she would!"

"Yes, I did. That way I won't have to lug all those books back and forth from his place to mine when I want to read them." Olivia grinned up at Shel.

"And," Shel said, "she's always home, so she can take care of Columbo, and I won't have to train another dog for her."

"So you see, it'll be a marriage of convenience for both of us," Olivia said.

"Oh, baloney! It'll be a lot more than that," Alyssa said. "Oh, Livvy, I'm so happy for you. You, too, Shel. I totally, wholeheartedly approve!" She motioned Olivia over to her so she could give her a hug.

"Have you set the date yet?" Collin said.

"We're thinking sometime this fall. I can't get married until my best friend can stand up with me. So Lissy, you and I have our work cut out for us, getting on with your therapy to get you up and on your feet."

"That gives me all the more incentive," Alyssa said. "Oh, I can't wait to start making wedding plans!"

* * * * *

Later that evening, Shel and Olivia sat on her front porch discussing their future together.

"Shall we live in your house or mine?" Olivia had been wondering about that since she'd accepted Shel's proposal.

"I vote for yours," Shel said. "You can't beat the views from here, and I'm ready for a change. I probably should've moved long ago, after Sandy died, but I just couldn't let go. Now I'm ready."

"I have an idea you might like," Olivia said.

"And what would that be?"

"Well, you know Lissy's been looking for a house. I think yours would be just about the right size for her. What if we were to run the idea by her?"

"I think that's a great idea. We'll see what she thinks about it in the morning."

237

"Shel," Olivia began, "There's one more thing I need to ask you."

"What?"

"Now that we're getting married, don't you think I should know your first name?"

"I suppose I can tell you now. But you have to promise not to laugh, and if you ever tell anyone else, I'll arrest you for giving out classified information."

As the sun kissed the mountaintops good night, with a promise to return in the morning, he leaned over and whispered, "My first name is…"

– The End –

ABOUT THE AUTHOR

Jeanine Fricke was born and spent most of her childhood in Montana where this story takes place. She has a BA in journalism from South Dakota State University and is a former cultural affairs reporter for SDSU. She is also a retired piano and voice instructor. She and her husband, Dan, have two married sons and six grandchildren. They currently live in southwestern Minnesota.

CPSIA information can be obtained
at www.ICGtesting.com
Printed in the USA
LVHW031754060420
652381LV00007B/646

9 781643 456782